214
PALMER
STREET

BOOKS BY KAREN McQUESTION

Wish Upon a Christmas Star

The Moonlight Child

Dovetail

Missing Her More

Good Man, Dalton

Half a Heart

Hello Love

Easily Amused

A Scattered Life

The Long Way Home

For Young Adults

THE EDGEWOOD SERIES

Edgewood

Wanderlust

Absolution

Revelation

From a Distant Star

Favorite

Life on Hold

For Writers

Write That Novel

For Children

214
PALMER
STREET

KAREN McQUESTION

**GRAND
CENTRAL**

NEW YORK   BOSTON

Grand Central Publishing
Hachette Book Group
1290 Avenue of the Americas, New York, NY 10104
grandcentralpublishing.com
twitter.com/grandcentralpub

First published in 2022 by Bookouture, an imprint of StoryFire Ltd.
First Grand Central Publishing edition: February 2023

Grand Central Publishing is a division of Hachette Book Group, Inc.
The Grand Central Publishing name and logo is a trademark of Hachette Book Group, Inc.

The publisher is not responsible for websites (or their content) that are not owned by the publisher.

The Hachette Speakers Bureau provides a wide range of authors for speaking events. To find out more, go to www.hachettespeakersbureau.com or call (866) 376-6591.

Library of Congress Cataloging-in-Publication Data
Names: McQuestion, Karen, author.
Title: 214 Palmer Street / Karen McQuestion.
Description: First Grand Central Publishing edition. | New York : Grand Central Publishing, 2023. | "First published in 2022 by Bookouture, an imprint of StoryFire Ltd."—Title page verso. | Summary: "When Maggie saw the beautiful linen curtains moving in the Caldwell's front window, she went on high alert. Her wonderful, friendly neighbors Cady and Josh are away, so who is in their house? The woman who answers the door tells a convincing story. She's the house-sitter. Just here for a month. An old friend of Cady's who needed a place to stay. She's pleasant and warm, and Maggie wanders back to her house thinking she might have made a new friend. But when Sarah closes the door she knows she must do something about Maggie. She didn't want anyone to know she's living at 214 Palmer Street. She doesn't want anyone to know her name, to find out about her husband, or how she really knows Cady. And she definitely doesn't want anybody walking into the house . . ."— Provided by publisher.
Identifiers: LCCN 2022042097 | ISBN 9781538725054 (trade paperback)
Subjects: LCGFT: Thrillers (Fiction) | Novels.
Classification: LCC PS3613.C58754 A615 2023 | DDC 813/.6—dc23/eng/20220909
LC record available at https://lccn.loc.gov/2022042097

ISBN: 978-1-5387-2505-4 (trade paperback)

Printed in the United States of America

LSC-C

Printing 1, 2022

For MaryAnn Schaefer

ONE

At first, Sarah disregarded the knocking on the front door. She was in the back of the house in the kitchen, out of the sightlines of any of the neighbors. All of the blinds were closed. As far as anyone outside could tell, no one was home.

Even as the rapping on the door became more insistent, she kept sipping her tea. They'd go away eventually. Most likely it was someone wanting to talk about security systems or lawn services. In this day and age, it was hard to believe that businesses tried to gain new accounts this way, but they did, clipboard in hand, ID badges hanging from their neck. When she'd encountered door-to-door salespeople in the past, she tried to be polite in saying no, because it had to be a miserable job.

The knocking continued. The person at the door was persistent, which made her think ignoring them was no longer an option. As she drained her cup, she mulled over the repercussions of showing up at the front door, much less in her bathrobe. It was still early in the morning on a Saturday, so it would be perfectly reasonable not to be dressed just yet.

When the rapping turned to pounding, she sighed, put her cup in the sink, and reluctantly made her way down the long hallway. At the front door, Sarah peered through the peephole and recognized Maggie Scott, the old lady who lived next door. Too bad. She'd been hoping not to cross paths with any of the neighbors.

"Yes?" she said, opening the door with a warm smile.

"Oh." Maggie took a step back in surprise. "I don't know you."

"No," Sarah said in pleasant agreement. "I'm the house sitter. You must be Maggie Scott. I've heard so much about you."

Poor Maggie looked as stunned as if Sarah had smacked her. Behind the lenses of her glasses, the old woman's eyes narrowed in confusion. She turned her head to stare at the house numbers to the left of the door, as if trying to confirm she was in the right place. Finally, she said, "I'm sorry. Who are you again?"

"I'm house sitting for Cady and Josh. They'll be back at the end of the month." Sarah had the definite advantage here, and not only because she was a head taller. Maggie Scott was someone Cady had referenced often, so Sarah was well versed on their relationship. According to Cady, the old lady periodically brought over flowers and baked goods. In the fall, Maggie could often be seen cleaning out the leaves that accumulated over the street's sewer grate at the end of the block. She was observant too, calling with a warning when suspicious vehicles went down their street or letting them know when they'd left their garage door open for what she deemed a long time. A raised garage door was something Maggie Scott found particularly troubling. She'd told Cady that an open garage door was an invitation to petty thieves, something Cady thought was hilarious. She gave the impression she found Maggie to be a lovable nuisance.

Sarah fidgeted with the sash of her bathrobe. "Is there something I can help you with?"

"No, I . . ." Maggie seemed flustered. "I thought I saw movement in the house, and it confused me because Cady told me she and Josh were going to be gone for four weeks."

She saw movement in the house? Sarah had just arrived the

night before and she'd been extremely careful to mask her presence. The fact that Maggie noticed meant she was even more observant than Sarah had anticipated. Clearly, she needed to be more careful. "You're right. They'll be away for a month."

Maggie's brow furrowed. "But I talked to Cady right before they left and she didn't say anything about a house sitter. In fact, just the opposite. She was worried about the house being empty and asked me to keep an eye on the place while they're gone."

Sarah tilted her head and nodded sympathetically. "I can see why you're confused. The arrangements for me to stay were made very last minute. I flew into town just as they were leaving. We might have even crossed paths in the airport." She smiled. "I'd just messaged Cady to let her know my mom was dying. My mom loved Cady like a second daughter, so I knew she'd want to know. Mom is over at Angel's Grace Hospice right now and I was certain Cady would want to visit her. I'm sure she would have, but the timing with their trip didn't make it possible."

"Oh, I'm so sorry to hear about your mother."

"Thank you. It's been difficult." A tear came to Sarah's eye and she brushed it aside. "Colon cancer."

"It's so hard to lose someone you love."

Sarah sniffed. "And you know Cady, when she found out I was going to rent a hotel room, she said that was ridiculous, that of course I should stay at her house, that it was just sitting here empty. I offered to pay her but she said there was no need. That knowing I was here would bring them peace of mind. That I should consider myself their house sitter. She's so kind."

"That does sound like Cady." Maggie looked visibly relieved. "Always so generous."

"Always so generous," Sarah repeated. "She's been that way as long as I've known her."

No one who knew Cady could deny it. She was the first to organize a meal drive when a co-worker or neighbor became seriously ill. She was an expert knitter who donated scarves and hats to the local homeless shelter. Until recently, she and Josh had trained service dogs. Right after she graduated from the university she'd done a stint in the Peace Corps, which was where she'd met Josh. Once married, they carried on with their philosophy of service to others. As if that wasn't enough, they trained for marathons while keeping a full-time work schedule. Cady did more in one day than most people did in a week. Sarah added, "I feel like I know you. She's mentioned you to me so many times. All good things. I hear you make the most delicious banana bread."

Maggie perked up. "I do feel better knowing someone is in the house," she said, her hand on the doorframe, leaning in. "The Caldwells are my favorite neighbors. We're very close." She craned her neck, trying to look past Sarah.

Sarah got the impression she was hoping for an invitation inside, but there was no way that was going to happen. "So you don't need to worry about the house anymore. I've got things covered."

Maggie didn't move. "If you're sure . . ."

"I don't want to be rude," she said, "but I really need to take a shower and go see my mom. I'm sure you understand." Her hand went up to her hair, which was always messy in the morning.

"Oh, of course. Well, if you need anything, I'm right next door." She gestured toward her house, which was unnecessary because Sarah knew exactly where she lived. In fact, she knew the color of the area rug in her living room, and where the framed Japanese prints of long-necked birds hung in her dining room. Sarah knew how many years the older woman had lived in her home, the name of the company she hired to replace her furnace, and the rating she'd given them on Yelp. If Maggie had any clue how much Sarah knew, she'd be horrified. "Anything at all, just come by. I'm always glad to help."

"I'll keep that in mind," Sarah said, taking a step back. "Thanks so much for stopping by."

"How did you say you know Cady?"

Sarah turned her head. "Sorry, but I hear my phone ringing. It might be the nurse from Angel's Grace, so I've got to go. Nice meeting you."

As the door was closing shut, Maggie called out, "But I never got your name!"

"Take care now!" Sarah pushed the door closed and locked it. She leaned with her back against the wall and closed her eyes, giving a sigh of relief. When a minute or so passed and she didn't hear anything else, she snuck a look through the peephole. Maggie was gone, which meant things were fine for now, but her appearance at the door and the following questions were too close for comfort and she knew it wasn't over yet. Judging from things Cady had said, Sarah knew Maggie could be persistent.

The old woman's intrusive nature was a problem to be solved.

Luckily, Sarah had a plan in place to cover this very scenario.

Honestly, she'd hoped it wouldn't come to this, but Maggie's appearance at the door had forced her hand. Sarah sighed. She'd have to make a phone call. It was an unfortunate turn of events, but she'd come too far to let one old lady stand in her way.

TWO

SIX MONTHS EARLIER

Disoriented, Sarah managed to open her eyes, but only slightly. She was outside, ground-level, flat on her back. The pain in her head was as intense as if she'd been hit by a sledgehammer. Next to her, two men talked between themselves, saying things she couldn't quite grasp. They rolled her onto her side, then pressed something against the back of her head and put a brace around her neck. Her eyelids were heavy, but she managed to open them just wide enough to see she was lying on the patio behind her house. The men, she realized, had to be EMTs. A second later, she mentally corrected herself. Not EMTs. They were paramedics. Was that the right term? EMTs. Paramedics. The two words overlapped in her mind, making her realize she didn't really know the difference.

The pain, though, that was a certainty. It felt like her skull had exploded and shards of bone had penetrated her brain. Complete and utter agony.

What happened? Thinking back, she remembered coming home after work and heading out the back door. And then the sound of the dog next door barking like crazy, which was completely out of character for him. Buster was a sweet dog and almost never barked. She remembered walking toward the fence to see what was making him so upset.

And then a sudden jolt to the back of her head. After that, nothing.

Until now.

Where had these men come from? Nothing made sense. A light drizzle fell on her face; she was cold and wet now, her clothing clinging to her body. One of the men noticed her eyes tracking his movements and gave her a reassuring smile. "My name is Darren and this is Chris. You're going to be fine. Can you tell me your name?"

With much effort she managed to say, "Sarah Aden."

He said, "Do you know where you are?"

"My house. Backyard."

"Good." From the color of the sky she got the sense that it was late. Kirk should be home by now. Where was he?

"Do you know what day it is?"

"Thursday. End of March." She racked her brain but couldn't come up with the exact date. "The twenty-second. I think."

"Can you tell me what happened to you?"

Not a clue. She seemed to have a gap in her memory. How did she go from setting her purse on the counter, to opening the screen door and being out on the patio to having EMTs arrive? "I...something...in my head." She struggled with how to describe it and settled on, "It went off."

Darren turned to look at the other man. "She's confused." He returned his attention to Sarah. "You've had a head injury. We're transporting you to the hospital."

A head injury? The pain kept her from thinking it through, but the idea that she had a head injury sounded unlikely. People's heads got injured playing sports or getting hit by a car while bicycling. Not by stepping out into their backyard.

The two men lifted her, her body supported by a stretcher she hadn't even known was underneath her.

As they carried her around the side of the house, she heard hurried footsteps and the sound of her husband's voice. "What's going on? What happened? I'm Kirk Aden. That's my wife, Sarah." The words ran together, his voice panic-stricken. The men didn't slow their pace, so Kirk walked alongside them.

Sarah couldn't keep her eyes open any longer. One of the men said, "Your neighbor called 911. She was upstairs when her dog began barking and alerted her that something was wrong. From the second-floor window she noticed your wife lying on the pavement. Sarah wasn't conscious when we arrived, but she's spoken since. She seems confused. Did you want to accompany her in the ambulance or follow in your car?"

He didn't even hesitate. "I'm staying with my wife."

The ambulance ride was a blur. She felt Kirk holding her hand and heard all three men's voices: Kirk's beseeching and worried, the EMTs' calm and professional. When they got to the ER, the movement of being shifted off the stretcher onto another surface caused so much pain that she cried out and clutched her head. "It hurts," she said.

"Can't you give her something?" Kirk asked. "She's in terrible pain."

As usual, he knew her so well. The pain was horrendous and the movement intensified her suffering.

"They'll give her something soon," a woman's voice said, a promise that sounded tenuous at best. Didn't they understand what she was going through? She needed relief *now*. When a doctor arrived and they rolled her onto her side to look at the back of her head, she felt as if her brain had been pushed against her eye sockets. The pressure was unbearable, so much so that she couldn't even manage the words to tell them what she was experiencing.

Thank God Kirk was here to advocate for her. What would she do without him?

THREE
NOW

After answering the door, and talking to Maggie Scott, Sarah went back to the kitchen and got out her burner phone, the one she'd purchased just a month before. When Phil answered, she said, "It's me. I just got a visit from the old lady next door."

"Oh no." His voice had the sympathetic tone she'd come to know. Thank God for Phil. When she first met him, a barrel-chested man in a navy blue tracksuit, she never dreamed he'd become the one person she could count on, but now even hearing his voice was reassuring.

"Oh yes. I really hate to ask, but will you get her out of the way for me?"

"Not to worry. I've got this."

"Do you have enough to cover it?"

"More than enough. Which reminds me," he said. "I need to give you the rest of the cash after I make the arrangements. I feel funny about having so much of your money."

"I trust you. Just hang on to it." She ran a fingertip around the edge of the tabletop and glanced out through the glass of the patio door. A bird flew out of the woods that lined the back of the property and landed on one of the dirt mounds in the yard.

"Okay, if you say so."

"Thanks. You're the best."

By the time the call ended, her worry about Maggie had melted away and tension had left her shoulders. Sarah, who'd initially felt odd about being in someone else's home, became bolder that morning, using the deluxe shower with the multiple jets as if it were her own, luxuriating in the warmth of the water and using Cady's high-end shampoo and shower wash. The beige towels were upscale too, thick and soft. She used them to dry off and didn't even feel guilty. It wasn't as if she was stealing. When Cady and Josh returned, everything would be as they left it.

More or less.

She smiled at herself in the mirror. Not too bad considering the stress of the past few days. If she put on makeup and made some effort, she'd actually resemble the Sarah from six months ago, pre-attack, but there was no need for makeup. Not now anyway. She combed her hair and used Cady's hair dryer, blowing it out until it was nearly dry, then decided that was good enough. She'd let it air dry the rest of the way. Later tonight, she'd surely have to take another shower anyway. It didn't make sense to wash twice, but it was force of habit. Taking a shower was part of her morning routine and not doing it would have felt wrong. It was bad enough being in a strange environment. Being in a strange environment and not feeling yourself would just make it worse. Besides, she had time to kill before it got dark.

She headed down the stairs, trailing her fingers as she went. The original 1950s banister had been replaced with a sleek black railing, the wooden spindles removed and taut wires put in their stead. So many updates that she barely recognized the place.

When she arrived the night before, she'd explored the house, starting with the kitchen. Except for condiments, Josh and Cady's fridge was empty. They'd left a full freezer, however, including two loaves of bread and assorted microwave meals. Not the standard grocery store microwave meals, but some gourmet, organic version, low in sodium and flash frozen to stay nutrient rich. The kind from a subscriber delivery service. Sarah smiled. So typical of Cady to only eat quality food. She did everything the right way. Sarah didn't need to wonder if Cady had remembered to cancel delivery of the meals during their trip. Of course she had.

Knowing there was food in the house was one problem solved. Between Cady's provisions in the freezer and the protein bars in her bag, she was covered for a few days. Hopefully it wouldn't take any longer than that.

Sarah walked from room to room, opening drawers and inspecting framed photos. One of them seemed to be a family reunion of about twenty people, all of them with big smiles on their faces. An older photo showed a young woman who was presumably Cady's mom holding an adorable toddler girl on her lap. The one of Cady and Josh on their wedding day was in the living room next to one showing the two of them in Hawaii. Taken during their honeymoon? Sarah wasn't sure, but Cady's hair was the same length and color as in the wedding photo, so maybe. In every picture Josh had his arm casually slung over Cady's shoulders. In a few of them, she smiled up at him, their eyes locked in love. It would be hard to fake that kind of devotion. Not impossible, though.

Cady and Josh were a tight-knit couple, but not to the point of shutting out the world. They still maintained a social circle of couple friends and each had their own one-on-one friendships as well. Both were from the Pacific Northwest, but when they moved to Wisconsin for Josh's job, they made new friends easily, something Sarah envied.

In Josh's home office the bookcases were noticeably devoid of novels, but he had plenty of textbooks and medical journals. His diplomas were framed and hung above his desk. So many degrees. Josh, she decided, was a bit of an overachiever. "Dr. Caldwell, I presume," Sarah said aloud. Cady often mentioned her husband's work on Facebook, but only in passing. He was a scientist, a researcher whose work involved something with the environment. Sarah didn't know the specifics, but knew his work was the reason the two of them were now on a ship, out to sea for a month. It was the opportunity of a lifetime. It was one thing to work in a lab, but another to do field work. Josh had been asked to replace one of the researchers who canceled at the last minute, and Cady had gone along for the ride. She'd posted: *You know he couldn't be without me for that long. LOL.* All of her friends agreed that Josh would be lost without Cady. *He wouldn't last a week without you, much less a month,* her friend Jocelyn commented.

You got the last good one, one of her single friends added.

Because she led a charmed life, Cady was easily able to take a leave of absence from her job, and so off they went. Luckily for Sarah, the remoteness of the ship's route did not allow for easy communication. Cady promised she'd be checking for messages, but added that the Internet would be spotty at best.

Don't plan on hearing from me, she'd said. *I'm going to be nearly unreachable. In fact, I might be taking a complete social media break and just live in the moment. What do you think of that?*

Sarah was all in favor.

In the kitchen, Sarah heated water for her tea in the microwave and returned to her spot at the kitchen table, staring out the glass doors leading to the backyard. Sarah had seen photos Cady had posted of a big tree being removed, a victim of the emerald ash borer beetle. Once the tree was gone and the remains of the stump ground down, Josh had decided to start fresh with new landscaping. Cady had commented, *I don't think anything has been done to the yard since the house was built in the '50s.* They were halfway through the process when they got the news about the trip. The landscapers could have kept going, of course, but that's not how the Caldwells operated. They were such perfectionists that they wanted to be there to oversee things. So the project was put on hold and the yard was now a mess. The old grass had been scraped off and piles of dirt dotted the edges of the property.

To Sarah it looked perfect.

After having toured every room in the house, she decided to head out to the garage to check out what really mattered.

FOUR

THEN

Sarah woke up and blinked. Everything hurt. It took a few moments to remember how she'd gotten there. She sized up her surroundings, noting the side rails of the bed, the ceiling tiles overhead, the television in the upper corner softly playing a news program. She was still in the hospital, but no longer in the emergency room. She had a vague recollection of having her head wound cleaned and stitched up, and getting a CT scan. Somewhat later, she had memories of being wheeled down a long corridor, but the actual end of the trip, arriving in this room, drew a blank. Not being able to account for every minute was alarming.

It was only after she shifted her head and saw Kirk in the chair next to the bed that her fears were put to rest. Her husband was here, which meant her ordeal wasn't hers to bear alone.

When he realized she was conscious, his eyes widened, and he leaned forward in excitement. "Oh, baby, it's so good to see you awake. How're you feeling?" His hair, usually neatly combed, stuck up at odd angles. She imagined him running his fingers through it, the way he did when nervous.

"I've been better." She grimaced. "What happened?"

He frowned. "Apparently, you were hit on the head. Hard."

She tried to process the words, but couldn't make sense of them. "I got hit by something?"

"Yes." Kirk gave her hand a gentle squeeze. "The police were here a minute ago. They're coming back in a little bit to ask you a few questions. Is that okay?"

She nodded and closed her eyes, opening them a few minutes later when a doctor entered followed by a gaggle of young people in white lab jackets. He said, "Mrs. Aden, do you mind if the students observe while I ask a few questions and examine you?"

"No, I don't mind."

He turned to the group. "Sarah Aden is twenty-nine years old and was brought in by ambulance yesterday with a head injury." He went on from there, pointing out her vitals on the monitor and explaining that her CT scan showed a hairline crack on her skull.

A cracked skull. That explained the spiky ball of pain bouncing around in her brain.

From there he changed his focus to Sarah. He asked her to do a few simple tasks. She was able to follow the doctor's moving finger with her eyes and squeeze his hands. She could count and add, and knew her address and where she worked. When they asked who the gentleman was sitting next to her, she was able to say, "My husband, Kirk Aden."

Kirk's eyes lit up with love when she rattled off the date of their anniversary and both their birthdays. She noticed then how worried he looked. Behind his glasses, his blue-gray eyes were marked with concern.

"That's my girl," he said, reaching over to caress the knuckles of her hand.

Sarah seemed to remember everything, except what had happened to put her in the hospital. As the doctor and his entourage left the room, Kirk called out, "Thank you."

The exchange with the doctor, easy as it was, left her exhausted. She closed her eyes again, and didn't wake until the police arrived an hour or so later. After they introduced themselves, giving names that didn't stick in her head, she answered their questions as best she could. "I remember that it was windy. Really windy." She thought hard, remembering the howling, and the way the trees in their backyard swayed, the branches of the willow actually whipping back and forth. She'd noticed that the patio table umbrella was open, which was odd, since they'd always kept it closed except when it was in use. She knew it had to be closed before the whole thing blew over. "I had just gotten home from work and was in the kitchen when I noticed the patio table umbrella was open. My husband was in the garage, I think?" It was so hard to remember.

Kirk leaned over. "No, honey, I had to work late that night, remember?" He turned his attention to the detectives. "I own the Aden Luxury Car dealership, so my hours vary. I was delayed because I'd been wrapping up some paperwork in my office."

"You were late that night?" Sarah asked.

"I sent you a text, remember?"

A text. The fog in her head cleared long enough for her to recall the ping of her phone. He *had* sent a text. It had come in around the time he usually arrived home. *Lost track of time. Will be home soon.* That's right. He hadn't been home yet, which was why the chore of closing the umbrella had fallen to her. The table and chairs were new, a top-of-the-line set. The umbrella had a solar panel on top, which powered the lights on the underside. If it had gotten ruined, it would have been a shame. More than a shame really. They'd both been excited about getting it. Sarah had anticipated sitting outdoors after work together, drinking wine and sharing the events of the day. When it was delivered she'd told Kirk, "We can shut out the world and just enjoy each other's company."

"I went outside to close the umbrella," she said slowly. She remembered a gust of wind had caught the screen door. In her mind, she heard the crack when it slammed behind her. The sky had been angry, with dark clouds that blocked the sun, which had made it seem later than it was. Usually, at that time of year, it was light outside until seven or so. "It was so windy," she repeated. Judging by the faces of the two police detectives, she sensed this wasn't what they wanted to hear. "I started to close the umbrella . . . I had some trouble with the crank."

Her pause was long enough that one of the detectives, a young woman with sharp features, prompted her, "And then what happened?"

"I don't know," Sarah finally admitted. "I heard the dog next door barking and I went to go see what he was going on about. Then I felt a terrible pain in the back of my head. And that's all I know." Calling it a terrible pain was an understatement.

"Did you see anyone?" the male detective asked. "Anyone at all?" He was the older of the two, bald with dark-rimmed glasses.

"No." She shook her head slightly. "It was really windy."

"Okay, it was windy," the male detective said patiently. "That we know. But someone else was there. Did you notice anything different in the house or the yard when you came home from work that evening?"

"I don't think so." Sarah saw them exchange a glance and felt as if she'd let them down. "Everything was the same as usual."

The woman detective asked, "Did you hear anything outside? Footsteps, maybe?"

"No."

"Any problems with neighbors or anyone at work? Friends, family members? Any disputes or fights?"

She'd thrown so many questions at her at once that it took all of Sarah's concentration to think it through. "No problems. No disputes," she said finally. "Why are you asking all these questions?"

"Just standard procedure." Her tone was reassuring. "We wouldn't be doing our job if we didn't ask."

Her partner asked, "Has anyone made any threats recently?"

She started to shake her head, then remembered something.

"In our mailbox," she said. "I got an odd note once. It was unsigned."

"It was more than once," Kirk chimed in hurriedly. "It happened four times. And on one occasion someone left a dead rat on our porch."

Four notes and a dead rat? Sarah had no recollection of a dead rat and she only remembered one note. She'd found it in their mailbox. The outside of the envelope was unmarked. Inside was a plain piece of white paper with capital letters scribbled in marker. It said:

I KNOW WHAT YOU DID. HOW CAN YOU LIVE
WITH YOURSELF?

Reading the words had taken her breath away. She couldn't even imagine what this referred to. The person who wrote these words was clearly confused and meant the note for someone else.

The woman detective's brow furrowed. "What did the notes say?"

"They were crazy," Kirk said. "Talking about how the truth will come out and people will know what you did. We couldn't make sense of it."

"There were four of them?" Sarah asked. She closed her eyes, trying to think.

"Four in all, yes." Kirk took off his glasses and gave them a polish.

The male detective asked, "Can we see them?"

"I handed them over to the police," Kirk said. "Chief Kramer is a friend of mine. He handled it personally." He restored the glasses to his face and took Sarah's hand.

The detective nodded. "How long ago was this?"

"About a year ago. We got them every few weeks and then

it just stopped. Gavin didn't think it was anything serious. He thought that it was probably just neighborhood kids with nothing better to do. Either that or an unhappy customer from my car dealership." Kirk smiled ruefully.

"We'll look at the notes as part of the investigation."

The lady detective jumped in with another question. "How about your job? Is anything happening at work that might seem contentious?"

"No," Sarah said. "I do marketing for Garden Design Landscaping. There're only eight of us and we all get along. We're friends."

"If we want to follow up, who would we talk to at your office?" She had a sympathetic tilt to her head.

Sarah closed her eyes and thought. "My boss, Brenda. Or my friend Clarice. Either one." She was on good terms with all of her co-workers, in fact, she'd often mentioned to Kirk how amazingly drama-free it was at her office. She was particularly close to Clarice, who served as the liaison between clients and the work crews. Clarice was a bright light, always bringing in treats and telling juicy gossip about some of their wealthier clients. The two of them had gone out to lunch the previous Saturday. Sarah hadn't laughed so much in years.

"What about family members?" the male detective asked.

Kirk said, "Sarah doesn't have much in the way of family. Her parents are both dead. But she gets along great with her cousins and sister. They all live on the East Coast. And my family adores her."

The detective nodded. "You didn't recognize the handwriting on the notes?"

"No." Sarah closed her eyes. "I only saw the one note. All I remember is that it was written in marker in capital letters. I don't know about any other notes but that one."

Kirk said, "My wife is very tired." His voice had lost its softness. "Can we resume this later?" He was so protective of her. They'd been married for three years, and his devotion had never wavered. Sarah's friends were in awe of the way he still ran around to open the car door for her, and sent flowers on the seventeenth of each month, to commemorate the day they'd met.

"I am really tired," she said, shooting Kirk a grateful look. "I can barely keep my eyes open. And my head is killing me."

Kirk said, "You should probably go now. My wife needs to rest."

The female detective pulled out a business card and handed it to Sarah. "If you think of anything else, anything at all, give me a call." The wording was right out of a TV show or movie.

Through bleary eyes, Sarah read the card, taking in the woman's name. Erin Nolan. Easy to remember under normal circumstances, but given what she was going through, the card was a good idea. "Thank you."

After they were gone, Kirk grinned and said, "I thought they'd never leave." A joke to make her smile, but she wasn't up to it. He stood and adjusted her covers, then stroked her cheek with his knuckles. "Don't worry about anything, honey. I'm not leaving your side for even a minute."

She closed her eyes, giving in to the fatigue. One final question came to the surface—something that had been nagging at her. Sleepily, she asked, "Why were they asking all those questions?"

"To help find the person who did this to you."

Her eyes widened. She was suddenly awake. "The person who did this to me?"

"We discussed this. Don't you remember? Someone attacked you. They think that Buster's barking interrupted them."

"Someone attacked me?"

"Sarah, we talked about this an hour ago. Don't you remember?"

She shook her head. An hour ago might as well have been a lifetime ago. Between the pain and the exhaustion, she was experiencing life minute by minute.

"Buster was going nuts. He was facing our property, barking continuously. Mrs. Sullivan saw you from the second-story window and called 911. At least that's what the paramedics told me. She came across our yard and was standing over you when they arrived, and they had to send her home because she was so upset she was getting in the way."

Kirk had never cared for Mrs. Sullivan. After they'd first met her, he'd said her high-pitched voice put him on edge. He continued, "I came home right after that. The cops said you were hit on the head with a solid object, possibly a rock."

"A rock?" Sarah couldn't make sense of this. She reached up to the back of her head, which was covered with some kind of wrapping. "It was windy. Maybe something blew into me." She imagined a broken tree limb flying through the air, or maybe a lawn ornament, one of those reflecting balls that Kirk thought were so tacky.

"No, they didn't find anything like that. They think you were deliberately struck with a hard, heavy object."

"I don't understand."

"I don't understand why someone would do this either," he said sympathetically. "You're the best person I know. Whoever did this to you has to be a lunatic." He gave her a sad smile.

Sarah tried to make sense of this, but couldn't. Their yard was enormous, with a wrought-iron fence, and although the gate was never locked, they'd never had anyone trespass. The neighboring lots were close by, but not easily visible. The previous owner of their house had planted rows of arborvitae on each side, which covered the fence and screened them from the neighbors.

She didn't have any reason to worry about anyone attacking her. She had no enemies. Everyone at work was friendly. It wasn't like she was the subject of jealousy or resentment. "Are the police sure that's how it happened?"

Kirk nodded. "They're treating it as a crime, so they must be sure. Why? What are you thinking?"

"I can't believe someone would do that," she said. "Maybe I had a brain aneurysm?" It was the only thing that explained the feeling of her head imploding, followed by losing consciousness.

"No," Kirk said. "The wound was on the outside, babe. This was definitely done to you."

"But why would someone do that?"

"I don't know." He shook his head. "You don't have to think about that now. The police will handle it. Just get some sleep."

"Maybe just for a little bit." She closed her eyes and felt herself begin to drift away.

The last thing she heard was Kirk saying, his voice cracking, "Can you imagine how horrible it would have been for me if I'd lost you? Sarah, I hope you know that you're my everything."

FIVE

HER

You know how sometimes you run into someone you haven't seen for a long time and the sight of them healthy and happy brings joy to your heart? Well, the time I saw Kirk Aden out to dinner with his fiancée was nothing like that. I hadn't seen the guy for a few years, so spotting him, dressed in an expensive suit and looking better than ever, was a complete shock. I watched as he sat at the white-linen-covered table with his date, a lovely young woman, the two of them drinking wine. She appeared content and happy, while he looked full of life and pleased with himself. A dagger to my heart. To think he could have caused so much pain, and still attain such happiness? Believe me, I was fuming more and more with each passing minute. It wasn't just his success—it was also how much he imposed himself on others, as if his existence was more important than anyone else's. When he ordered, he spent a lot of time discussing his options with the waiter, like he was the only customer in the place and the server had all the time in the world.

Selfish. So very selfish. Of course that was the least of his faults.

I didn't know that the woman was his fiancée at the time, but

I couldn't help but notice she appeared much younger than him and out of his league. I found out later that her name was Sarah and that she wasn't from around here. That night she wore a floral wrap dress. Her curly hair was left natural, falling in waves around her shoulders, and she wore silver hoop earrings. She had a sweet look and seemed enamored of him, resting her hand on his arm, laughing at what had to be lame jokes.

He hadn't changed much—still had wire-rim glasses and uncooperative hair. When he saw me staring, he looked away sheepishly like he'd been caught doing something wrong, and nervously ran his fingers over his scalp. Good. I was glad I made him uncomfortable.

That evening my mother and I were dining at the same restaurant, a fancy establishment called Golden. We were celebrating her birthday, and dinner was on me, a considerable expense for someone with my salary. For Kirk Aden, though, dinner at Golden was just a drop in the bucket. Life had been good to Kirk. In high school, he'd lived in a standard 1950s home on Palmer Street and his family was nothing special. If anything, having just the one child made the Adens seem a little incomplete. At least in my eyes.

When I read in the news about his parents becoming suddenly wealthy, I was livid. It wasn't even something they'd earned. Bert Aden had bankrolled the development of various medical devices, one of which grew in value until it was worth millions. So it wasn't him. Some other dude had the brains to develop this thing and Bert and Judy got rich just by being nearby when it happened. The Adens: one minute they were middle-class suburbanites, the next they were multi-millionaires. What the hell? Why do some people go through life with problems and tragedies, while others less deserving wander into good fortune, served on a platter? I know the answer, of course. Life isn't fair. Still, it made my blood boil.

When Kirk opened his dealership, a luxury car dealership

no less, I could have spit flames. There's no way Kirk came up with the funds or the game plan to pull that one off. His parents had to have supplied the financial backing. It wasn't the money that irked me, though, it was the acquired status. After so many years of being Gavin Kramer's sidekick, he finally one-upped him, and everyone else for that matter. Now while Gavin was the local chief of police, Kirk was socializing with the elite, employing dozens of people, and making major bank with minimal effort. Not to mention driving the best-performing, most expensive automobiles. Not my thing really, but I know that's important to a lot of people. I was sure he was a great boss, guiding his team so they could be the best version of themselves and being supportive when they needed time off due to family problems or whatever. Blah, blah, blah. He was always good at blowing smoke.

Everyone always loved Kirk.

If I sound bitter, it's because I am.

I was sure Kirk's successful business made Gavin angry too. He wasn't the kind of friend who would be happy at someone else's good fortune. We had that in common anyway. No, Gavin had to be secretly seething. On the surface, though, he'd be all "so happy for you," and "couldn't happen to a nicer guy," when actually he was hoping Kirk's business would fail. Gavin was as two-faced as they came.

When we finished our meal at the restaurant that evening, Mom wanted to head out, but Kirk and his date had just been served dinner, so I said, "What's the rush? It's your birthday!" I flagged down the server, the same poor man who'd had to hear Kirk prattle on about the wine list, and told him it was my mother's birthday and we wanted to order dessert and coffee. When they brought out her flan, it had a lit candle in it, which delighted her. The staff didn't circle the table and sing, though, because this wasn't Applebee's, but a fancy restaurant. Or more accurately, and this is according to their website, "a unique, upscale dining experience."

We lingered over coffee, Mom telling me repeatedly how much she appreciated the birthday outing, that it wasn't necessary, but so thoughtful of me. My mother had gotten more than her share of misery in her life, and so I tried to make it up to her. She had a philosophy of "live and let live," which made her the better of the two of us. She always gave everyone the benefit of the doubt. It was her most admirable attribute, but also her biggest shortcoming. "I don't know what I'd do without you," she said, sighing and patting my hand. Since my dad died, it had been just the two of us. "You're the best daughter. Thank you for this lovely dinner. I'm so grateful. I believe I will feast on this memory for months."

Those statements illustrated my mom perfectly. She was the kind of woman who feasted on memories and was grateful for everything. Just a good soul. She volunteered at our church and gave out sincere compliments. Once, I heard her tell a homeless man that she liked his backpack. "Very colorful!" Mom had exclaimed, making him smile. When she said she'd pray for someone, she actually did. In fact, she prayed twice as much, to make up for those who promised to pray, then promptly forgot. Like me.

I took her hand. "You don't need to thank me, Mom. It was my pleasure." Seeing her face light up with a smile was its own reward.

I knew Kirk and his date would have to come past us when they left and I lucked out that the row farthest from our table was blocked by a waiter carrying a large tray, forcing him to walk right by us. He didn't make eye contact, of course, but I wasn't going to let him off the hook. Right as they approached, I called out, "Kirk! Kirk Aden! Imagine seeing you here." I hadn't realized how hushed the conversation in the restaurant was until my own voice rang out, drawing attention to me.

His face flushed red, and I saw it in his eyes—there's no way you can disguise guilt, not when a reminder of your crime is staring you in the face. The moment passed and he managed to say,

"Hi, nice seeing you." His lady friend paused, but he took her by the elbow and they continued on.

I watched him go, willing my eyes to bore two holes into his back. How dare he go about his life, blissfully happy while I sat here, still stuck in the past? I turned to Mom. "Notice how he couldn't even stop to exchange pleasantries? What does that tell you?"

She said, "You can't make assumptions. Maybe they had somewhere they had to be." Which was so like her, making excuses for deplorable human beings. Mom couldn't help herself; she was just too good.

"Too busy to talk for two minutes?" I raised my eyebrows.

"It's been a long time," she'd said gently. "Maybe you need to let it go for your own peace of mind."

I didn't want to upset her, so I let it drop, but that was the moment that I decided that since life wasn't fair, it was up to me to even things out. Enough already.

SIX

THEN

Exhausted from talking to the police and the doctor, Sarah was only vaguely aware of the staff coming and going, checking her vital signs, and talking among themselves. She could barely open her eyes. When they asked questions, she could nod or manage a word or two. For the most part, she slept.

The next morning, she woke to find Kirk by her side. He hadn't been there during the night, so his appearance was like a welcome magic trick. "You're here," she murmured.

"Of course I'm here," he said. "Where else would I be?" He stood up and gently kissed her cheek. "I love you, Sarah."

"Love you too." Sarah returned his smile, glad to see he looked less distraught than the day before. Despite being ten years older than her, Kirk had a boyish look she'd always found appealing. He had a slender build and was only a few inches taller than herself. His thick brown hair had two modes. It was either combed like a fourth grader on picture day or disheveled from his nervous gesture of running his fingers through it. His glasses were forever sliding down his nose, and even when they weren't, he pushed them upward out of habit. On their first date, he talked too much and too quickly, coming off as nervous and trying to impress her. This, despite owning and successfully running a large business.

Kirk was a contradiction that way. Outwardly confident, but inwardly always doubting himself.

Later, she found out that his anxiety was real and could be debilitating. He took a prescription medication that would periodically require tweaking. Sarah had never known anyone so troubled or so honest about their fears and worries. At his worst, he didn't want to get into elevators that were too crowded. During heavy snowfalls he'd asked if she minded driving. During evening thunderstorms he'd sometimes retreat to the bedroom and crawl under their weighted blanket. But he usually returned from his monthly visits to his psychiatrist as if a load had been lifted. And somehow he managed to run the dealership and be a good husband, all the while putting on a good front for everyone else in the world. Only she and his parents were privy to his anxieties. He opened his soul to her, which was no small thing.

Once, she asked him to explain how it was to live with depression. He sighed and said, "There are times I can feel it building. Other times, it just arrives unexpected. I wake up and it's like I'm encased in sadness and my arms are pinned to my sides. Sometimes it takes everything I have to psych myself into doing the simplest things. I really hate being this way."

His dark moods lifted after Sarah came into his life. His parents noticed it, and his mom, Judy, had taken Sarah aside to tell her as much.

Very often Sarah caught Kirk looking at her, regarding her with incredulity. "How did I get so lucky?" he'd say, shaking his head. When he said things like that, she could actually feel his love washing over her like a wave.

There were long stretches where she forgot all about his anxiety, times where nothing bothered him. They talked and laughed and made plans for the future. Being with Kirk was effortless.

Of course there were times when he became furious over the smallest things. Bird droppings on his car. Employees who didn't show up on time. Rude drivers. Once during their dating days, they'd been on the expressway heading to a nice restaurant when a pickup truck cut off their car, forcing Kirk to slam on the brakes. In a flash, his face darkened in rage. He'd pointed and said, "Someone should kill that guy." Sarah had been shocked at how her mild-mannered boyfriend had transformed into someone menacing. Just as quickly, though, he calmed down and apologized for his outburst. Sarah told herself that he was entitled to be frustrated on occasion. It happened infrequently and was never aimed at her. To his credit, Kirk claimed it as one of his shortcomings and told her he was working on it. She understood. No one was perfect.

Her sister, Maren, had advised her not to marry him. "His problems will become your problems. There are lots of other guys out there. Find someone else, someone who doesn't have mental health issues."

"Everyone has something. Besides, lots of people have depression and manage it just fine." What she didn't tell Maren was that she herself had gone for grief counseling after her previous boyfriend's unexpected death. Maren prided herself on being tough. She'd never have understood. "I actually admire that he acknowledges his depression and anxiety and is facing it head-on."

Maren had shrugged then. "It's your life."

She'd responded, "The heart wants what the heart wants." Emily Dickinson had said something similar back in her time, and it was as true now as it was then.

The idea of finding another guy was unthinkable. There was no one like Kirk. He was genuine and he really listened when she talked, something she found wasn't the case with other men she'd dated. When they weren't together, she missed him so profoundly that she physically ached.

If Maren could see Kirk sitting next to her hospital bed right now, his adoration and concern fully on display, she'd understand. A person couldn't fake that kind of love.

Sarah was eating her hospital breakfast, a cheese omelet with orange juice, when someone rapped on the door. A man's voice called, "Hello?" and Kirk responded, "Come in." When she saw it was Gavin Kramer, in his police chief uniform, she gave him a smile.

Kirk got up and gestured to him to take his chair, but Gavin shook his head and stood bedside. "I can't stay long, but I wanted to see you, Sarah, and assure you that my people are doing everything we can to find whoever did this to you." Gavin's dark eyes peered at her intently.

"Thank you." She set down her fork.

"Natalie sends her love. She's visiting her mom right now, but I called her as soon as I heard. We're both devastated and outraged."

Kirk said, "We appreciate it." Despite the fact that the two men were the same age, when they stood side by side, Kirk looked like his little brother. Gavin's hair was slicked back, with gray at the temples. He was built like a lumberjack with wide shoulders, big biceps, and massive torso, while Kirk had the slight, wiry build of a man who occasionally went running, but didn't hit the gym.

Gavin reached over and gave her a pat. "I know my detectives gave you their cards, but feel free to call me directly if you prefer. Friends get special priority. You and Kirk are family to me."

"We feel the same way about you and Natalie," Kirk said, which wasn't entirely true—at least not on Sarah's part. They were Kirk's friends and she found them pleasant enough, but family? No, not at all.

She had to admit, though, that Gavin Kramer was a presence. He had a loud laugh and a way of pulling people into conversations. His signature look consisted of wraparound sunglasses, a neatly trimmed goatee, and a wide smile, revealing straight, bright white teeth. If you spent any time with him at all, you'd hear him proclaim his love for his wife, his country, and his SUV.

But despite Gavin's big personality and good looks, there had always been something about him that Sarah found off-putting. She had no reason not to like him; in fact, he and his wife, Natalie, had welcomed her into their circle of friends with open arms. But something was off and she couldn't quite work it out. Maybe it was the way they always insisted on having dinner at their house, but found excuses not to come to Kirk and Sarah's. Or the way Gavin had of bragging about his exploits, his most recent golf game, a big arrest at work, the woman brought in for questioning who blatantly hit on him even though, he said, she was under suspicion of burglary and he was happily married. He'd pulled Natalie into a hug after saying this. "When a man comes home to a woman like this, all others pale in comparison."

Natalie had rolled her eyes and leaned in toward Sarah. "Don't believe a word he says."

Gavin told countless stories, all of them for entertainment value, and he had a killer sense of humor. Despite herself, Sarah found herself laughing. He told jokes too and did impressions. People remembered Gavin. Of the two high school friends, Kirk might have turned out to be a bigger financial success, but when it came to having standing in the community and important connections, Gavin had him beat.

The man also had a fondness for things—oddities and collectibles. During her first visit to their house, while his wife was getting the table ready for dinner, he'd insisted on showing Sarah all the treasures located in his den. Kirk had unenthusiastically followed them down the stairs to the lower level. "I'm not sure this is Sarah's kind of thing," he'd said.

"She's going to go crazy when she sees." Gavin's tone was firm. "Everyone does."

The room, with its black-and-white motif, large-screen TV, and leather furniture, had a man-cave vibe. What made it unique were the items he kept displayed in glass cabinets and framed shadow boxes. She was taken aback at the shrunken head and the display of white mice dressed in clothing and arranged as if they were playing a miniature round of golf. "The magic of taxidermy," he'd said, proudly showing it to her. Some of the items he'd gotten during their travels, but he also came across things at estate sales and antique shops.

One wall was covered with weaponry: antique firearms and numerous swords. Taking in the display, she said, "Looks like an entire fleet of ninjas could battle it out here."

Gavin took her comment as encouragement and went around, telling her about each item. Everything had a story. One antique pistol he'd gotten after a bidding war with another guy. "A real yokel," he'd said. "Right off the farm, but not stupid. He clearly knew the value of the piece. It's one of a kind. He desperately wanted it, but I got it." He grinned.

Kirk must have sensed her boredom because he said, "Shouldn't we be heading back upstairs? Natalie must be ready with dinner by now."

"She'll call us when it's time, believe me," Gavin said with a wave of his hand. He kept going, ignoring Kirk and focusing on Sarah. Even though they'd barely known each other at that point, he was overly familiar, resting his hand on the small of her back and leaning in close when making a point. She could see the whiskers on his face and smell breath mints as he spoke.

Because Gavin was Kirk's best friend, she ignored her unease, making sure to smile and exclaim over every piece. Still, she was relieved when they'd gotten to the last one, a black-framed shadow box holding a silver knife.

"And this one?" she'd asked lightly. "Did it belong to Julius Caesar?"

"I can smell dinner," Kirk said before she got her answer. "Shall we go up?" He made a point to take hold of her hand, as if reclaiming her.

"I am hungry," Sarah said, turning to Gavin. "And Kirk has raved about Natalie's cooking."

"In a minute," Gavin said. "I need to tell you about this knife because it's my favorite."

"Oh, man," Kirk groaned. "Can't you see that Sarah is bored? Give her a break."

Sarah felt her cheeks flush in embarrassment. "No, no, it's fine," she assured him. "I'm finding this all very interesting. Tell me about the knife."

"It wasn't owned by Julius Caesar," Gavin said with a laugh, "but it's still very special. It's a machete made from Damascus steel."

She leaned in to take a closer look. "I don't think I've ever heard of that kind of steel."

"You can tell it's made with Damascus steel by the wavy light-and-dark patterns in the metal. See?" Gavin pointed. "Besides being beautiful, it maintains its razor-sharp edge. It's superior to weapons forged from iron. Both hard and flexible." He raised one eyebrow.

"Nice."

"The handle is decorated with espresso wood and held in place with brass pins. Very unique."

"Let me guess," Sarah had said. "This piece is one of a kind and someone else wanted it, but you got it?"

Gavin nodded, a smile stretching across his face. "Correct." He turned to Kirk. "She catches on quickly. Pretty soon she'll know all your secrets."

Sarah thought she'd caught a flash of irritation cross Kirk's face, but it was gone in an instant. Perhaps she'd misread him. "Time to go upstairs," Kirk had said, gently pulling on her hand. At the time she'd wondered if Gavin was needling Kirk by trying to hit on her. Kirk had never struck her as competitive, but Gavin definitely had a superior air to him.

The rest of the evening was so lovely that it made up for the awkward beginning. Natalie's beef Wellington was delicious. The wine flowed and the conversation, punctuated with a lot of laughter, was light and easy. On the way home, she'd asked Kirk if there had been tension during the tour of Gavin's collectibles, and he'd shrugged and said, "Gavin gets a bit full of himself at times. You were being a good sport about it, but I could tell he was getting tiresome."

"I didn't mind," she'd said, and that was the last they spoke of it. After that, the two couples got together every few months. She grew to enjoy their company, even if neither Natalie nor Gavin was the type she'd have befriended otherwise.

Seeing him now, at the hospital, gave Sarah a new appreciation for Gavin. As he and Kirk talked about her injury and what had transpired since, she thought she saw Gavin blink away tears. He said, "I promise you, Sarah, that we will not stop until we find the person who did this to you." He leaned over and smoothed her blanket. "You just work on recovering. I'll take care of keeping you safe and getting you justice."

"Thank you," she'd murmured, feeling a surge of warmth toward Gavin. Yes, he could be full of himself, but he was Kirk's oldest and closest friend, so clearly he had his good qualities.

Maybe she hadn't given him enough credit.

SEVEN

Clarice opened the door to her apartment, a smile crossing her face. "Chief Kramer, how unexpected! Do come in." She waved him inside. "And in uniform too. My, my, this looks official. To what do I owe the visit?" She didn't wait for him to answer, but beckoned, then turned and went into the kitchen, hips swaying as she walked. To Clarice the world was a stage and she was the star of the show.

He followed her, watching as she took two tumblers out of the cabinet, then filled them with ice. Typical of Clarice to start everything with a strong drink. The last time he'd visited her, he'd come home smelling like a distillery. After leaving her place, he realized that no amount of gum-chewing or mouthwash would obliterate the odor. It was actually oozing out of his pores, the smell so pervasive he'd had to tell Natalie that one of the guys at work had gotten engaged and he'd stopped at a bar for happy hour to celebrate with the gang. This was completely out of character. He had a policy of never socializing with his guys, something Natalie knew, but she accepted the story without question. No guarantee he'd be that lucky again. He'd vowed to be more careful in the future.

"Take a seat," she said, gesturing to the bar stools at the island. "Whisky or gin?"

"None for me," he said gruffly.

"You don't want a drink?" Without waiting for a response, she got down a bottle of Jim Beam and poured two fingers into a glass. "More for me, then."

"Actually, I'm here on police business."

"Really?" She raised her eyebrows. "And what would that be?"

He fished in his pocket and pulled out a silver hoop earring set with alternating sapphires and diamonds and slid it across the counter. "I believe you lost this?" Now he was the one with the raised eyebrows, deliberately mimicking her facial expression.

"You darling man!" she exclaimed, picking it up and holding it in her palm. "I never thought I'd see this again. Wherever did you find it?"

"Funny story," he said, leaning against the counter. "I was at a crime scene. Kirk Aden's wife was attacked in their backyard. This earring was on the ground near where the first responders found her lying unconscious. You know anything about that?"

"Sarah was attacked? Oh no! What happened?" She set the earring on the counter and covered her mouth with her hand.

"You tell me, Clarice. Seeing as you were there, I think you'd know best."

"I was there?" She frowned, forehead wrinkling. "I'm sorry, what?"

"Oh, come on." He pulled out a bar stool and took a seat. "This is me you're talking to, Clarice. I just covered for you"—he pointed to the earring—"and now I'm here giving you incriminating evidence. You might as well tell me the whole story."

"What exactly are you implying? Sarah is my friend."

"That doesn't mean much. I know how you tend to cycle through friends."

She frowned. "What happened to Sarah?"

"Someone hit her in the head with a rock and knocked her unconscious," Gavin said, his eyes narrowing. "Kirk told me that the doctor said it could have been worse. She'll probably come out of this just fine."

"Oh, what a relief." Her hand went to her heart. "I'll have to organize something at the office. We'll send flowers. And maybe a fruit basket." She took a sip of her drink and looked up to see Gavin staring at her. "What?"

"You seem pretty nonplussed considering your friend was attacked."

She shrugged. "Kirk is with her and you said she's fine. Plus, you're on the case. It sounds like she's in very good hands."

Gavin tilted his head and gave her an appraising look. He'd been so certain of her guilt, but now he didn't know what to think. "I don't believe you answered the question. How is it that your earring wound up in Sarah's backyard?"

"I must have lost it when I was at her house, visiting."

"I talked to Kirk at length. He never mentioned that you'd visited."

Clarice folded her arms. "Sarah and I went out to lunch last Saturday and I drove. Kirk wasn't home when I got to their house, but she invited me in and showed me the new patio set before we left for the restaurant, so I was in their backyard. Come to think of it, I noticed the earring was missing later that afternoon."

"Can anyone back that up?"

She laughed. "Back up that I lost an earring? I doubt it. But Sarah can vouch for everything else."

"Sarah's a little confused right now, so I've been talking to Kirk."

"Like I said, Kirk wasn't home. Maybe he didn't know we went out to lunch."

"You know better than that. You know how fixated he is on Sarah. There's no way she did something he didn't know about."

Clarice scoffed. "I don't pretend to understand you married people. I have no idea what she told him. But I can tell you we had a fabulous lunch over at Café Vin. I actually got Sarah to order a glass of wine, believe it or not. The service was outstanding." She ran a finger around the edge of her glass. "We had this hot waiter, Cole, who was most attentive. And Sarah and I had the best conversation. She actually got the giggles, which made me start laughing. You should have seen the two of us. An old woman actually stopped by our table to tell us that hearing our laughter brightened her day. We had so much fun."

"Sounds like quite the lunch."

"It was." She smiled. "If you ever go to Café Vin, I recommend the poulet Breton."

"I'll keep that in mind," Gavin said and sighed. Clarice was a piece of work. She still thought of herself as a head-turning beauty, but under the pendant lights hanging over the kitchen island, he had a more accurate view. The lines around her eyes were prominent, and her eyeliner created dark slashes against her pale skin. His mental image of her had always been that of the popular girl in high school, all fresh-faced and dewy-eyed, but time had passed, and her drinking, cigarette habit, and occasional pot smoking had taken its toll. Of course they'd all gotten older, he just didn't notice it most of the time, least of all in himself. With Clarice, though, life had been a wild ride and it showed clearly on her face. He said, "I'm going to let this go now, Clarice, but you should know that no one saw the earring but me and I also got rid of the incriminating rock."

She set the glass down. "I appreciate getting the earring back, so thank you for that, but I have no idea why you'd get rid of an incriminating rock. Just out of curiosity, why would you think I'd hurt my friend?"

"Because of your fixation on Kirk."

"My fixation on Kirk?" She shook her head and gave him a

sad smile. "We had a thing years ago, but once he met Sarah, I cut him off. Frankly, I find Kirk and all his moods to be really tiring. Sarah's got her hands full with that one."

Gavin's years in law enforcement had brought him into close contact with a fair number of criminals seemingly without a conscience. Earlier in his career, when he'd worked in a big city, he found himself driven to even out the odds. One criminal, an asshat named Blake Starkey, looked good for the murder of his girlfriend, but he was one cool customer and wasn't giving anything up. They didn't have concrete evidence to pin on him, so Gavin had to exert some force to get a confession out of the guy. Not his finest moment, but it got the job done. The expression on Clarice's face reminded him of Starkey's when he'd been sure he was going to get away with it. Confident, smug.

Starkey's confession had been a defining moment in his relationship with his dad, who, upon hearing the news, gave him a rare compliment. "Well done, son," he'd said, nodding approvingly. "I'm proud of you." Gavin had waited a long time to hear those words. Before then his father had made it clear that he thought Gavin had fallen short in so many ways. For one thing, his dad hadn't approved of his friendships in high school, saying, "Why are you hanging around those losers? You can do better." But Gavin hadn't believed that to be the case. Besides, he was the king of these losers and what could be better than that? If his dad was still alive, he'd probably be disappointed that Gavin still socialized with Kirk and Clarice, but old habits were hard to break.

Giving Clarice a steely eye, Gavin asked, "So you don't have any interest in hooking up with Kirk?"

"God, no. There's a whole world of men out there. Trust me, Kirk Aden isn't even on my radar anymore. I'm too busy looking for new conquests."

That part had a ring of truth to it. He'd never known a time when Clarice hadn't landed on her feet. In her early twenties, she'd romanced an older man, a widower with no children, and when he died a year later, she'd inherited his entire estate. She'd certainly played that one right. If he was certain of anything, it was that Clarice took care of Clarice.

She gestured to her empty glass. "Looks like I need to top this one up. Are you sure you won't join me in a drink?"

Grudgingly he said, "Maybe just one."

EIGHT

NOW

The garage, a standard two-car, wasn't especially spacious, which was typical for a house built during the 1950s. Josh's Audi was parked on one side of it, leaving Sarah to think they'd driven Cady's Jeep to the airport. The space was sparse and clean. The side wall was well organized, with one long shelf holding a red metal toolbox and a plastic sprinkler. Hooks below it supported gardening equipment: hedge trimmers, shovels, a hoe, and two rakes, one for cultivating, the other for gathering leaves. An electric lawn mower, the kind that used a rechargeable battery, stood in one corner, but it was the pickax alongside it that was the real find.

Sarah gave the pickax the once-over before lifting it up. It was heavy, which was good. With the backyard dirt already loosened by the landscapers, and a pickax with this kind of heft, she should be able to do some serious digging.

Yes, the pickax would do just fine.

If she'd been thinking clearly, she'd have brought one along, just in case the Caldwells didn't own one. She'd given so much thought to everything else, but oddly enough, overlooked that one important detail. Well, no matter. She had what she needed.

Sarah went back inside, where she found herself at loose ends. She walked through the house, mulling over everything that had happened since her injury six months before. Sarah's body had recovered completely since then; the back of her head had healed nicely and the headaches had stopped. Her emotional state, though, that was another story. She'd lost her confidence and there were times when she thought she'd lost her mind. She'd taken so much time off work that they'd hired a temporary replacement. When it came time for her to return, Kirk had talked her out of it. He was a persuasive man, born to make friends and win people over. When they'd met, she'd thought he was a nice counterpart to her own shy personality. All of his arguments regarding an extended stay at home made sense, and at that point she was starting to doubt her own mental capacity. It would be awful to not be able to keep up at her job, to let her boss and co-workers down. Why not take a year or two and wait until she was really ready? It was hard to say no to that.

So she gave her notice, which made her replacement, a young woman with school-aged kids, very happy. Everyone in the office said they understood. Even her best office buddy, Clarice, had taken the news well, saying, "I'll miss you, Sarah, but I'm happy you can stay home to recover. Kirk told us how hard it's been for both of you." Her boss had said she was welcome back anytime, that if they had an opening, it was automatically hers.

Without her job, she felt relieved but adrift. Not counting brief conversations with neighbors and various store clerks, the only outside contact she'd had was with her physical therapist. Kirk was there for her, though, every step of the way.

It had taken months, but eventually she'd found herself again. An epiphany had dawned on her one day when she realized how dependent on Kirk she'd become, something he seemed to relish. In time, his assumption of her neediness had made her less trusting and suspicious of him. She found herself assessing everything Kirk said and did, until she was so turned around she didn't know what was real anymore. Once she'd come up with the idea to dig into his past, she made a plan, and having a plan gave her a sense of purpose. It was definitely a crazy idea, but Phil, while not entirely on board, agreed to help. Sometimes all you needed was one person to have your back.

She watched TV for about an hour before losing interest, then scanned the bookshelves looking at the novels that belonged to Cady. She knew Cady belonged to a book club, a group made up of the ladies in the neighborhood. They called themselves The Book Sisters, and joked that they spent less time discussing the book than visiting with each other. *It's more of a wine club*, one of the women commented on a photo of the group. Another had added, *But that's fine with me!*

It was only midday. The sun would be out for hours now, giving her time to see if The Book Sisters' last selection, a novel called *The Snow Child*, lived up to the hype. It was the only book that all the neighborhood women had enjoyed, which was no small thing.

Still, Sarah was through with taking other people's word for things. She'd decide for herself.

Settling down on the couch with the book, she took a look around the room. Cady's house was so Cady. Everything—the photos, the furniture, the brightly covered wall hangings—was exactly as Sarah would have expected. So unlike her own home, which was perfect, but not necessarily to her taste. Kirk had wanted their home furnishings to be classic, and since she didn't have strong feelings either way, she'd gone along with his preferences. Guests always exclaimed over their decor, which confirmed his good taste. Now that she was in the Caldwell house she could see the difference.

A person could be very comfortable here.

During her stay she'd intended to make herself at home, but she wasn't going to be foolish about it. The night before, she'd slept on the couch and going forward she would continue to do so.

Sleeping in another couple's bed was too intimate. Besides, being in the living room made her feel less vulnerable. If someone came into the house while she slept, the lower level had three exits, while the upstairs only had one. She kept her backpack nearby so she could grab it quickly if need be. Ever since her injury she'd assessed every situation with safety in mind and always had an exit strategy.

Her whole life had become an exit strategy.

NINE

When Kirk came home from work that night to find Sarah gone and a note on the counter, he was dumbfounded. He stood in the kitchen, clutching the lined paper, and read it several times trying to make sense of the words.

Dear Kirk, I've decided I need some time to myself, just a little break from my usual routine, so I've taken a short vacation—just for a few days. I'll be in touch. Love, Sarah.

At first, he thought it might be a joke and he'd find her upstairs with a surprise. He even called out, "Sarah? I'm home!" as he climbed the stairs. He imagined finding her standing in the bedroom with a smile on her face, holding an early birthday present, or better yet, posed seductively on the bed, ready to give him the gift of herself. Since her injury, their sex life had dwindled down to almost nothing, but he'd been patient, knowing that she'd come around once she felt physically better.

The bedroom was empty. She'd made the bed and perfectly arranged the pillows. Everything was in place. She just wasn't there.

After searching the house, he began to think it through, methodically checking the closets, her jewelry box, and their luggage. Her bathrobe still hung on the hook in the walk-in closet, and from what he could tell, her entire wardrobe was there, looking the same as when he'd left the house that morning. Her purse was gone, but none of the luggage had been taken.

In the bathroom, nothing was amiss. Sarah hadn't taken any of their travel-sized toiletries. The drawer she used for cosmetics was perfectly organized and nothing appeared missing. This wasn't an exact indicator, though, because he knew she kept makeup basics in her everyday purse.

He went online and checked their bank account for debit card transactions and there was nothing new since she'd gone grocery shopping the day before. Sarah didn't use a credit card, so this would be her only source of money. All of the cars were parked in the garage, undisturbed. Kirk ran his fingers over his scalp, trying to make sense of this. He couldn't remember the last time they'd had a disagreement. Why would she leave him? What exactly did she need a break from?

Making it even more puzzling was her phone. When Kirk called, it went straight to voicemail. Next he tracked it, only to find it was in the top drawer of her nightstand, underneath a pair of striped fuzzy socks. He held the phone loosely in his palm, wondering why she'd leave it behind. It didn't make any sense. He thought of all the problems she'd had over the last year—the times she'd forgotten a word, or worse yet, substituted the wrong one; the occasions when she'd lost her house keys, or mixed up dates for things like doctors' appointments—and he got a cold chill up his spine. Something was seriously wrong here. She would never randomly take a little vacation, not so suddenly and especially without him.

Kirk thought back to the last few days, but couldn't come up with anything out of the ordinary happening between then and now. He'd gone to work, and come home to dinner, and they'd talked about their respective days. Granted, Sarah's days at home weren't all that thrilling, but he took an interest, like a good husband should. They had a solid marriage. Other guys complained about their wives being mentally absent, eyes on their phones, immersed in social media and texting, but Sarah was never online when he was home and only seemed to take a cursory interest in keeping up with friends and former co-workers. She used one of his old laptops, but he hadn't seen it around in a while. He went through the house, opening drawers and cabinets, looking for the laptop, but not finding it anywhere. She left her phone, but took the laptop? His sense of foreboding deepened.

He went back downstairs and paced, frantic with worry. Sarah was not the type to do things impulsively. Had she left of her own free will?

Worry gnawed at him, a claw at his throat. Why would she leave? He had a bad feeling.

When he calmed down enough to talk to someone, he settled onto the couch and called the one person who always had his back. His mother. Per usual, she answered after one ring. "Kirk!" Always so happy to hear from him. It was a shame to bring her down with his troubles, but that's what mothers were for.

"Mom, something is seriously wrong." He glanced around the living room, the blinds in each window up one third of the way, just the way Sarah kept them. From outward appearances all was perfect in his world, but inside he felt hollow.

"Oh no, Kirk. What happened?"

He poured his heart out, reading the note aloud and telling her what he'd discovered so far. "I just don't understand. This is not like her at all."

"Let's think this through," his mother said, her voice calm. "The note was definitely in her handwriting?"

He glanced down at the paper in his hand. "Yes, absolutely."

"And she was fine when you left this morning? Not upset about anything?"

"She was more than fine. She made me an omelet for breakfast and gave me a kiss before I headed out the door. We were like a married couple in a 1950s sitcom." As he'd backed the car out of the garage, she'd even stood in the open doorway and given him a wave and a smile. Nothing indicated she was planning to go on a trip. Could it have been a completely spontaneous, spur-of-the-moment decision? Possible for someone else's wife, but not for Sarah. He knew in his heart she wouldn't do such a thing. She was thoughtful and kind. Not one to just take off and leave him wondering and worrying.

"Well," his mother said, "there are a few possibilities here. It might be she really just decided she needed a getaway and wanted to be alone. Lord knows there were times I could have used a break from your dad." Kirk heard his father voice an objection in the background. "Or," she continued without acknowledging his dad's remark, "possibly it's related to her head injury."

"You always blame that." He had trouble keeping the irritation out of his voice.

"You don't need to snap at me, I'm only trying to help."

"I know. I'm sorry. It's just that the doctor said her injury wasn't that severe. It was only a hairline crack."

"I would think a cracked skull is serious enough. You've been telling me how erratic her behavior has been lately. Her moodiness, and the problems she's having with brain fog. She told me herself she's had trouble sleeping."

"I know. She told me the same thing."

"Sleep deprivation can exacerbate emotions. Ask any mother of a newborn."

He exhaled. "It's been hard on her being home during the day by herself. I thought she was getting better, though."

"The doctors did say recovery time varied from person to person."

"I know what the doctors said, Mom. You're just repeating what I told you." After a long pause, he said, "I keep thinking there's something I'm missing."

"I guess it's possible someone coerced her into leaving, either talked her into it, or threatened her somehow." After a few moments' silence, she added, "I think you should call Gavin."

This was the second time in a year that his connection with Gavin was proving to be helpful. His friend's job as the head of the local police force came as no surprise. Even as a boy Gavin talked about guns, jail, and arresting criminals, and no wonder— law enforcement was woven into his DNA. Gavin's dad had been the chief of police, and when he died unexpectedly of a heart attack at fifty-three years old, Gavin was his natural successor.

Despite a falling-out in their teen years and the occasional disagreement, their friendship had been a constant in Kirk's life. They'd been on the same sports teams all through school, went to the same college, and had been in the same fraternity. Sometimes the closeness had felt like too much, but whenever Kirk tried to ease away from the relationship, something happened to pull him back into Gavin's orbit. They had a connection impossible to explain to anyone else, and as Gavin liked to remind him, it was in Kirk's best interests to stay on his good side.

When Gavin had gotten married, Kirk was his best man. Seeing Gavin and his wife, Natalie, standing together at the altar stirred something inside of him, made him want what they had. By the time the cake was cut, Kirk had decided it was time for him to settle down as well.

He'd met Sarah in a doctor's waiting room. She'd made a comment about the book he'd been reading, *The Cider House Rules* by John Irving. Turned out that she'd read it too. "One of my favorites," she'd said. The conversation flowed from there and they'd never stopped talking. If he'd been able to create a woman from scratch, it would have been Sarah. Pretty, sweet, smart, agreeable.

Gavin and Natalie had given Sarah their vote of approval and even helped Kirk pick out an engagement ring. The two women had hit it off, and they often had dinner at the Kramers' house. Natalie loved to cook, so it seemed to make sense.

His mother was right. If anyone knew what to do right now, it would be Gavin. "I'll give him a call after we're done talking."

"Did you check the doorbell footage?" his mother asked abruptly.

"No, but I didn't get pinged at all today. Nothing, not even an Amazon delivery." In thinking back, this was unusual. Even when there weren't deliveries, he always knew when Sarah had gone to the street to the mailbox, or left to go on a walk through the neighborhood. In the last year, he hadn't made it through a day without getting alerted by the doorbell cam at least once. And today, on the day she left, there was nothing? Odd.

"I'd check it anyway. And try texting, Facebook messaging, and calling her friends. Make sure and ask Gavin if you can report her missing. He'll know how to handle it. Mention her head injury. She's vulnerable."

TEN
HER

Police Chief Gavin Kramer was a big deal in our town. He was in the local news occasionally, and his wife, Natalie, owned a fancy boutique downtown. I stopped in once and tried on some cocktail dresses, but didn't make a purchase. She didn't know who I was, something I found of interest.

I was nothing to her, but that didn't really matter to me. My eye was on Kirk Aden. As soon as I made eye contact with him at that dinner, I could see that he was twitchy. Easy to startle and to catch off guard. Like a man with something to hide.

I was a virtual stalker at first—googling from the comfort of my home was my favorite mode—but that only satisfied me for a while. Cyberstalking gave me information, but not the day-to-day details I craved. At some point I began tracking both Kirk and Sarah in person—actually venturing out of my house and watching them in real life. I knew I was spiraling down a dark hole, but I couldn't seem to help myself. If only they weren't so damn public with their bliss. That was what set me off initially, the fascination turning to contempt, and from there the act of watching began to feed itself. The more I knew, the more curious I became. I wanted to know everything—what they did in their free time, who they socialized with, how much money they had, what they talked about when it was just the two of them. But most of all I wanted to know if this young woman had any idea what kind of man she'd gotten involved with.

I thought of warning her, but women in love don't usually listen. If I had attempted to talk to her, Kirk would have painted me as a lunatic and she would have believed him.

My obsession actually started before they'd married, when I read an article about their impending nuptials in the local paper. They used the word "nuptials" like they were in Bath, England, in a Jane Austen novel, and not in a small town in Wisconsin. After the article, the nightly news channel featured a segment on them as well. A local citizen profile piece, they called it. How they were chosen to be featured was beyond me. If you must know, the whole thing really pissed me off. People got married every minute of every day. Since when was this news? The expression "must have been a slow news day" was created just for this kind of thing.

Turned out that Kirk's bride had experienced a lot of tragedies in her young life. She was from the East Coast originally, New Jersey to be precise. Her parents had died in a car accident when she was in college. There's never a good time for something like that, but she was only twenty-one and in the middle of her senior year, which admittedly had to be difficult. Even so, she continued with her studies, graduating on time with honors, then moving with her boyfriend to Wisconsin where he'd gotten a job with Kimberly-Clark. Then the boyfriend *died* of some kind of fluky heart problem, of all things, at the age of twenty-four. He'd had this heart defect since birth, but never knew it. They were both home when it happened. She'd left the room for a few minutes and came back to find him lying on the couch, eyes still open, but no longer alive, the televised football game still in progress. I imagined the scene: his head propped up on a pillow, legs crossed, the remote control balanced on his abdomen. I pictured her coming out of the kitchen with a tray of snacks and drinks and finding him nonresponsive. From there would be the 911 call, and the teary pleas to the paramedics, begging them to save him. Even thinking about it made me miserable. There's so much pain in the world, it's a wonder all of us keep going the way we do.

The story went on from there. Instead of returning to the East Coast after this tragedy, she'd stayed in Wisconsin. "I was paralyzed with grief," she'd said by way of explanation.

As much as I had it out for Kirk, my empathy for her was grudgingly sincere. She walked onto the stage in the third act and had no way of knowing what came before.

Of course the interview used the boyfriend's untimely death as a jumping-off point for the real story—the happily-ever-after of their upcoming marriage. At thirty-six, Kirk was ten years older than Sarah, and he explained his bachelor years by saying, "All those lonely nights make sense now. I was single for so long because I was waiting to meet Sarah." He had his arm draped around her shoulders and had pulled her in closer, smiling down as he'd said these words.

Oh, puke.

Is it petty to begrudge evil people happiness? If so, I'll readily confess to being petty.

At first, I was just curious about this particular aspect of their lives—it wouldn't help me much with what I wanted to do. I checked out their bridal registry online and read over the pages on The Knot website. The story of how they met, which was supposedly in the waiting room of their therapist's office. Who'd admit to such a thing? The interviewer thought it was adorable, though. Other notable items on the wedding website? The listing of the names of the wedding party, which was small to say the least—each one having only one attendant. Sarah's sister, Maren, was her maid of honor, and Kirk, predictably, had Gavin as best man. I could have guessed that one. What I couldn't have guessed was the size of the wedding. Considering the enormous diamond ring on her finger and his family's wealth, a gathering of one hundred people might be considered modest. They called it a backyard wedding, but who were they fooling? I knew plenty of people with backyards, but none of them had room for a hundred guests, a gazebo, a constructed-for-the event dance floor, and linked tents housing enough tables and chairs to serve an elegant dinner for all of the attendees.

Please. This was no backyard. It was an estate.

Would you think it was creepy if I admitted to driving by his parents' house the day of the wedding? I couldn't see much, since the house was so far back from the road. Still, I parked nearby and watched as the guests arrived in their shiny, expensive cars. Not a dent or rust spot on any of them, which made my car stand out. I didn't care. I wasn't doing anything wrong. It's not against the law to park on a public street.

After all the guests had arrived, I waited awhile, my car windows down to catch a breeze. When I heard the sounds of a string quartet floating through the air, I realized that the ceremony had started. She'd gone ahead and done it.

God help her, because I sure couldn't.

ELEVEN

THEN

After Sarah came home from the hospital, everything became hazy. Everything she'd taken for granted had changed. She had to move cautiously, for fear of a sudden bout of vertigo. Headaches plagued her, and the pain pills made her thinking fuzzy. Besides that, the house itself was disorienting, the rooms not quite right. The first day, she went to get a drinking glass for water and opened the cabinet to find dishes and bowls on the shelf instead. She stood there puzzled, then tried the cabinet where she remembered the dishware had been stored, finding the glasses instead, but lined up in their usual familiar way.

The two cabinets had swapped their contents. Or at least that's how it seemed.

Calling out to her husband, who was sitting at the kitchen table, she asked, "Did you rearrange the cupboards?"

Kirk stopped shuffling through the stack of mail to look up and meet her gaze. "No. Why would I do that?"

"No reason. I just wondered."

"Do you *want* them rearranged? I can do that if you want. It wouldn't be a problem."

"No, everything's fine."

"If you need anything done, just say the word. I want you to be happy."

"I know." Sarah knew she was a people pleaser. She'd once taken an online test which told her as much. In her marriage, this was a skill that came in handy. Kirk was a sensitive soul who seized the most innocuous comment and assigned value to it. She'd learned to downplay her own concerns or he would knock himself out to make her happy. She held back from admiring things because he'd insist on buying them for her. At restaurants if she made an offhand comment about the food being too spicy, he'd have the server bring her another plate despite her objections. He surprised her with expensive clothing and jewelry for no reason at all. It was not uncommon for him to whisk her away for romantic weekends, where he'd already made reservations for dinner and a couples massage.

Her friends at work were envious of Kirk's devotion. "If only Sam did half of what Kirk does, I'd be overjoyed," her friend Lauren had said, shaking her head sadly. "But it would take a miracle."

Every time flowers were delivered to the office, at least one other co-worker would tell her she was a lucky woman. She always agreed, but something about his excessive generosity nagged at her, making her wonder if his motivation wasn't her happiness, but something else entirely. Some insecurity that made him want to prove his love to others? Or maybe a public display of his wealth? She never dwelled on these doubts, though, because it seemed disloyal. Kirk had always been good to her. His arrival in her life had been a godsend. Her parents' death while she was in college left a vast emptiness in her life. Her sister, Maren, was eight years older and consumed with her own life. She had a high-powered job that took her on international business trips. In her free time Maren enjoyed scuba diving, running marathons, and rock climbing. Sarah was more of a homebody, whose interests lay in gardening, cooking, and reading. Hard to believe two sisters could be so different.

Sarah had been lonely before Kirk. Now she was part of a family once again. Kirk's parents adored her and had made her feel at home from the moment she'd met them. They were down to earth, considering their wealth. But, of course, they hadn't always been rich. When Kirk was growing up they lived a regular suburban life. It was only after Kirk's father sold his business for an astronomical amount, and they made some good investments, that they were able to scale up so dramatically. From what Kirk said, she got the impression they were sitting on about twenty million dollars, some of which came in handy when Kirk had the opportunity to buy the car dealership.

By the time Sarah met them, the older Adens lived in a house larger than Sarah's apartment building. Kirk had been their only child, and the fact that they approved of her meant a lot to him. Theirs had been a whirlwind romance. It started with an accidental meeting in a doctor's waiting area, which led to a dinner date. After that, it was Saturday morning hikes, and outings to art galleries and museums. Within a month of meeting him, she was his date to a wedding, where he introduced her as his girlfriend. Six months later, they were engaged, and six months after that, they married in a private ceremony in a gazebo on his parents' property. After that, life had been a dream. She didn't have to work, but she enjoyed it and liked having her own money. Kirk himself put her needs above all else. She really had nothing to complain about. He'd never raised his voice to her. If anything, the opposite. He watched her facial expressions for any sign of displeasure and apologized for things he hadn't done.

Really, he was perfect.

Lately they'd been talking about having a baby. "I would love it if we had a little girl who looked just like you," Kirk had said once during a conversation right before falling asleep. They were snug under the covers and had finished talking about their days, when he broached the subject out of the blue. He'd mentioned it before, but she'd never felt ready.

More recently, it was starting to feel like the right time. "Maybe it will be a boy," she'd answered. "With blue-gray eyes and uncooperative hair."

"Poor kid." Kirk reached over to stroke her cheek. "Doomed to have bad hair and terrible eyesight. I think it's better if our children take after their mother."

She'd gone off her birth control pills that weekend, but didn't tell him, thinking that it would be fun to surprise him when she was actually pregnant. Now that she was recovering from an assault, she was glad she didn't get pregnant right away.

The first evening after her arrival home from the hospital, she headed into the master bathroom to take a shower, and did a double take when she saw the towels. The ones folded neatly over the towel rack were the same color, sea foam green, but were striped not solid. When drying off, she noticed they were thicker and fluffier than the previous set, which she appreciated especially when it came to her hair.

"I like the new towels," she said, heading into the bedroom. Kirk was sitting up in bed, the covers over his legs as he read a book. He often waited for her that way.

He glanced up over his reading glasses. "What new towels?"

She gestured back with a jab of her thumb. "The striped ones. I approve. They're nice and absorbent."

Kirk's forehead furrowed. "Those are the same towels we've had for a while now. They're not new."

"No, they . . ." Sarah stopped, confused. "Didn't we used to have solid-colored towels? Same color, though."

"We did about six months ago." He gave her a concerned smile. "Did you *want* solid-colored towels?"

"No, I'm not asking for something different. That's not what I'm talking about. I'm asking if you bought new towels while I was in the hospital."

"No, Sarah," he said with a smile. "I did not buy new towels when you were in the hospital. These are the same ones we've had for quite a while."

She slowly came around to her side of the bed and slid under the covers. "I feel like I'm losing my mind. I could have sworn we had different towels. I can even picture what they looked like."

"I'm sorry. That must be frustrating, but give yourself a break. You're remembering the old towels." He reached over and squeezed her hand. "You've had a head injury. Things will be muddled for a while."

"The doctor said the injury wasn't that extreme, though. And you'd think I'd remember something as simple as towels." She sighed. "I'm sorry for bringing it up."

Kirk put his bookmark in between the pages and closed the book. "I'm actually flattered that you thought I had time to go towel shopping on top of being camped out at the hospital." He took off his glasses, folded them up, and put them in the case on his nightstand, then meticulously set the book next to them. "I was a little busy being out of my mind worrying about you. I could barely breathe, much less anything else."

"I know." Sarah nodded. He'd been at her side the entire time. The nurses even looked the other way when he didn't budge from his seat at the end of visiting hours. Sometimes she woke up to find him watching her intently and stroking her arm.

"I know this recovery isn't happening fast enough for you, but soon enough you'll be back to normal."

"I hope you're right." The physical problems, the never-ending ache in her head, the dizziness that came on suddenly, the pressure behind her left eye, none of it was nearly as bad as her cognitive issues. "The worst part is feeling like I'm losing it. Now I know how it must feel to have dementia." She reached back and adjusted her pillow. "Like those threatening notes. Except for the first one, I have no recollection of them, and you'd think I'd remember finding a dead rat on our porch. I've racked my brain, but nothing comes up. That's so alarming. Why don't I remember?"

"Maybe it's your mind giving you a break," Kirk said, leaning over to give her a quick peck on the lips, before turning off the lamp on his nightstand. "You've repressed a painful memory. You were distraught at the time. Better just to forget it."

In the dark, Sarah aimed her gaze at the ceiling, barely making out the ceiling fan overhead. "Maybe if I read the notes again, it would jog my memory. Before you leave for work tomorrow, could you get them out for me?" There was a long pause and then she heard her husband sigh audibly. "You still have them, don't you, Kirk?"

"Now why would you want to read something so horrible? It's better to let it go, Sarah. It'll just get you upset."

"I think I'm more upset not knowing." She pulled the covers up to her chin, then slid her hands underneath. "So you don't have them anymore?"

"I gave them all to Gavin. When I filed the police report."

Sarah waited a moment. "Do you think we could get them back? Or maybe get copies?"

Kirk took a deep breath. "I don't think we can get them back. There might be a connection to the notes and your attacker, so the police need them. They're evidence now. If it helps, all of the notes were similar to the first one, the one you remember seeing. Block letters saying things like you're going to get yours, and you think you're so great. Rambling crazy stuff, Sarah." He turned toward her, and reached over to stroke her hair. "It makes me angry even thinking about it. Please don't dredge it up again. It was bad enough the first time around."

"It's not that I want to read hateful notes. I just think it might help jog my memory."

"I get it. It has to be frustrating."

"It is." She settled back into the pillow and took a deep breath.

"I'm going to take care of you, so no more worries. You trust me, right?"

Before drifting off to sleep, she managed to answer, "Of course I do."

TWELVE

Without having to go to work, Sarah would have thought her days would be empty, but recovering turned out to be a full-time job. The doctor made it sound like she'd had a minor head injury, but nothing about it felt minor. The things she'd previously done almost on autopilot now required enormous amounts of effort. Showering was equivalent to an hour's hike. Leaving their bedroom and walking down the stairs to the first floor required extra energy. Naps were a common part of her routine. Truthfully, she felt like sleeping all the time. If not for Kirk prodding her to go for walks, and pushing her to get out, she'd have checked out of life completely. It was depressing being less than her former self. Kirk recognized her emotional state and bolstered her spirits. For the first time in their married life he put his business in second place, ignoring phone calls and letting other team members make decisions about the dealership. She'd hear him on the phone saying, "I'm with my wife right now, so you'll just have to handle it."

Because she couldn't trust herself to drive safely, Sarah agreed to temporarily give up her car. "There's no point in it sitting in the garage for the next few months," Kirk said. "You can drive mine whenever you want, and when you're back to driving on a regular basis, we'll get you a new one. You can have the pick of the lot." It made sense. Besides, they had a five-car garage, which held three vehicles, even after hers was taken back to the dealership. Two of the spots in their garage held what he called his babies: a vintage Ferrari, the exact model Kirk had yearned for in his high school years, and an Aston Martin, similar to one driven by James Bond. Not that Sarah ever drove either of them, but she knew where Kirk kept the extra set of keys, so in a pinch she had access to a car.

After she'd been home from the hospital a week, Sarah and Kirk established a routine. Kirk came and went from work, but was always there to drive her to doctors' appointments and to her physical therapy sessions. She couldn't even imagine how physical therapy could help her, but as it turned out, it was exactly what she needed. She'd been told to dress comfortably, so she wore yoga pants, a T-shirt, and her most comfortable athletic shoes. When she and Kirk walked into the room, the space resembled a private gym more than a medical facility. Phil, her physical therapist, greeted them with a smile. He was in his forties, with graying hair and a slight paunch, which she found surprising for someone in his line of work. "You must be Sarah Aden. Welcome," he'd said. "I'm glad you're here." He had a toothy grin, the kind that looked over-the-top silly in pictures, but endearing in person.

As they made their introductions, Phil shook hands, first with Kirk, then turning to grasp Sarah's hand. He held her gaze for a moment before letting go.

"My doctor suggested physical therapy, but I'm not really sure how you can help me," she told him honestly.

"I'm familiar with your medical history," he said. She imagined him poring over a folder, then flipping through the doctors' notes, maybe making a few notations of his own, but, of course, no one did that anymore. He probably accessed her health chart online. "As I'm sure you're aware, everything in the body is interconnected. Exercise has physical and mental benefits. There's also been studies that show that physical activity speeds healing. Beyond that, we'll be addressing your issues with vertigo by doing exercises to improve your balance, which will help avoid falls. What do you say? Are you willing to give it a try?" Again with that toothy grin, one canine tooth overlapping its neighbor.

"That's why we're here," Kirk said, clasping his hands. "Let's get started."

Phil lost his smile. "There's a waiting area right outside those doors. The Wi-Fi password is posted on the bulletin board."

Kirk said, "I don't want to be rude, but I'm very protective of my wife, as I'm sure you can understand, considering she was attacked on our own property. I want to be part of her recovery, so if you don't mind, I plan on staying right here." He folded his arms.

"Of course," Phil said. "Not a problem."

Sarah had thought the first appointment might be more of an introductory session, but Phil didn't hold back. He went right to work, putting her through her paces. He demonstrated exercises that looked easy enough, but when she finished repeating them, doing three reps of eight each, her limbs felt sore and rubbery. Every time she felt like saying she couldn't do another one, Phil would push her, and when she completed them, he'd say, "There you go, Sarah, now you're doing it." He sounded genuinely excited, which made her want to do a little bit more.

From the side of the room, Kirk kept a watchful eye. When she noticed him frowning partway through the session, she winked, which made him smile.

By the time the hour was over, Sarah was drenched in perspiration. "Next time I'll bring a towel of my own and a change of clothes," she said, dabbing her face with a towel Phil had handed her.

"Might be a good idea." He nodded. "Be prepared to sweat. Believe me, it's not going to get any easier."

On the drive home, Kirk said, "I'm not sure I like that guy."

"Why do you say that?" Her gaze was on the printouts Phil had given her—diagrams showing exercises for her to do at home. She stared at the rudimentary drawings of people demonstrating each exercise with arrows indicating movement. Her earlier self would have remembered the exercises, but now she was grateful to have the visual reminders. Phil's email and phone number were printed across the top.

"He seemed to take a perverse pleasure in making you work so hard. I wanted to step in several times, but admirably, I held back."

Sarah tilted her head and thought about what he'd said. Kirk wasn't completely wrong. At the time she'd felt as if Phil had pushed her to do more than she was capable of, and yet, that hadn't been the case at all. To avoid embarrassment, she'd soldiered through, doing each exercise a few more times than she would have thought possible, impressing herself with her own fortitude. "I took it as encouragement. I mean, it's his job."

"I have to tell you, Sarah, I'm not fond of someone who considers it his job to torture my wife."

"Torture?" She laughed. "That's a bit of an overstatement, don't you think?"

He ignored her question and went on. "There are other physical therapists in the world. It doesn't have to be *that guy*. Maybe we should hire someone to come out to the house? You could handpick the therapist and we could let them know that you need to work at your own pace."

Intuitively she knew that given the opportunity to work at her own pace she'd never recover. Left by herself, she'd take naps and watch Netflix. No, she needed Phil or someone like him, and why not him? The doctor had set it up, so apparently he felt Phil was competent. "No, I want to keep doing this." She held up the sheaf of papers. "I think he really knows what he's doing and for the first time I feel like I'm on track to eventually getting back to normal."

Kirk shrugged. "Suit yourself."

"I will. Thanks."

THIRTEEN

Over the weeks of Sarah's recovery, Kirk transitioned to going back to work, and Sarah began to use a ride service to get to her doctors' appointments. This small degree of autonomy made her feel like she was getting her life back.

One gray day, on a whim, she had the driver drop her off at a local coffee shop for a latte and a dose of normalcy. When she got into line, she was pleasantly surprised to see Phil up at the counter. As he walked past, cup in hand, she pinched his sleeve, making him pause. When he turned, she said, "Imagine meeting you here."

"Sarah! What a nice surprise," he said, his smile widening. Sarah had just finished the last of her physical therapy sessions the week before. She'd actually been sad to have it come to an end, but she'd regained her sense of balance, and she was more than capable of doing the exercises at home. He asked, "How have you been?"

"Doing well," she said, which was only partly true. She rarely had vertigo anymore, but the headaches had persisted and there were some afternoons when a nap was the only thing that got her through the day. The doctor had said her symptoms would be resolved now, so she felt embarrassed to still be struggling.

A young woman with a baby on her hip got in line behind her, and Phil stepped away to make room. "Good to see you, Sarah."

After she'd gotten her drink, he waved her over to his table and she pulled out a chair to join him. "No work today?" she asked.

"No, I have Thursday off because I work Saturdays." He took a sip and then smiled at her over the rim of the cup.

Behind them, one of the employees, a young woman with purple hair, called out, "An iced white-chocolate mocha for Charlie!" Out of the corner of her eye, Sarah saw the woman push the cup toward the edge of the counter. Charlie, a thirtysomething with glasses and a scruffy beard, came to claim his drink. She noticed he was wearing faded gray sweatpants. Charlie apparently valued comfort over style.

"An iced white-chocolate mocha," Sarah repeated. "That sounds good."

Phil shook his head. "Too sweet for me, but it sounds like something my husband would like."

"I didn't know you were married!" Sarah said with delight. In all the hours they'd spent together, he'd never mentioned anything about his personal life. For some reason she'd pictured him going home alone to a lonely apartment. She was glad to be wrong.

"That's because my husband doesn't hover over me every second like yours does," Phil said, a twinkle in his eye.

"Kirk is a bit overprotective," she acknowledged. "It's because I was attacked. He'll loosen up in time."

"I hope you're right."

With all the hours they'd spent together, there was an ease in being in Phil's presence. Still, she realized she didn't know much about him. "So did you always want to be a physical therapist?"

He grinned. "Not really. My original major was art history."

"So was mine!" Sarah couldn't believe it. "I switched when I realized how impractical it was."

"Me too. I figured out early on that I wasn't going to be able to pay my student loans with an art history degree." He drummed his fingers on the surface of the table. "So what made you choose art history in the first place?"

She looked down at her cup, then sheepishly met his gaze. "In all honesty, it started when I was about fourteen and I first saw the movie *Ferris Bueller's Day Off.*"

Phil nodded in understanding. "The part where they're at the Art Institute of Chicago and Cameron is standing in front of Georges Seurat's painting, *A Sunday Afternoon on the Island of La Grande Jatte?*"

"That's it," she said in amazement. When she'd discussed the movie with Kirk, he hadn't even remembered that scene. "I was so taken with the pointillist style. It was like magic to me. When you stand close to the painting, it looks like nothing but colored dots. And then when you back up, it all comes into view. Absolutely mind-blowing! After I saw the movie, I read a biography of Seurat, which got me interested in some of his contemporaries. One thing led to another and I became obsessed with all of it—everything from the Old Masters to modern art. I went through a period where I took some drawing and painting classes, thinking I might have some hidden talent." She sighed, thinking about that phase in her life.

"And did you?"

"If I did, it was so hidden I couldn't find it." She laughed. "My artwork was rubbish, but if anything, that made me admire artists even more. It's amazing to me that it all starts with an idea in someone's head and then they manifest it so we can all experience it."

Phil nodded in agreement. "I always thought pointillism was a metaphor for life. When you're too close to something, you lack perspective. It's only once you have some distance that you see things the way they really are."

"That's deep," she said, taking a small sip of her latte.

"So when you first saw Seurat's painting at the museum, did it live up to your expectations?"

"I've never actually seen it in person," she admitted.

"You've never seen *A Sunday Afternoon on the Island of La Grande Jatte?*" he asked incredulously. "But Chicago isn't that far away."

"I keep meaning to go," she said, knowing how lame that sounded. "I just haven't gotten to it yet."

"We have to rectify that," he said, leaning back and folding his arms. "If your husband won't go with you, I'd be happy to be your road trip buddy."

"Oh, Kirk would take me if I asked him to," Sarah assured him. "It's just not his thing, so I wouldn't ask. If we went, would your husband want to come along?"

"Are you kidding?" Phil snorted. "Only if he had to. Trust me, an art museum isn't his idea of fun."

Having found common ground, they grinned at each other. "Your husband sounds like a monster," Sarah joked. "I say we make him go."

"I say we leave both the husbands at home," Phil said. "We don't need them dragging us down." He downed the last of his drink and then asked, "So is it a plan? We're taking a day trip to the Art Institute?"

"Count me in!" she said, her spirits lifting. A line from another movie came into her head just then: *I think this is the beginning of a beautiful friendship.*

FOURTEEN
HER

Everyone does irrational things from time to time. Our emotions get the better of us and we blurt out a rude comment we don't really mean or dump a bag of dried dog food in the front seat of a cheating boyfriend's car. (Really, he should have locked the doors.) We're human beings. Sometimes we go off track in a bad way. Usually, there's some remorse, and even if that's not the case, these kinds of things run their course. Sometimes you just have to get it out of your system.

That's what I thought would happen with Sarah and Kirk. I honestly thought my obsessiveness would run its course. That's not what happened.

Instead, I went from my interest in him to becoming emotionally entangled in his wife's life. Why was she still working when they were so obviously wealthy? The other couples in their league ran charitable foundations or worked in the family business. Sarah's mundane job, doing marketing for a small landscaping firm, was the kind that kept people buying lottery tickets. From what I could tell, she thrived at her job, but besides lunching with the other office ladies, she didn't socialize with anyone but Kirk.

Odd.

When they visited a bistro on Saturday mornings, I'd get a table on the other side of the decorative barrier. Out of sight, but within earshot. Their conversations were light, discussing buying new patio furniture, what movies they wanted to see, plans for his mother's birthday. To the casual listener their discussions might even seem pleasant but uninteresting. I, however, could see the subtext. Kirk steered the ship. What sounded like a conversation was actually him overriding her ideas and getting her to go along with what he wanted. They traveled to his chosen destinations, ate at the restaurants he decided upon, and went to see the movies of his choosing. She always went along with whatever he wanted. Why? Was she afraid of him or just agreeable?

I feared the worst.

By the time they'd been married nearly two years, I felt a responsibility. Someone needed to shake Sarah. Someone needed to wake this woman up.

The first time I left a note in their mailbox it was done on impulse. I waited until the street was quiet and no one else was in sight, then slipped the envelope inside and drove off quickly, trying not to speed. I knew there might be hidden security cameras in the area, but I didn't care. I imagined Kirk opening the envelope and reading my message, knowing that I knew what he'd done and that he wasn't off the hook. Let him sweat. I didn't even care if he guessed it was me.

Later at home, I waited for the knock on the door. The one you see in movies when the police come to call and they take the suspect away in handcuffs. It never happened, which was both a relief and a bit of a letdown. Over the next week or so, I looked to see if it came up under the police reports in the local paper. It never did.

At first, the lack of response infuriated me. Had I been ignored? And then it emboldened me. I continued keeping watch and eventually left three more notes. All of them anonymous, of course. I was making a point, not trying to get myself in trouble.

When I drove downtown one day and saw a dead rat by the side of the road, it called to me. An opportunity to do something truly shocking. I picked it up using a plastic bag and threw it in the trunk. That time I waited until after dark to visit the Adens, dumping the rodent corpse on the porch and running like hell back to my car, which was parked down the block.

I waited for something. A phone call from Kirk, where I'd get a chance to either deny it was me or defend my actions. I wanted to hear raw emotion in his voice; whether it was terror or anger was up to him. Or perhaps I'd see Sarah packing her bags and leaving. That would serve him right. But nothing. Another day went by and then two and three. The Adens continued to be a good-looking, happy, and rich family, all of which was missing at my house.

And then Sarah began seeing another man on the sly.

I didn't know what to think. The guy drove a dinged-up Ford Focus with a plastic hula girl suctioned to the dashboard, so he was as far from Kirk Aden as a man could be. At first, I thought it was an affair, but their outings said otherwise. Each time he parked around the corner and she exited the house through the patio door on the side of the house, cutting through the neighbor's yard to meet him. Why the subterfuge? My guess is that she was evading a security camera.

The first time this happened he drove her to City Hall, where she went inside while he waited in the car, windows open, tapping on the dashboard to the beat of '90s pop music. She returned with a smile. I watched as she flung open the door and scooted inside, as happy as a teenager escaping her parents for the night. Something good had happened.

Another time, he picked her up and the two of them drove around my old neighborhood, lingering in front of Kirk Aden's childhood home. "What are you up to, Mrs. Aden?" I mused aloud, my hands gripping the steering wheel.

My curiosity was at an all-time high, so after he'd dropped

her off near her house, I followed him, back to a place called Body Mechanics Physical Therapy, a place where I'd seen Kirk drive Sarah on numerous occasions after her regrettable injury. Later, I looked at their website and matched his face to one of the therapists. Phil Schaefer. According to the reviews online, his clients loved him and it seemed like Sarah was no exception. My guess? Kirk didn't know they were friends. She also didn't want Kirk to know about these outings, which made me curious.

She was up to something.

Maybe there was more to Sarah than I'd thought.

FIFTEEN
THEN

When Kirk announced he was going to a two-day convention in Chicago, Sarah thought it was a good opportunity to tell him about her own Chicago-related plans. "I ran into Phil the physical therapist this afternoon when I stopped for a coffee," she said.

Before she could finish, Kirk had said, "Oh no, not that guy. I hope you didn't get stuck talking to him."

"Actually, we sat and talked for quite a while and I really enjoyed his company. Turns out we were both art history majors at one point."

"Sounds about right," Kirk said and then launched into the details of his trip to the Chicago Auto Show. The opening to tell him about the Art Institute was gone, overridden by his plans. "My mom was hoping to spend some time with you, if you're agreeable." Her guess was that he was nervous about leaving her alone for two days. "If you don't want me to go, I can cancel."

"No, you should go," she said, giving him a smile. "You'll have fun, and I'll be fine."

Sarah's mother-in-law had called it a girls' day, which just meant that her father-in-law, Bert, was free to go golfing. She suspected that Kirk had asked his mother to keep her occupied while he was away, but she didn't mind. Judy was easy company and at this point Sarah was feeling better. Not quite well enough to return to her job, but increasingly more restless at home. She wondered if she should try working part-time, but Kirk didn't think it was a good idea. "What's the rush? You're just now feeling more like yourself. Another week or two won't make a difference." He was rubbing her shoulders as he said it, which made it all the more convincing.

That morning Kirk had dropped her off at his parents' house, getting out of the car only briefly to say hello to his mother and kiss Sarah goodbye. When Judy asked him to come in for a cup of coffee, he shook his head. "Chicago traffic is brutal in the morning. I need to leave now if I want to get there on time."

Sarah knew Kirk well enough to know that his calm demeanor masked his small-child excitement. Going to the auto show was Christmas in July for him. She'd accompanied him the first year of their marriage and had loved seeing the new models on display in McCormick Place, but as the day went on, her interest waned as Kirk's had grown. After hours of following him mutely while he made small talk with business reps and arranged for dinner meetings, she declined to join him for dinner and instead spent the evenings with room service and a novel. He'd invited her the year after, but both of them knew she'd be happier at home.

This year, he'd opted to go for only two days, but only after checking in with her. "You really don't mind?" he'd asked. "I can send Eric in my place."

"I really don't mind," she'd said. Shortly after that, Judy had called.

Judy was a whirlwind, a chatterbox with a big laugh, which was a nice counterpoint to Sarah's quiet nature. Judy talked enough for the two of them, so Sarah didn't have to fill the pauses with small talk. Her mother-in-law made plans for mani-pedis for both of them. Afterward, there was a reservation for lunch at the Manna Café, a new vegetarian restaurant. "I took Bert here once," she'd told Sarah, laughing. "After we got home, he made himself a salami sandwich. Said he was still hungry."

The morning passed pleasantly enough. The mani-pedi included a foot massage that felt like heaven. Their lunches— an exotic salad for Sarah, a vegetable stir-fry for Judy—were just right. "I can almost feel my body thanking me for the nutrients," Judy said, lifting her chin and chuckling.

When they returned to her in-laws' house, Sarah followed Judy into the living room and watched as Kirk's mom went to a cabinet and pulled out a stack of books. "I thought it would be fun to show you some family photos of Kirk as a kid." She chuckled. "The ones from his awkward years, the ones he'd rather you not see."

Judy settled on the sofa, patted the seat next to her, and opened a photo album on the coffee table. "The dreaded middle school years!" she proclaimed. Judy chattered away telling stories of family vacations and pointing out her son's unflattering hair-styles. "Believe it or not—Kirk with bangs! At the time he thought this was a great idea." She laughed again. "I tried to talk him out of it, but my opinion didn't carry much weight back then." She shook her head. "Teenagers."

Flipping through the pages of photos, Sarah watched as her husband aged from prepubescent adolescent to young man, his face morphing gradually from chubby cheeks and chin to strong jaw and sharp angles. In high school, the pictures transitioned from family photos to friend photos. School events. Base-ball games. Young Kirk with a gang of kids around a bonfire. In another, they were playing video games back in the Adens' old house.

Turning another page, she came across a grouping of photos showing what appeared to be the same cluster of kids sitting on bean bag chairs, a concrete block wall in the background. The quality of the photos was poor, dark around the edges, with the faces of the kids lit up by the camera flash. In each image one person was missing, as if they'd taken turns with the camera. Mentally Sarah counted and came up with five in all, including the kid taking the picture. Kirk and Gavin she knew, of course. It was within character that Gavin wielded some kind of toy weapon in all of the shots—a curved gray knife, from what she could tell. With his arm held out, only half of the knife was in the pictures. She studied the other three faces, then sat up straight, recognizing one.

"Is that Clarice Carter?" She turned to Judy.

"Sure is," she said with a nod. "You know her?"

"Yes, I do. She works with me." Sarah tried to process the idea that Clarice, her friend from the office, was in these photos from Kirk's teenage years, sitting cozily between her husband and Gavin, her outstretched arms slung tightly around their necks. Such an intimate sight that it was jarring, even if it did happen a long time ago. "I knew she went to their high school, but I didn't know she hung out with Kirk."

Why hadn't her husband mentioned this? She'd talked about Clarice countless times after she'd been hired. She specifically remembered telling Kirk a story Clarice had shared with the office. Apparently, Clarice had befriended an elderly gentleman when she was in her twenties. The man had been all alone in the world, and in desperate need of help, so she'd moved in with him and tended to him as he lay dying. Clarice had tears in her eyes when she said, "Can you imagine my shock when I found out he'd left me his entire estate? I just couldn't believe it. I had the attorney do a search for family members, but he couldn't find any relatives. I donated a good part of the money to a charity Ralph really believed in. It just seemed like the right thing to do."

It was a noteworthy story, one that had impressed Sarah. If anything, this would have been Kirk's opening to talk about his connection to Clarice, but he'd only commented that he'd known her in high school. He'd said it so casually that she'd envisioned them as acquaintances, giving a nod as they passed in the hall or making small talk before the start of class. Finding out they'd been friends was a shock. And not just friends, but close friends by the looks of it.

It was odd that Clarice had never mentioned it either. Very odd.

"That summer she and the boys were thick as thieves. Her parents got divorced a year or so before and then her dad moved out of state and dropped out of sight. Her mom had a new boyfriend and wasn't home much. Poor thing. I always got the impression that Clarice was trying to fill the gap," Judy said. "Looking for love anywhere she could find it."

"She told me about her parents' divorce," Sarah said.

Judy nodded. "She was flirty with all the boys. I think Kirk may have been sweet on her, or maybe Gavin was the one with the crush, but who knows?" She sighed. "You'll see when you have kids—they don't want you to know anything. Girls are usually more communicative than boys. I was left out of a lot of it."

Sarah pointed. "And who were the other two?"

"The boy was a good buddy of Kirk's from the time they were little guys. Jeremy Bickley. The girl next to him is his little sister, Stephanie. Now *that* was a sad story. The two of them came from a troubled family. Alcoholic father, a mother who tried to cover it up to keep the family intact. One night after his father beat him up, Jeremy just took off. He was eighteen by then, so he left a note in their mailbox saying he'd had enough. It sounded like he'd been planning to do it for a long time. He said that once he got settled somewhere, he'd contact them with his new address. His mother was about out of her mind with worry, poor thing. And all these years later, they've never heard a single word from him. His parents reported his disappearance to the police. They went on TV pleading with him to come home. They sent out flyers, posted a reward for information, created a website. Basically, did everything they could, but never heard anything. I heard the parents separated, and shortly after that, the dad died. So sad."

"When did this happen?"

"The summer after Kirk's junior year. Jeremy was older than the other boys, already eighteen."

Sarah asked, "What do you think happened to Jeremy?"

Judy shrugged. "I don't know. Something awful, I'm afraid. Back then there were reports of young people disappearing while hitchhiking, never to be found. I would guess it was something like that. Otherwise, I would think he'd have called. He was devoted to his mother and he and Stephanie were very close."

"How awful."

"He didn't have a car or take a bus, so he must have decided to hitchhike. That's all I can come up with anyway. After that, it's anyone's guess."

Sarah nodded, staring at the picture of Jeremy and his sister. Anyone could see they were related. Their dark eyes, thin nose, and smiles were nearly identical. In one of the photos, she'd rested her head on his shoulder. They had to have been close.

"I pray for the Bickleys every night. I can't imagine what they went through. What they're still going through. You don't ever get over something like that."

"It must have been terrible for Kirk too. I can't believe he's never mentioned it." She thought of all the hours she poured out her heart to him, telling him about the day she got the news of her parents' death in a car accident. She and Maren had to go identify their bodies. The experience had been horrendous, and after that, they'd had to plan the funeral. And just when she'd found happiness again, fell in love and got engaged, her fiancé, Trevor, had died of a heart attack. For months afterward, she'd had nightmares. It was only through counseling that she'd been able to move on. She'd experienced so much pain in her life and hadn't held anything back from Kirk. Why wouldn't he tell her about his own loss?

"It's probably just too painful," Judy said, by way of explanation. "He and Gavin were both gutted when it happened. I know that Kirk cried in his room some nights. He came down in the morning with red eyes, said he was fine, said he was getting a cold, but I knew better. The whole thing was just so odd and unexpected."

"What about the police? They never came up with anything?"

"No." She shook her head. "They questioned all his friends, talked to the neighbors, checked the bus station. No one knew anything."

Sarah stared down at the photo album. Inexplicably, she felt like crying. Since she'd been attacked, her moods had swung wildly, mostly from frustration and fatigue. Now she experienced a sadness for the family of the lost son, coupled with a troubling sense of unease. Why would Kirk keep this from her? Awash in emotion, she was only dimly aware of Judy's voice, speaking as if from a distance.

"I'm sorry," she said, raising her head. "What did you say?"

"I said that it seemed to help once we did away with the bomb shelter," she said. "They spent so much time down there playing Risk and writing screenplays and what have you. When Kirk said he and Gavin wanted to fill it in, Bert and I understood. Too many memories."

"You had a bomb shelter?" Sarah's eyes widened.

"In our backyard." Judy frowned. "I can't believe Kirk never told you about that either? It came with the house. The original owner built it himself. I'm sure there was no building inspector involved." She chuckled. "They constructed it during the Cold War era. Back then people built them so their family would have a place to go in case of a nuclear attack. It was all the way in the back of the property, smack-dab in the middle, close to where our property abutted the state park." She pointed to the concrete block wall behind the kids in the photos. "These were taken down there. Kirk and his friends made it into a sort of clubhouse."

Sarah felt her breath catch in her chest. "And why did Kirk and Gavin want it filled in?"

Judy said, "I was the one who wanted it filled in right from the start, if you must know, which is what put the idea in their head, I think. From day one I thought it was a disaster waiting to happen. It had these steep concrete stairs that were super narrow. The floor was originally sand when we bought the house, but after we moved in, Bert covered it with pieces of plywood. And the bugs!" She shuddered. "It just smelled damp and closed up. Like a musty basement, but worse."

"Sounds awful."

"After we bought the house, I only went down there once and that was enough for me. Bert slipped on the stairs and nearly broke his neck. After that, his back was never the same. Then when Kirk's friends claimed it as their own, I worried about the usual things teenagers do when parents aren't around. Once, I went to call Kirk for dinner and I got a definite whiff of pot when I opened the door. After that, I worried they were going to start a fire down there, get trapped, and die of smoke inhalation. Or burn alive. I tried to make a rule about no girls allowed, but as you can see, that happened anyway. Bert thought I was getting worked up for nothing, but it never left my mind. When Kirk and Gavin came in one day and said they wanted to fill it in with concrete, I was relieved."

"Then you went ahead and filled it?"

"No. We looked into doing it that way." She ran a finger over the edge of the page. "But it would have cost a fortune and the truck would have torn up the lawn. So one day Bert had the boys clean their stuff out of there, then he padlocked the door, and they covered it up."

"With what?"

"Dirt. Bert bought bags of garden soil and put those boys to work. He said they were old enough to take care of it and he wasn't going to strain his back." Judy laughed. "I never saw Kirk so sweaty or red in the face. His clothes were wet by the time he was done."

Sarah pursed her lips in thought. "I can't really picture this. If the bomb shelter was underground, why did they need to cover it up?"

Judy nodded. "The metal door was flat, but not quite level with the yard. Once they'd covered it with dirt, and the grass grew in, though, you'd never know it was there. Kirk took care of seeding and watering too. Did a good job."

Sarah's forehead furrowed in thought. "Why did they say they wanted it closed up?"

"Because it wasn't the same without Jeremy there. I guess they outgrew it. And Gavin's dad thought it was a hazard. He recommended we seal it up."

"I see."

Judy shrugged. "I didn't care what their reasoning was. I was glad to be done with it." She waved her hand as if whisking away a fly.

Sarah sat quietly, considering everything her mother-in-law had told her.

When Kirk came home from the car show, they were definitely going to have a conversation. She wanted to know why he'd kept his friendship with Clarice from her, and just as importantly, why had he never mentioned the disappearance of one of his best friends? She hadn't held back about anything in her life, thinking that there should be no secrets between a husband and wife. Unlike most of the guys she'd dated, he'd always been forthcoming about everything, telling her stories about his childhood, sharing opinions on everything from restaurants to employees. He'd answered every question she'd ever asked. Nothing seemed off limits between them. Her heart sank, realizing that Kirk hadn't been completely honest with her.

Her mother-in-law cleared her throat. "I'm sorry to bring you down." She smiled apologetically.

"Oh no," Sarah assured her. "I've found this very interesting." She tapped one of the photos. "I see Gavin hasn't changed much. Always with the weapons. Probably why he wound up in law enforcement."

Judy leaned over to take a closer look. "I never noticed that before." Her brow furrowed.

"I hope when they cleaned out the bomb shelter, he remembered to take his knife."

"It wasn't his and it wasn't a knife." Judy's voice became more serious. "It was a machete made of Damascus steel. Bert's. Kirk borrowed it without permission and the boys lost it. Bert was furious. Gavin's parents offered to pay for it, but we didn't accept, of course. It had belonged to Bert's dad. It couldn't be replaced."

A machete made of Damascus steel. Sarah felt a cold chill go up her spine. She swallowed a knot in her throat. "Did you ever find out what happened to it?"

"No. We heard varying stories about who had it last. I imagine one of those kids walked off with it and couldn't bring themselves to admit it." She sighed. "Live and learn, right? That's how it is with kids. A hard lesson for all of us."

SIXTEEN

After her conversation with Judy, Jeremy Bickley and his family were on Sarah's mind. She couldn't imagine what it would be like to lose a child with no clue as to what had happened. How would a mother cope? The grief had to be crushing.

Besides feeling sympathy, she also found it puzzling. How was it that a young guy about to start his last year of high school just takes off and is never seen again? He had to go somewhere and in doing so, leave traces behind. No one just vanished. Judy seemed fairly accepting of the circumstances of Jeremy's disappearance. The story played out in a believable manner, at least on the surface. It began with a drunken, abusive father who beat his children, or at least his son. The son finally has enough and takes off, leaving a note in the mailbox.

A note in the mailbox. The thought nagged at her. It was too close to the troubling note left in her own mailbox. Besides that, it was an odd way for a teenager to notify his family that he was leaving and starting a new life. Wouldn't he have told his friends of his plan? She thought back to her own high school years. Friends were everything then, and in a case like this she imagined his friends would take him in, or at the very least give him money and drive him to the bus station.

Judy implied that something terrible had happened to him after he left, that perhaps he'd been murdered while hitchhiking. That was plausible, but there were other possibilities as well. What if he had been killed before he'd even left town? Perhaps his own father had killed him and covered up the death by saying he'd run away. Or maybe Jeremy had an argument with friends, an argument that got heated and led to violence and his death.

With a shudder she recalled the machete seen in the photos of the bomb shelter. Damascus steel, just like the one Gavin had displayed at his house. What were the chances there would be two of them? Her heart raced as she went over all the possibilities. Could the machete somehow tie in with Jeremy's disappearance? No. That meant that Gavin and Kirk would have been involved, which didn't connect with what she knew of her husband. Kirk could fly off the handle at times, but he wasn't capable of committing violence. He rarely even raised his voice. And Gavin? He always seemed like he had something to prove, but murder? No. He was a decorated police officer. Natalie had once bragged about a time earlier in Gavin's career when he'd outsmarted a hardened criminal, getting him to confess to a murder. Natalie had said, "Blake Starkey would still be walking the streets if not for Gavin. He's a hero."

A hero.

Kirk and Gavin were good men. She knew this, so why was her mind going to this dark place? Her imagination was out of control.

It was a long time ago and the situation had nothing to do with her, but somehow she couldn't shake the feeling that she and Jeremy were connected.

When Kirk came home from the auto show, she didn't waste any time. He'd barely set down his messenger bag in the foyer when she asked, "Why didn't you tell me you were friends with Clarice Carter in high school?"

In one second his friendly demeanor became guarded. "I wouldn't say we were *friends*."

"I saw some pictures and you looked pretty friendly to me."

He ran his fingers through his hair and lifted his shoulders. "You know how it is in high school. Sometimes you hang out with people for a while, but they're not really your friends. Clarice had a thing for Gavin and so she just kept coming around. It was only one summer, thank God. She's annoying."

His words made sense, but Kirk was a bad actor. His tone was disingenuous. Alarm bells went off in her head. *He's lying.* "And you didn't think to tell me this when Clarice started working with me?"

"It was a long time ago, Sarah. I didn't actually think too much about it, frankly." He sighed. "Can I at least get in the door, put my feet up?"

She followed him into the living room. "Kirk, it just doesn't make sense to me. Why wouldn't you say something?" He sat on the sofa and patted the space next to him. She took the chair opposite. "And why didn't you ever tell me you had a good friend in high school that went missing? We've been married three years and I had to find out about this from your mother. Why are you keeping secrets from me?"

He rested his hands on his knees. "Listen, Sarah. I'm sorry you had to find out from my mom, but this isn't a big secret. I just don't like to talk about it. That was a painful era in my life. Jeremy taking off like that was the worst. He was my best friend and then he was gone."

"I thought Gavin was your best friend."

"That's what he'd have you think." He gave her a sad smile. "But no. Gavin's always been a friend, but not like Jeremy. Jeremy and I were close. Really close. We had plans to room together in college."

"So no one knows where he went?"

Kirk shook his head. "He told his sister he was coming to see me when he left home that day. But he didn't come to my house. The note he left in his parents' mailbox said he was going away, but didn't give any details about where he planned to go. His family blamed me for a long time and it really weighed on me. I was just a teenager." He took off his glasses and dabbed at his eyes with his fingertips. "As for Clarice, I did tell you she was bad news in high school."

He had, but she'd assured him Clarice was fine. People changed. Everyone at work liked her. She hadn't thought it was fair to judge her based on how she'd been half a lifetime ago. Maybe she should have listened to him.

That could have been the end of it, but she couldn't let it go.

The next day, after Kirk had left for work, she got out her laptop and googled Jeremy Bickley's name, immediately coming upon a website devoted to his disappearance. The home page had what looked like a school photo, and beneath it his statistics. Hair color: brown, Eye color: brown, Height: 5'8", Weight: 156 lbs, Distinguishing marks: none. She studied the photo. Jeremy Bickley had a shy smile and hair that fell over his forehead. He wore a button-down shirt and tie in the picture, like he was heading out to a wedding.

"You look like a sweet boy," she said aloud.

The website was poorly done, with wonky formatting, making it hard to read. She imagined that the family had set this up in the early days, and as the years went by with no news to report, it hadn't been updated. She wondered why. Creating websites was so easy nowadays that it wouldn't take much to revamp this one. Had the Bickleys given up hope?

There was a video clip of the family being interviewed on a local news station. She clicked on the link and watched as the female anchor introduced the segment, saying, "An eighteen-year-old local man has gone missing. Jeremy Alan Bickley left his family home the night of June nineteenth, after an argument with his father. He hasn't been seen since. A note from Jeremy left in the family's mailbox said: *Dear Mom and Stephanie, I've had enough of Dad and his drunken rages. I need to get away and find myself. I'll be in touch once I get settled somewhere. Love, Jeremy.*" She faced the camera. "Understandably the family is worried about their son and would like him to call or come home. Dale Pittman visited with the Bickley family recently."

The view switched to a shot of the family being interviewed in their home. Dale Pittman asked, "What would you like to say to Jeremy if you could talk to him now?"

Mr. Bickley said, "I'm sorry, son. Come home and give me a chance to make this right. Things will be different, I promise you."

Jeremy's mother, tears streaming down her face, said, "You know how much I love you, Jeremy. I haven't been able to sleep since you left. Please call."

The parents looked tired and beaten down. Sick with worry, Sarah thought. Even his dad, who was the supposed cause of the trouble. His sister, though, had a stern look on her face.

The clip had been filmed twenty-one years ago and was grainy, as if it had been videotaped from an airing on TV, but even so, it had a powerful effect on Sarah, who could still feel the emotion behind the words. Jeremy Bickley's parents were worried. His sister was angry, and she was also right. Someone, somewhere, had to know something.

Sarah watched the clip over and over again, looking for clues, but it was just a family missing their son, wanting answers. Returning her attention to the website, she read comments from people in the community expressing their sympathies, and saying they were praying that the Bickleys would hear from Jeremy soon. One woman said she was having Catholic Masses said in his name and Mrs. Bickley responded: *This comforts me more than I can say.*

Another page on the site contained family photos of Jeremy, starting when he was a baby and going forward in time from there. He looked to be about three in the one where he held his little sister, Stephanie, a newborn. The caption said, *Jeremy took to her right away, saying, "This is my baby!"* In all of the photos of every age, he had the same sweet, unassuming smile. When he reached his teenage years, he wasn't too cool to hang out with his little sister, posing with his arm around her shoulder. In one of the last pictures, he was with a group of friends. The way they were clustered together was similar to the photo taken in the bomb shelter, but in this case they were sitting on a plaid couch, with Jeremy and Clarice in the middle, Kirk and Gavin on either side. Off in the background, face slightly blurred, Sarah caught sight of Stephanie.

Some newspaper articles had been scanned into the site. Most of them were straightforward, just reporting the facts of the case. She did a quick read, taking note of the statement from the police. Captain William Kramer had said he'd personally interviewed Jeremy Bickley's neighbors, friends, and relatives. His men had also canvassed the area. "I am convinced that Jeremy Bickley left of his own accord and will be heard from in time. I know this is difficult for his family, but I've assured them that we will still be available if need be. Jeremy has not been forgotten."

The first time Sarah read this she concentrated on the meaning behind the words. Clearly, the police force considered the case closed and was only placating the family. She scanned it again, and the name jumped out at her. Captain William Kramer. A relation of Gavin's? It had to be. Otherwise, it would be a pretty big coincidence.

Further googling brought up an obituary for Gavin's grandfather and the confirmation that Captain William Kramer was indeed Gavin's father. Apparently, law enforcement was the family business. Now that she thought about it, Gavin *had* mentioned something about growing up around guns and going target shooting with his dad as a kid. It hadn't interested her all that much, so she'd listened politely, not really heeding his words. At the time she'd assumed he was talking solely about hunting.

Odd that Kirk hadn't mentioned that Gavin's dad had also been the chief of police.

Sarah went back to the home page and surveyed the text that went from one edge of the screen to another. On the photo page, some of the captions extended to adjacent pictures. She'd designed the Garden Design Landscaping site and knew, with only a few hours' work, she could improve this one as well. A good hosting site had templates, which would make it easy. If the family didn't want to pay for it, she was sure Kirk would be happy to finance it. It was his friend, after all.

Impulsively she went to the contact page and filled out the form, leaving her name and phone number. In the message, she wrote:

I'm so sorry for your loss. I'm married to Kirk Aden and would like to help update your website at no charge to you (if you're interested).

She entered her name and phone number and pushed submit.

About an hour later, her phone buzzed while she was emptying the dishwasher. She didn't recognize the number, but stopped what she was doing to answer and put it on speakerphone. "Hello."

A woman's voice said, "Sarah Aden?"

"Yes?"

"Is this some kind of joke?" Barely contained anger came through the speaker as clearly as if she were in the room.

"Who is this?" Sarah's finger hovered over the button, ready to end the call.

"Stephanie Bickley." And as if that wasn't enough, she added, "Jeremy's sister."

Sarah felt her breath stall in her chest. It was clear from Stephanie's tone it had been a mistake to fill out the contact form. By trying to help she'd made things worse. "You got my message about the website," she said, her voice trailing off at the end.

Stephanie said, "Yes, I did, and I didn't appreciate hearing from you. I'm glad my mother didn't see it first. She doesn't need more aggravation in her life."

"I'm not sure what you mean. I was only offering to help revamp the website. I have the skills and the time. I wanted to help." After what seemed like a long silence, she said, "Are you still there?"

"I'm still here. Look, I'm sorry if I came off as nasty. You sound like a decent human being, but like I told Kirk at my dad's funeral, we don't need any more help from the Adens, monetary or otherwise. If he doesn't want to tell us what happened to my brother, I have no use for him."

"Wait, wait, wait! I have no idea what you're talking about. I only know that your brother went missing."

"Your husband is the one you should be asking about this."

"I will, but could you explain your side of things for me?" Sarah leaned her elbows onto the counter, her heart pounding. "Please?"

"Look. All I know is that when my brother left the house that night, he wasn't talking about running away. He was going to go to Kirk's house to hang out in the bomb shelter until my dad sobered up. Next thing I know, there's a note in our mailbox and he's gone." She gave a heavy sigh. "No way would my brother leave like that, knowing how my dad was. He *never* would have left me behind. Kirk saying he didn't see or talk to Jeremy that night is total bull. He can cry in public and pretend to be devastated all he wants, but he knows what happened and I *know* he knows. So I'm sorry if you and I aren't going to be friends, but frankly your husband is a piece of human garbage. So good luck with that."

"Was the note in the mailbox written by your brother?" Sarah didn't know how she managed to keep her voice steady.

"I'm done talking to you."

The phone went dead, leaving Sarah with a sick feeling knotting in her gut. Stephanie's anger, her revelations, were like a smack to the face. All these years later and she was still convinced that Kirk was involved? And why wouldn't she answer the question? According to everything Sarah had heard, the family had accepted the note as having been written by Jeremy. Wasn't that proof that he'd left of his own accord?

SEVENTEEN

HER

For a few weeks after she left the hospital, I only spotted Sarah Aden when she was going for walks in the neighborhood or riding in the car with Kirk at the wheel. Her forays into the world were so mundane that I nearly lost interest in her life. Maybe my mother was right and it was time to let go. I'd read about these two people, unleashed my anger in writing, and followed them. I'd had these bottled-up feelings for so long now and accomplished nothing except for creating even more misery. It was a miracle that I hadn't been spotted so far. Why push my luck?

I was on what I was thinking of as my last Sarah Aden spy mission, when I spotted Phil's green Ford parked around the corner of her home, engine idling. Luckily for me, Phil was looking at his phone, so I was able to pass him and park farther ahead. In my rearview mirror, I watched as Sarah came out of the neighbor's yard and climbed into his car. I ducked down as they came by, then waited until they were a safe distance and followed them.

They headed down a busy road in the direction of my old neighborhood and I kept two cars behind them, annoyed when a pickup truck cut in between us. They turned off and I didn't notice in time. I wound up going another half mile before I could turn back. It was possible I'd lost them completely. I had a feeling, though, that I knew where they were going. Traffic thinned once I turned off the main road into the subdivision. I went past my old house, which looked curiously bare now that our large, leafy oak tree had been reduced to a stump in the middle of the front yard.

More than a block away, I saw Sarah Aden on foot, heading up the driveway of the Adens' former residence. Phil's car was nowhere in sight. I pulled over to the curb and turned off the engine, then feigned looking at my phone, while keeping my eyes ahead. She knocked on the door and peered through the sidelight window. While waiting, she nervously shifted from foot to foot. Finally, she turned and stepped off the porch. Just when I thought she might give up and leave, she picked up a garden gnome from the landscaped bed close by and turned it upside down. I couldn't see what she was doing, but after she'd returned the gnome to his spot, she went back to the entrance, unlocked the door, and disappeared inside, and it all became clear. She knew where the new occupants of the house kept their hidden key.

They must be close friends if they trusted her that way.

Still, that didn't explain all the sneaking around. Such peculiar behavior. I couldn't understand it and I couldn't let it go.

I got out of the car and started walking in that direction, stopping just short of the driveway. As I looked around, everything was familiar, but different since I'd lived here. Houses were different colors. Saplings had grown and now towered overhead. At one point this subdivision had been my world. Now it was part of a painful past. I couldn't see Sarah inside the house. The blinds were down. From all outside appearances, no one was home.

I went to the neighbor's house and knocked on the door. When it opened, I peered into a familiar face. "Mrs. Scott?" I said. "I don't know if you remember me, but I used to live down the block—"

Her face lit up. "I know exactly who you are! How nice of you to stop by. How is your mother?"

"She's doing well, thank you." We faced each other for a moment, sizing each other up. Maggie Scott had always seemed old to me, so she hadn't changed much at all.

"Where are my manners? Come in, come in." She held open the door and beckoned for me to enter.

I followed her into the house, taking a seat in her living room. When she offered me a drink, I accepted a glass of water to be polite. "Thank you." I took the glass and rested it on my knee. "I'm sorry for coming unannounced, but I was in the neighborhood and thought I'd say hello."

"I'm glad you did. I don't get many visitors nowadays and it's good to see a familiar face." She pushed her glasses up her nose as if to get a better view of me.

"It's a good thing you were home."

"Oh, honey, I don't go much of anywhere lately." She chuckled. "You know, I always had a soft spot for your family. Your mom was my favorite neighbor. Always with a smile, always lending a hand. I was sorry when she had to sell the house, but, of course, I understood. It's a lot of property to keep up. I've had to hire a high school boy to mow the lawn and half the time he doesn't get around to it. Then I have to call and beg him to come do the work. Honestly, kids today don't have a work ethic."

"I'll tell Mom you asked about her. She's mostly recovered from the stroke, but still has some mobility issues. We live in a condo now." I took a sip of water. "I was wondering about the house next door." I gestured in that direction. "Who lives there now?"

"The Adens' old place? It was bought by the nicest young couple, Josh and Cady Caldwell. No kids yet, just the two of them."

"I spent so much time in that house in high school. I wonder if they'd let me take a look around. You know, a trip down memory lane?"

"Oh, I'm sure they would, but just between us, they're out of town." She leaned in as if sharing a secret. "For a whole month, out on a ship in the middle of the ocean. For his job. He's some kind of environmental scientist or something. Cady explained it to me." She put her palm to her forehead. "But I didn't quite grasp it. Anyway, when they get back, I'd be glad to ask for you."

"So no one is home?"

"Nope!" she said happily. "Completely empty. They asked me to keep an eye on the house. My lawn boy is going to mow the grass in front when he finally comes around to do mine. Their backyard is all torn up, so that's all he'll need to do."

"That's funny. I could have sworn I saw a woman go inside while I was waiting for you to come to the door."

Her forehead furrowed in thought. "No, that couldn't be. The house is empty."

"Huh." I wiped a droplet of condensation off the side of the glass. "I guess I was mistaken."

We talked until I'd finished the water. By that time, she'd exhausted the litany of stories about the comings and goings of the residents in the area. On the front porch before I left, she gave me a hug. "Tell your mother I say hello and that I'd love to see her."

"I will," I promised. As I walked to my car, I glanced back. She wasn't looking at me, but had her gaze on the house next door. My comment about seeing a woman go inside had bothered her. I knew she'd keep on top of it.

That night, I had an epiphany. My eyes opened and I was instantly wide awake, with a realization. I suddenly knew, just knew, why Sarah Aden was in that house.

EIGHTEEN

NOW

Sarah spent the day indoors. She had always intended to wait until dark, but now she realized that she also needed to be certain Maggie wouldn't be around to spy on her. She read Cady's books, watched her television, and heated up one of her organic meals in the microwave. Sitting at the island at lunchtime, eating one of the Harvest Bowls, she imagined what it would be like to have Cady's life. Josh, by all accounts, was the perfect husband, thoughtful, kind, full of fun.

For Cady's thirty-fifth birthday Josh had created a "this is your life" video, showcasing her childhood home, all the schools she'd attended, and clips of friends and family saying how they knew Cady and what she meant to them. Now that was a gift. When he was putting it together, Josh had messaged Sarah, thinking she was Cady's old friend, and asked if she'd wanted to contribute, but she declined, saying her schedule was too hectic. His reply sounded decidedly disappointed, which gave her a twinge of guilt, but there was no way she could tell him the truth.

Cady had posted the video on Facebook, along with another

video of her crying while she watched the first video. Sarah had watched both of them over and over again. Even Maggie had made an appearance in the birthday video, saying that Cady was a wonderful neighbor, and that she enjoyed their talks.

Seeing all of Cady's friends send virtual love for her birthday made Sarah realize how few true friends she had. None, really, if she were to be honest with herself. She and Kirk were a party of two, so close that no one else had been needed.

After she'd been hospitalized, friends from work had been there for her: cards, flowers, short visits, and phone calls. So much love and attention at once and she wasn't even in a good place to appreciate the attention. By the time she was feeling better, the outpouring had dwindled to texts and messages on social media. And finally, as the weeks went on, complete silence. Nothing at all.

Even Clarice, who she'd once considered her closest friend, became strangely distant, answering her texts in a friendly but dismissive way. *Want to do lunch one day this week?* she'd text, and Clarice would answer, *Great idea! But this week isn't good for me.* She'd insert a sad face for illustration, then add, *Been thinking about you a lot lately. Hope you're doing well!* A generic sort of response. Sarah noted that there was no offer of an alternate plan—no suggestion to meet on another date or get together for dinner instead. With a pang of sadness, Sarah realized that all of her friendships had been workplace based, and now that she no longer went to the office, she was literally out of sight and out of mind.

She imagined all of her office mates driving off together in a party bus while she stood at the curb, completely forgotten. It was a lonely thought.

Cady's friends, on the other hand, came from a mix of sources. Besides the usual work and school friends (high school and university), she'd kept in touch with people from her Peace

Corps days, and also knew people from her volunteer stints, the neighborhood, and the gym. From the looks of it, Cady picked up people wherever she went. Some people, Sarah decided, just exuded likability and she was one of them. Once you met Cady, you wanted to be her friend. And once you were her friend, you were friends for life.

As the hours passed, Sarah felt more comfortable being in the Caldwells' house. She went upstairs and looked through the couple's walk-in closet, a feature that had been added during the recent rehab, with space borrowed from an adjacent bedroom. Pushing hangers aside, she assessed each item of clothing as if she were shopping. All of Cady's clothes were simple and classic. She dressed casually when not at work, mostly leggings and cute tops, which could be matched to an assortment of athletic shoes. Her work attire was an assortment of pencil skirts, tailored button-down shirts, and classy pants.

In the back of the closet, Sarah came across an evening gown. She pulled the dress off the hanger and examined it closely, then took it to the full-length mirror in the bedroom, where she held it against herself and turned from side to side. For a second, she considered trying it on, then shook her head, knowing that would be taking things too far. It was bad enough that she was staying at the Caldwells' house without their knowledge. Wearing Cady's clothing was another thing entirely. Reluctantly she returned the dress back where she'd found it.

Sarah spent the evening in the living room, occasionally peering through the blinds when she heard cars approach, then exhaling as they drove past. She ate another one of Cady's organic meals, along with a can of coconut water. She wiped down the counters when she was through, then checked her new flip phone. Considering only one other person had this number and she'd been carrying it with her, it was unlikely she'd miss a call. Still, it was good to keep on top of things.

At the end of the day she settled down on the couch, aware that if not for Maggie's intrusive appearance, she'd already have started working in the yard. So frustrating to have to wait.

She wondered what Kirk had thought when he found her note. She'd spent countless hours deciding on the wording, hoping it would sound perfectly reasonable for her to duck out for a few days' vacation. Her goal was not to arouse any alarm on his part. After several attempts, she sighed. There was no wording in the world that would keep him from being upset, so in the end, she decided just to keep it short and to the point.

Dear Kirk, I've decided I need some time to myself, just a little break from my usual routine, so I've taken a short vacation—just for a few days. I'll be in touch. Love, Sarah

---

Sarah had purposely left the door open for her return. What if she was wrong? Nothing would make her happier than finding out she'd concocted this crazy idea, spun it from speculation and paranoia, and not a bit of it was true. A byproduct of a head injury and too much time on her hands. If only.

When Kirk found the note, he would be worried and angry, she knew that, but hopefully he'd leave it be and not take any action until a few days had gone by. The day before she'd left, she met their neighbor Doris Pisanelli at the mailbox, and casually mentioned taking a trip by herself. Doris had been surprisingly supportive, nodding and saying, "I think most women could use some time to themselves. Men so often hover." Sarah found that to be just the right response, and knew that it ensured that Doris would remember the conversation.

To make her intentions even more public, she'd texted Clarice with virtually the same message right before she'd left the house. She hoped this would prevent Kirk from spinning some tale—that she'd left in a huff, or been abducted or whatever. She imagined him organizing a search party, saying her head injury had made her irrational and susceptible to foul play. When her imagination took it a step further, she envisioned her photo being broadcast on the news. The idea made her cringe. At least Clarice and Mrs. Pisanelli would back up her version of events. If asked, they'd say that she left willingly and seemed to be in her right mind.

All she needed was time, a few days at least. But first she had to wait until Maggie Scott was gone.

That night she managed to sleep, albeit fitfully. In the morning, as light streamed in through the blinds, she got up from the couch, folded the borrowed blankets, and returned them, along with the pillow, to the linen closet.

After she showered and changed into fresh clothing, she pulled a chair up to a second-story window in the front of the house and watched the neighborhood from up above. When a white van pulled into Maggie Scott's driveway, she stood to get a better look. From that angle the logo on the side of the van wasn't visible, but she could see an attractive young woman exit the van and walk confidently up to the door. Within a few minutes, the woman came back out, followed by Maggie. Both women had luggage in hand, Maggie carrying a small overnight case and the woman pulling a slightly larger suitcase. They chatted while they walked. Sarah watched as they loaded the luggage and Maggie was helped into the van.

Phil had assured her that his plan would work, but she still found it unbelievable that a woman would accept an offer from a complete stranger and get into a vehicle with someone she didn't know. How could Maggie be so naïve? Didn't she know evil lurked everywhere? In a way, Sarah found it reassuring that there were still trusting souls out in the world and that one of them was Maggie. Lucky for her that the old woman was so gullible, because it got her out of her house and away from the Caldwells' backyard.

A car coming down the street slowed noticeably as it passed, then sped up again. People could be so nosy.

As the van sped off, Sarah put her hand up against the glass. "Goodbye, Maggie. Enjoy your trip. Don't hurry back."

NINETEEN

THEN

Kirk tried ignoring her texts, but it got his attention when she sent one that said:

We need to talk. It's about Sarah.

He was fairly certain this was just her usual cry for attention, but the fact that she now was bringing his wife into her craziness made him livid. This had to end.

There were some back-and-forth messages between them after that, but ultimately he agreed to meet. He set the terms. It would be during the day and in public: lunch at a local family restaurant far enough away from his business that it was unlikely he'd see anyone he knew. Even if he did, he had a ready explanation: he'd been running some work-related errands, stopped for a bite to eat, and ran into an acquaintance from high school. They'd chatted and she insisted on joining him for lunch. Ever the gentleman, he'd agreed. A convincing story, he thought, and completely plausible.

Sometimes he wondered if he'd ever be rid of Clarice. He'd go months or even a year or more without seeing or hearing from her and then suddenly, at the most inopportune times, she'd show up. When Sarah came home from work talking about the new hire, Clarice Carter, he felt a sudden pain in his chest. His initial thought had been that he was having a heart attack, and wouldn't it be ironic if Clarice caused his death? The physical pain passed soon enough, but the horror of knowing Clarice was back in his life stayed, a dull throb that never quite went away. This was no coincidence. She'd deliberately gotten the job because Sarah worked there. Another way to insert herself into his life. When Clarice and Sarah became fast friends, that prolonged the pain. He wanted to warn his wife, but couldn't be completely forthcoming, so all he'd said was, "If I remember correctly, Clarice had a bit of a reputation for being two-faced in high school."

Sarah, sweet Sarah, who always saw the best in everyone, had answered, "But that was a long time ago. People change. She seems really nice now."

Some people only wanted what they couldn't have, and that was Clarice. Always grabbing for the brass ring. He was pretty sure she was hooking up with Gavin again. He would have thought that would be enough for her, but for some reason she wanted to have Kirk panting after her as well.

When he pulled into the parking lot of the family restaurant, he could see Clarice already waiting in a booth by the window. He walked inside, bypassing the front register and the glass pie case with the revolving shelves, and went straight to the booth. He slid into place on the vinyl-clad seat opposite her without saying a word.

She winked at him. "Hey, Kirky, you're late."

"Were you worried I wouldn't show?"

"Oh, I knew you'd show. Some things in life are certain." She lifted her chin triumphantly and snapped her fingers. "You said you'd come and you're a man who is true to his word." A young woman with a friendly smile came with two glasses of water and a pair of laminated menus. "I won't need a menu," Clarice said. "I know what I want."

"Just coffee for me," he said.

Clarice frowned. "No. We're having lunch. That was the agreement." She turned her attention to the server. "A Caesar salad for me and my darling *boyfriend* will have a cheeseburger medium rare with fries, and a side of ranch dressing. And I'll have a diet cola." Addressing Kirk, she asked, "Did you still want coffee with your burger?"

Kirk sighed. "Forget the coffee. Just the burger and water will be fine." He glanced up at the server. "Just for the record, she's not my girlfriend. We're just friends from high school." He held up his left hand. "I'm happily married."

The waitress, clearly not interested, said, "Alrighty then," and gathered up the menus.

After she walked away, Clarice said, "You're so quick to disown me, but who else would have known exactly what you would have ordered? How many people in the world know about your penchant for dipping French fries in ranch dressing?"

"First of all, I'm not and never have been your boyfriend. Secondly, I rarely eat red meat and I haven't had fries in years. You don't know me nearly as well as you think you do." His eyes darted around the restaurant, checking for familiar faces. When he didn't see any, he relaxed, but only a little. "The only reason I agreed to see you is to impress upon you how serious I am about ending whatever this is between you and me." He waved a finger between the two of them. "It's over. If I never see you again, that would make my life complete."

"Oh, Kirk, you don't mean that."

"I do." He leaned forward to meet her eyes. "Look, we've had some fun over the years. I'll give you that much. But I'm married now."

"You were married the last time, but you still went up to my hotel room." She pinched the end of the paper straw covering and pulled it free. "Seems to me like Sarah wasn't even on your mind that evening." She stuck the straw in the water, lifted the glass, and took a long pull.

He felt his face flush red. "That was a mistake." The biggest mistake of his life, unless you counted meeting Clarice in the first place. When he said his marriage vows, he'd meant every word. And then one evening he'd taken his top sellers—Veda and Marcus—out for a celebratory dinner to commemorate an outstanding quarter. He'd let Marcus pick the place, and he'd chosen Valentina, a fine dining restaurant located on the first floor of a downtown hotel. Sarah had been invited, but begged off saying she had a bad headache. After dinner, the three of them had ended up at the bar for a few more drinks. Marcus called it quits first, with Veda soon following.

Kirk had just gotten off his bar stool and was assessing whether or not it was safe for him to drive when Clarice had appeared out of nowhere. She sidled up behind him, running her hand down his back and between his legs. She whispered in his ear, telling him she had a room at the hotel. To further illustrate, she held up her key card. "Join me for a private drink?" She turned away and inexplicably he'd followed. He knew, with every step, that this was a terrible idea. His drunk mind rationalized it, thinking that he'd just go along with what she wanted to keep her in check. Otherwise, she might make a scene in the bar. He'd been meaning to have a serious talk with her anyway because she was a loose cannon.

They'd had a history of being friends with benefits, but that had been in their younger days. He'd spent the last ten years warding her off, not answering her calls or texts for days and then making excuses for not getting together. He thought she'd get the hint and give up, but that never happened. Now he had a chance to set her straight. Going up to the room with her didn't mean that it would necessarily lead to sex.

It did, unfortunately.

The sex wasn't even that good. The whole episode turned out to be a moment's weakness that led to only the tiniest bit of pleasure and a world of regret. Even though Sarah never found out, just the fact that he knew what he'd done tainted his marriage. His stupidity had sullied the best thing that ever happened to him. He couldn't go back in time and undo it, but he sure as hell could make sure it would never happen again.

"Look, Clarice." He jabbed at the table with one finger. "This has to stop. There's a lot at stake here for me and for you. Sarah thinks you're her friend. She'd do anything for you. Are you really willing to lose that? And clearly you can have any guy you want. All I'm doing is asking you to step away from me. You can do better, frankly."

Her lips stretched into a thin smile. The waitress returned with her drink, setting it down on the scallop-edged place mat. Clarice wrapped her hand around the glass. "Thank you." When they were alone again, she said, "You think I can have any guy I want?"

"Absolutely. You're the whole package. I'm surprised you never got married, frankly."

She laughed. "You're so conventional, Kirk, thinking I aspire for the traditional. Me, walking down the aisle in a white dress and veil? Making vows to some poor sap, promising to love and cherish him forever? Please. The truth is that I could have been married a dozen times over if I wanted, but I'm too smart to fall into that trap."

"You don't have to get married. I'm just pointing out that you have many choices besides me."

"This isn't news to me, Kirk."

He turned and gazed toward the parking lot for a minute before looking back at her. In a resigned way, he said, "I realize the ball is in your court, Clarice. I'm asking you, as a personal favor to me, to just let it go. Find someone else to set your sights on."

"A personal favor?"

"Yes, a personal favor. I can't do this anymore. I appreciate our past history and nothing will erase that, but everything is different now. Sarah means more to me than anything. When she was attacked and in the hospital, I was out of my mind thinking I'd almost lost her. I need to make Sarah a priority. I'm sure you understand."

Clarice scoffed. "You and Gavin have become so old. We used to have fun." She glanced out the window, distracted. "Remember?"

"Well, people change and grow, Clarice." To get her mind onto a different topic, he related a story about a former classmate of theirs who'd come into the car dealership looking to buy a Mercedes. "He married Fiona Berman. Remember her? One year younger than us? They came in together."

"How did she look?"

"I wouldn't have recognized her. She must have gained fifty pounds."

Clarice perked up then and smiled. There was nothing she liked better than good gossip, especially if it was about former classmates who hadn't aged well.

Even though the conversation had taken a positive turn, he was happy when the waitress—whose name tag identified her as Rhiannon—arrived at their table and set their plates down in front of them. "Here you go," she said cheerfully. "Ketchup's on the table. Do you need anything else?"

Clarice shook her head and Kirk said, "No, I think we're good. Thanks."

A moment or two later, Clarice reached over and took a fry off his plate, then dipped it into the cup of ranch dressing. Taking a bite, she said, "Yum, you're right." She nodded in approval. "It is better this way."

"So what do you think, Clarice? Can we part ways?"

Her eyes narrowed. "How's the investigation going?"

Her question caught him off guard. "What investigation?"

"Silly man!" Her tone was flirtatious. "You say Sarah is your everything, and yet you've already forgotten that she was attacked? And nearly killed, from the sounds of it. Have they found the man who did it?"

He shook his head. "No. They haven't found a suspect, but they're still working on it. Clarice, would you mind answering the question? I want to know if I can count on your discretion going forward. I'm asking that you please stop texting and calling me, and please promise you won't say anything to Sarah. This is important to me. I'm begging you!"

"Begging? I like the sound of that." She laughed. "Say it again, Kirk."

He set his napkin next to his plate. "I can see this isn't going anywhere."

"I have a thought," she said. "How about you lend me ten thousand dollars and I promise not to tell Sarah about that night at the hotel?"

"You're blackmailing me?"

"It's not blackmail. Just a loan between old friends."

"Why would you need a loan? I thought you were rich. Didn't you inherit some old fart's money?"

She waved a hand dismissively. "I did inherit his estate, but between the attorney's fees and everything else, it wasn't enough for a lifetime. I have to live, you know."

Kirk stared at her incredulously. "I'm not lending you money. Ever."

"So you don't mind your wife knowing about us?"

"There's no 'us.'" He crossed his arms. "And might I remind you that I have the goods on you too?"

The waitress paused by their table. "How's your lunch?"

Kirk glanced down at his untouched plate. "Delicious, thank you."

"Everything's fine," Clarice said.

Watching the waitress walk away, Kirk came to a resolution. He was weary. Tired of worrying. Exhausted by Clarice. Ultimately, he wanted to live his life without fear, and in order to do that, he had to be prepared for the worst.

Meeting her eyes, he said, "I asked you nicely, Clarice, hoping that you'd be reasonable and leave me be, but I can see that's not going to happen. I'm drawing the line right here and now. I'll be blocking you, and if I have to take out a restraining order, I'll be doing that as well. Leave. Me. Alone." He got out his wallet and threw a handful of bills on the table before getting up and striding away.

After a few steps, he heard Clarice cry out, "You can't get rid of me that easily, Kirk Aden. I'll tell Sarah." Her voice was loud and triumphant. Conversation in the restaurant stopped and heads swiveled in her direction. Damn Clarice, always having to be the center of attention.

He stopped, spun around, and said, "Go ahead. Do it." Turning back, he was shocked to see a familiar face, a man sitting at the counter, staring right at him. His mind shuffled through memories until he realized the guy's identity. It was Phil. Sarah's annoying physical therapist. Kirk quickened his pace, going around two women who were walking ahead of him, and darting out the front door of the building. Outside he felt a sense of having escaped, but for how long?

Sitting in his car he had a full view of the restaurant. Through the windows running the length of the building, he clearly saw Clarice sitting exactly where he'd left her, calmly eating her salad. Nothing seemed to faze the woman. He scanned the rest of the room, noticing that almost everyone had returned to eating and talking to their companions.

All but one.

Phil was staring at Clarice. As Kirk watched, he lifted his phone and aimed it in her direction. As Clarice took a sip of her soft drink, Phil had her in his sights. Kirk could almost hear the click, click, click of photos being taken.

From there Kirk's imagination went a step further, envisioning Phil showing the pictures to Sarah and telling her what he'd heard. He could only imagine what her reaction would be. Kirk rested his head against the steering wheel and hit the dashboard with the palm of his hand.

Damn. Could his life get any worse? He didn't think so.

TWENTY

A few months into her recovery, Sarah made the decision to visit the town hall. Spending so much time alone had given her time to think, and she'd found herself ruminating on the conversation with her mother-in-law and the follow-up discussion with Kirk. He'd lied to her. Why? She couldn't ignore her mounting suspicions. She had to know more.

She and Phil had begun to meet weekly for coffee, something she didn't share with Kirk. He certainly wouldn't have objected to the friendship, but he'd never hidden his dislike of Phil, something she didn't understand. Over the course of the last few weeks, she'd come to value Phil's opinions. He wasn't connected to her life and so he had some distance and could see things more clearly.

Some part of her wanted information about the bomb shelter. Where on the property was it located? How big was it? She wasn't sure how this fact-finding mission would help her, but at least it was a start toward getting some answers. When she'd talked all of this through with Phil, he'd suggested checking the official records. "You could check to see if there was a builder's

permit for the shelter. That would give you some information."
When he'd said he'd drive her, she took him up on the offer.

When he pulled into a parking space, she said, "Do you mind
waiting here while I run inside? It'll be just a few minutes."

"Take your time," he said, smiling. "I brought a book."

Typical of small communities, the town hall was in a huge brick
building that also contained the community center and the police
department. The library was in a separate building, but stood
adjacent and shared a parking lot. There was some comfort in
walking across the parking lot, since it felt so reminiscent of visiting the library.

Sarah went into the entryway, following the arrow down the
hallway, then entered through the glass double doors to the town
hall. She thought this would go quickly. After all, how long did it
take to peruse all the documents pertaining to one property? In
her mind, this was a quick errand. Heidi, a silver-haired woman
with reading glasses hanging off a chain around her neck, turned
out to be a major deterrent. The exchange started off well enough.
When she first walked in, Heidi stepped up to the counter with a
smile on her face and asked, "Good morning! How can I help you
today?" Implying, of course, that she wanted to be of service.

Just as she'd practiced, Sarah politely responded, "I'd like to
see everything you have pertaining to a certain property, a house
located at 214 Palmer Street." She felt her heart hammer against
her chest as if she were doing something wrong, which was ridiculous. People looked at public records all the time. It wasn't a
crime, so why did she feel so guilty? She took a deep breath to
steady herself.

Heidi wrinkled her forehead. "Is there something specific
you're looking for?" She must have sensed some hesitancy on
Sarah's part because she began to list off all of the records in her

department, as if it were inventory. "For a residential property we'd most likely have plats, builder's blueprints, any permits that were filed, maps, and documents pertaining to easements and zoning requirements. We also might have any written correspondence between the developer or builder and the building inspector. If you're looking for a deed, that would be at the county office." She leaned over the counter and smiled. "For some of the earlier homes in town we don't have much, but I believe Palmer Street was developed in the 1950s. By that point the planning commission was in full force, so there would be more documentation."

"I see." Sarah felt herself regaining some confidence. "Actually, I'm considering buying the property and I want to know everything about it." Back in an office out of view, she heard the faint one-sided conversation of a woman on a phone. Above her head a fluorescent light buzzed.

Heidi leaned against the counter. "Usually, we have real estate agents make this kind of request. I'm surprised yours isn't helping you out."

"I prefer to do things myself." She gave Heidi a winning smile. "I'm particularly interested in knowing if there were any permits issued for outbuildings or structures besides the main house."

"Outbuildings?" She lifted her glasses off her bosom and set them on her nose, peering at Sarah through the lenses. "You mean like a storage shed?"

"Any kind of structure besides the actual house."

"We might not have information for something like that. Back in the day they used to be more lackadaisical about that kind of thing. You wouldn't believe what people would do without permits. One guy put a whole addition on the back of his house and no one knew until twenty years later when they tried to sell it." Heidi shook her head. "One thing you might want to check out— we have an excellent website with aerial views. You can zoom in quite close. It might be able to tell you more than anything we have." She hadn't budged from her spot. Sarah got the impression she wasn't eager to go in back and search for old records. "Getting an online look might be your best bet."

This was not how Sarah had imagined this visit. She'd envisioned being handed a file or folder, leafing through it, finding what she needed, and being on her way, not facing this roadblock of a woman. She thought of Phil waiting in the parking lot. He'd said to take her time, but she was still aware of the inconvenience. "Can I just see what you have?" she asked. "Any information would be helpful."

"Just a minute," Heidi said, her mouth settling into a grim line. "Let me talk to my supervisor. I'll be right back." She walked away from the counter, then strode down a short hallway until Sarah could no longer see her.

She had to talk to her supervisor? Why? The woman's reluctance to comply with a basic request was unsettling. There was no reason for Sarah to get a bad feeling, and yet, there it was. A sick sensation rose from her stomach, followed by the fear that someone was going to ask for her name and identification.

Sarah heard Heidi speaking to someone, but couldn't make out the words. She wondered if Heidi found her request to be suspicious. The harsh light of the office made her feel exposed. She had a stray thought: Did the office or entrance have cameras recording her visit? Probably, she decided, with a sinking feeling. Didn't most places nowadays?

In a second of panic, she decided to abort what she'd been thinking of as "the mission." Turning away from the counter, she slipped out the door. In the hallway, she breathed a sigh of relief. This was the kind of idea that seemed great in concept, but terrible in execution. She walked purposefully, eager to leave.

When she got to the end of the hallway, the sight of Gavin Kramer coming out of the police department made her stop in her tracks. She'd momentarily forgotten that, as the chief of police, he worked in this building. There was no pretending she didn't recognize him. Even if they hadn't met dozens of times, he stood out, dressed as he was in his usual work attire, white dress shirt with a black tie, gold badge over one pocket. The patches on each shoulder made him look even more official. Sarah felt herself paste a smile on her face.

"Gavin!" she exclaimed as he came through the doorway. "What a nice surprise."

"Sarah?" With outstretched arms he pulled her into an embrace, making her cringe. When he stepped back, he still had a hand on her shoulder. "What are you doing here?"

Caught off guard, her mind shuffled through all the plausible reasons she could have for being here. "Looking for you, of course." She hadn't known she was going to say that exact thing until the words came out of her mouth. "I was just at the library and thought I'd pop in and ask a few questions." Mentally she gave herself credit for coming up with an explanation on short notice.

"What kind of questions?"

"About the threatening notes left in our mailbox? I've had some memory issues from my head injury and I thought seeing them might help." Her head injury was turning out to be a handy excuse.

"Of course." He smiled, then beckoned. "Why don't you come down to my office? I'm just heading out to a meeting, but I'll ask my assistant to get what you need."

She followed him into the office, past the front desk and into what he called a meeting room. With a wave of his hand, he offered her a chair. As she took a seat, he said, "Kirk said you're having some cognitive impairment. False memories, memory loss. I've never experienced anything like that. Feeling like you're losing your mind—that must be terrible."

He stood over her with folded arms, making her feel like a

child being schooled. Sarah said, "It's not as bad as all that. And I'm getting better every day." His expression showed he wasn't buying it, so she added, "I'll be back to my old self in no time at all."

Gavin gave a patronizing smile. "I hope so. Kirk sent me an email when you first came home and he was frantically worried, said you insisted that he'd replaced the towels and rearranged the cabinets. He was concerned that you had permanent brain damage."

Kirk emailed Gavin about this? Sarah felt a stab of betrayal. Smoothly she said, "The doctor said some confusion is normal. And I was still on pain meds at that time as well. Later on, I remembered everything." All true. Days later, she recalled buying the new towels and rearranging the cupboards to make emptying the dishwasher easier. The gap in her memory had somehow filled itself in, which had been a relief. She met his eyes. "You said you had a meeting?"

"Right." He nodded, smiling widely. "I'll have Christy bring you the file. It might take a few minutes. Are you going to be fine here by yourself?"

"Of course." He turned to leave, but before he left, Sarah said, "Just one thing. When I spoke to you about the notes and the dead rat, how did I seem?"

Gavin put a hand to his goatee, seemingly in thought. "Kirk was the one who brought the other notes in and he was the one who filed the report. He said you were too upset to talk about it."

"So I never discussed it with you?" she asked casually, tilting her head. "Maybe at one of our dinners?" She couldn't pin down the last time they'd gotten together, but if it was around that time, certainly the subject would have come up.

"Not directly, no." He shook his head ruefully.

She nodded. "One more thing. Any leads on my case?"

"I'm sorry, Sarah. We haven't made any progress at all." He gave her a sympathetic smile. "But that doesn't mean we've given up. I've seen cases solved years later. People call in through the tip line, or the victim suddenly remembers something that leads us to a suspect. If seeing the notes helps you remember something, please let me know."

"I will."

After he left the room, Sarah sat under the bright fluorescent lights built into the white ceiling tiles and checked her phone. The only ones who ever messaged her anymore were Kirk and his mother. Once in a great while, Natalie checked in with her as well, but those were drive-by messages. She sent Phil a quick text:

Sorry this is taking so long. Maybe another ten minutes?

He pinged back immediately.

No worries. Whatever it takes.

She put her phone back in her purse and examined the room. A large window in the hallway had proved to be a mirror on her side, leading her to believe she was actually in an interrogation room.

A few minutes later, Christy came in with a file in hand, saying, "Mrs. Aden? The chief said you wanted to see your file?"

"Yes, thank you."

"You need anything else? Coffee or water?"

"No, I'm good. I won't take long. I promise."

"Take as much time as you need. When you're done you can just leave it on the table and I'll take care of it later."

"Great, thanks." After the door closed behind Christy, she

opened the file and pulled out the paperwork. Finally, she was able to see the police report filed by Kirk, along with the four notes and a photo. The image of the dead rat, gutted and sprawled out on their porch, was the most shocking to her. Who would do such a thing? It was bold to leave a dead animal by their front door. Their house was far back from the road and fronted by a U-shaped driveway with a fountain in the center. Anyone leaving anything on the porch was taking a big chance of being seen. Added to this was the fact that most people in their neighborhood had a security camera. Her house hadn't yet been equipped that way, but that wouldn't be known by outsiders, so it was still a ballsy move.

The notes were inside a clear plastic holder and dated with sticky notes. Each of them was like the first one, written in marker on plain white paper. The wording varied somewhat, but all of them were printed in capital letters. She shuffled through the notes, organizing them in the order they were left in her mailbox.

I KNOW WHAT YOU DID. HOW CAN YOU LIVE WITH YOURSELF?

JUST YOU WAIT. YOU'RE GOING TO GET YOURS.

SOMEDAY EVERYONE WILL KNOW WHO YOU ARE AND WHAT YOU'VE DONE.

ENJOY YOUR LIFE OF LUXURY. SOON YOU'LL
BE EXPOSED FOR WHAT YOU ARE AND IT
WILL BE OVER.

Even though the words were crudely printed, the vitriol behind them felt like an assault. She remembered going to the mailbox and finding the first one. She'd been shocked then too, reading it over and over again, racking her brain, trying to work out what it meant. Some part of her did feel undeserving of the life of luxury she'd gained by marrying Kirk. Did she come off as conceited? She didn't think so. She never mentioned anything about her circumstances when talking to her co-workers. Clarice was nearly as privileged, but not quite as discreet. Clarice was known to show off expensive jewelry and talk about trips—the kind of travel most people who worked in their office couldn't afford. Clarice wasn't as tuned in to the feelings of others, but Sarah clearly remembered the days when she was just getting by and tried to be considerate of how these kinds of references might make others feel.

The notes were puzzling for other reasons too. I KNOW WHAT YOU'VE DONE. An accusation that didn't make sense. What were they referring to? She couldn't even imagine. Sarah was a rule follower through and through. She'd never gotten so much as a parking ticket and she tried to be nice to everyone she met. Another note: YOU'RE GOING TO GET YOURS. Definitely a threat, but nothing specific. Vague. Like something a kid would say. Maybe Kirk was right and there was no reason to it, just a crazy person venting over some perceived slight or imagined misdeed.

Maybe they'd erroneously targeted the wrong house.

She read over everything else pertaining to the notes. The police had questioned their neighbors and checked the security camera footage in the surrounding areas. Ultimately, they came up with nothing. They'd advised Kirk to get his own security cameras, and as far as the police were concerned, that was the end of it—until she was struck in the head in her backyard. It wasn't until that happened that he finally had the security cameras installed.

Even now that she was nearly recovered, thinking about her injury made the back of her skull throb. Was the attack somehow tied to the notes? There was nothing definite linking the two, but she thought it must be, because what other possible explanation was there? What were the chances the two events *wouldn't* be related?

Sarah took out her phone and took pictures of everything in the file, then reassembled the pages and left the folder on the table. On the way out, catching sight of Christy at her desk, she mouthed the words "Thank you." Nodding, Christy gave a friendly wave.

Sarah felt an air of triumph by the time she climbed into the passenger seat of Phil's car.

"What did you find out?" he asked, starting the engine.

"I bailed on getting the property info because the lady behind the counter seemed suspicious and I was afraid she'd ask for my ID," she said. "But then I ran into Gavin Kramer as I was leaving. I panicked for a minute, but then I recovered and told him I wanted to have a look at the threatening notes."

Phil gave her a quick smile. "Good thinking. How'd that go?"

"His assistant gave me the file. I still don't remember ever seeing three of the notes. And I definitely don't remember the dead rat." She held up her phone. "But I took pictures of everything."

"So what's your takeaway from all this?"

Dear sweet Phil. She knew he would never badmouth Kirk directly, but some of his questions had made his opinion clear: he thought Kirk wrote the notes and was gaslighting her. She wasn't convinced. "I'm not sure what to think, but I feel like I'm close to figuring it out."

TWENTY-ONE
NOW

Clarice didn't bother with a greeting. She answered her phone by saying, "What do you want?" Her voice through the speaker-phone conveyed her irritation.

Kirk could have anticipated this reaction. Yes, she'd tried to hit him up for money, even threatening to tell Sarah everything if he didn't, but he'd known she was bluffing. Clarice was always playing games, making unreasonable demands, pushing people away, and then trying to lure them back again. She was a walking nightmare. Of course she was irked with him. He hadn't played his part in the game. Frankly, he hadn't really wanted to call her, but she was Sarah's closest friend and the most likely to know where she'd gone.

"Really, that's where we're at now?"

"You said you never wanted to speak to me again, and now you call and expect what? That I'd be thrilled to hear from you?" She laughed. "I thought you were going to block me. Whatever happened to that?"

Kirk leaned against the kitchen counter and sighed. He didn't have the time or patience for games. "Please don't start with me, Clarice. I'm calling to ask if you know where Sarah is."

"You're her husband. Shouldn't you know where she is?"

"Can you just answer the question?"

"Oh, that would be too easy."

"Okay, never mind." His finger was poised to disconnect the call, but something kept him from it.

Clarice laughed. "Do you have any idea how much I'm enjoying this? Kirk Aden calling me, suddenly needing something. This is rich."

Typical. She hadn't changed much since they were teenagers. Technically she'd been Gavin's go-to back in the day, but she was nondiscriminatory, flirting with all three boys, smiling their way, laughing at their jokes, touching them playfully. Gavin thought the fact that she hit on all of them was a riot. Once, he'd told Kirk, "Trust me, you guys are just the warm-up act."

When the five of them hung out in a group, Clarice would wait until everyone's attention was elsewhere and do something provocative just for Kirk. Licking her lips. Leaning over to show him her cleavage. Winking in a suggestive way. Kirk tried his best to ignore her. One time Stephanie Bickley had noticed Clarice running a hand over Kirk's thigh and her eyes grew wide.

Later, Clarice had asked Jeremy, "Why does your sister always have to be here? Doesn't she have any friends of her own?"

Jeremy had shrugged. "She has friends, but none of them live nearby."

Kirk had to speak up then, of course. "Why do you care? She just sits and reads. It's not like she's bothering anyone."

"It's just crowded down here. We don't really need one more person taking up space," Clarice said with a pout. Clearly, she would have preferred being the only female in the group.

"She stays," Kirk had said firmly. His house, his bomb shelter, his rules.

So many years later, just when he thought he'd gotten Clarice out of his life, she started working in the office with Sarah at Garden Design Landscaping. He couldn't believe the nerve of her befriending his wife. And now, adding insult to injury, he had to ask her, of all people, for help. He could picture the gleeful look on her face.

Sarah had seemed enamored of Clarice, starting with her admiration of the older woman's sleek buttery-blond hair, cut to exacting standards. Clarice had an effortless way about her with her perfect makeup, coordinated outfits, and obviously expensive jewelry chosen to draw attention. Those who didn't know her well only saw her outward appearance and an outgoing, friendly personality that could light up a room. Clarice was someone you noticed, but the truth was that Clarice had nothing on Sarah, but an undeserved confidence and a love of shopping. Next to her, Sarah, with her unpainted nails and more casual clothing style, seemed less sophisticated, but anyone who knew both women could tell the difference. Sarah was the real deal, a quality woman with a big heart. Clarice was all show, no substance.

He sighed audibly. "I can tell this is going nowhere, so never mind. If you hear from her, tell her to give me a call. I'm worried."

He'd almost clicked off when he heard her voice from the other end of the line call out, "Wait a minute! I did hear from her. I got a text this morning."

Kirk leaned in to the phone. "This morning?"

"Yes, about nine o'clock."

"What did it say?"

"You want to come over and I'll show it to you?" Her tone was teasing.

"No, I don't want to come over." She had to be the most annoying woman on the planet. "Just tell me now. Seriously, Clarice, I'm crazy with worry over her. She just took off and you know that's not like her."

"All right. I'll send you a screenshot, but first you have to apologize to me."

"For what?"

"For everything."

He clenched his fist and looked out the window at their backyard, willing himself to keep it together. "Of course, Clarice. Whatever I've said or done to hurt your feelings, I regret. I hope you'll accept my sincere apology for my behavior."

"That's better." Her tone softened. "I think we might become friends after all, Mr. Aden."

Friends? That was never going to happen, but there was no point in contradicting her. "You said you'd send me a screenshot?"

"After we're done with this conversation," she said.

He was quickly losing patience with her, but tried to stay on an even keel. "Then I think we're done talking. I don't want to be rude, Clarice, but I have a few more calls to make." Sarah referred to this voice as his "smooth, charming guy persona." Anything to finish this discussion and get what he wanted. "If you'd send me the text as soon as you can, I'd really appreciate it. Thanks." After disconnecting, he waited for the ping, which thankfully came only a few minutes later.

And there it was. A text from Sarah sent exactly when Clarice had specified. Apparently, she could tell the truth on occasion.

Hey, Clarice! I know we talked about getting together this weekend, but I'm leaving for a few days out of town, just me. When I get back, I'll give you a call.

This was followed by a heart emoji. Kirk read the words over and over again. He knew that on the surface, this message was reassuring. It didn't sound like she'd been coerced, but it still nagged at him. Sarah wasn't the type to do things impulsively. She was reliable and responsible. Leaving without notice and not taking her cell phone? He had a sick feeling something was seriously off.

TWENTY-TWO

Kirk stood in the kitchen and took a deep breath. All around him were reminders of his wife. The paint color on the walls—a dove gray, that they'd chosen together. The espresso maker his mother gave her as a birthday present. The dishtowels she'd picked up at Kohl's the last time they'd shopped there together. He leaned his elbows against the countertop, and returned his gaze to his cell phone, willing it to ring, to be Sarah explaining what had happened. He blinked back the start of tears. Sarah was his whole world. Where could she have gone?

Once he had collected himself, he called her sister, Maren, and a few of her other co-workers, including her boss, Brenda. None of them had heard from her. All of them promised to let him know if they did. Finally, he scrolled through his contacts until he came to Gavin's name. His personal cell number, not the number at the police station. He pushed the button, and when Gavin picked up, he said, "Sarah left me." He thought he had tucked his emotions away, but now, despite his best efforts, his voice shook. He glanced down to see that the knuckles of the hand gripping the edge of the counter were white. "She left a note saying she just needed some time to herself, but I have a bad feeling about this."

"Relax." As usual, Gavin downplayed Kirk's concerns, even before hearing the whole thing. "What exactly did the note say?"

Kirk read it aloud.

Gavin scoffed. "In her own words. *A short vacation. Back in a few days. Love, Sarah.* I'd say she's fine. She's just doing what we'd all like to do."

"No," Kirk said. "This is more than that. Something's going on. I just can't figure it out."

"Kirk, you worry too much. I'm sure she's fine."

"You don't understand. She's been different lately. Argumentative." Kirk thought back to a recent evening when she'd confronted him after visiting the police station. He'd never have thought she'd go out walking on her own, especially not for such a distance. The therapist had suggested daily walks, but he'd been talking in terms of a few blocks. The police station was a mile and half from their house—a good walk under regular circumstances, but for a woman still recovering from a head injury, it was unthinkable. At home she occasionally had to grab the wall from dizziness. He tried not to think about what would have happened if she'd had an episode of vertigo while walking outdoors and passed out on the roadway. She'd taken a huge chance going it alone.

Kirk had said to her, "I can't believe you walked three miles. What if you'd collapsed along the way? Or been struck by a car crossing an intersection?"

She'd tilted her head and crossed her arms. "Why would I be hit by a car? Do you think I'd randomly wander into traffic?" From the look on her face she was upset by the inference she was incapable.

Truthfully, he *had* been worrying about how distracted she'd been lately, but he didn't dare admit it now. "If I had known how badly you wanted to see the notes, I would have driven you myself," he said. "You know I would have rearranged my hours. I'd do anything for you."

She'd softened then. "Yes, I know."

"So the notes upset you. It's understandable, but Gavin didn't think they were anything to worry about."

"I know that I never saw the last three notes. Just the first one."

"You don't *remember* seeing them," he clarified, and felt a pang of guilt at the lie. At the time, he hadn't told her about the subsequent notes, but had quietly passed them on to Gavin, who'd written up a report and thrown everything into a file. Kirk knew there would be no actual investigation, but wanted it on record in case it had escalated. He justified keeping it from Sarah because she'd been so upset upon seeing the first one. Honestly, his intent was to spare her, but he could see now that he'd made a big mistake.

"Don't play games with me, Kirk Aden. I know that I never saw those notes. I don't know why you're doing this, but I resent you telling people I have brain damage."

"I never told anyone you have brain damage."

"Gavin says otherwise."

"If he said that, he twisted my words. You know how he is— acts like he knows it all. I might have said you had some memory gaps, but brain damage? I know I never used those words."

Sarah nodded, making him think he'd put the issue to rest, but then the conversation veered in another direction.

She said, "And I'm still puzzling over why you failed to tell me about your connection with Clarice Carter in high school? Or that one of your best friends from back then went missing? Someone important disappeared from your life and you never shared that with me?"

And just like that, the argument was resurrected.

He kept his voice from rising as he came to his own defense. "I didn't mention it because nothing ever happened with Clarice and it was in another lifetime. There was a period when she hung around with us, but it didn't last long and then she got bored and moved on to another group of kids. She was always too cool for us." Damn that Clarice. She was a dark cloud in high school and was still casting a shadow. He couldn't seem to shake her. "As for Jeremy, that summer was a dark time for me. He was a good friend in a terrible situation. All of us knew his dad was an abusive drunk, but none of us knew how bad it was. I feel guilty for not helping him when I had the chance. Even saying his name still causes me pain. I let him down and now he's gone."

"And none of you knew where he went?" She folded her arms.

"And none of us knew where he went," he repeated softly. "We figured he took off to escape a bad home life. We were kids. Stupid kids."

"Why is it that I know your third-grade teacher's first name, but not this? Why, Kirk?"

He ran his fingers through his hair and sighed. "I don't have a good reason, Sarah."

"You have nothing for me?" Her voice was tinged with anger. "You're keeping secrets from me and can't tell me why?"

He shrugged. "Talking about it reminds me of Jeremy and that makes me want to cry. Once we covered up the bomb shelter, I felt such a sense of relief, I can't even tell you. After that, I buried the memories too. Honestly, this has haunted me all of my adult life. I'm not sure I was ever happy until I met you. And once you were in my life, I only wanted to look forward, not back." He could tell by the look on her face that without even trying, he'd said just the right thing. She took a step toward him and wrapped her arms around his neck. He kissed the top of her head and said, "I love you, Sarah. I'm sorry you felt like I was keeping things from you."

She pulled away as if suddenly remembering something. "But what about the machete?"

Panic raced through him. "Machete?"

"The one belonging to your dad. Damascus steel. Sound familiar? I saw a picture of Gavin holding it in the photo album. Your mom said it went missing, but Gavin has it displayed in his man cave, so obviously it's not lost. You want to tell me what that's all about?"

"Oh, that." He exhaled audibly. "That machete." Even to his own ears, it sounded like he was buying time. "The one Gavin has is similar, but it's not the same one. I was such a stupid kid back then. I took it without permission to show my friends. I left it in the bomb shelter overnight and the next day it was gone. My parents grounded me for two weeks after the machete disappeared. Gavin came across one just like it on eBay and bought it to torment me. He thinks it's funny."

She tilted her head to one side, considering his words. "I see."

"You didn't mention Gavin's machete to my mom, I hope?"

"No. I wanted to hear what you had to say first."

He nodded. "I appreciate it. I'd rather not get my dad all riled up again."

After that conversation, things had been fine between them—or at least they were fine on the surface. Every now and then, though, he'd catch her studying his face. When he met her eyes, she looked away, something that tore at his heart. He knew he'd broken her trust, and without trust, what chance did they have of making their marriage work? When he asked what was on her mind, she'd brush it off and change the subject. Clearly, thoughts had been churning in her head, thoughts she didn't want to share with him. She was a smart woman, insightful and curious. He doubted she'd let this drop so easily.

And now Gavin was on the other end of the phone, acting like her absence was no big deal. As if wives just left for getaways without warning on a regular basis. Kirk tried again. "Could you please give me the benefit of the doubt here?"

"What do you want from me?" Gavin asked, exasperated.

Kirk sighed. How many times had Gavin circumvented the law to his own advantage? Several that he knew of, and probably a lot more. And then there was the time he bragged about slamming a guy's head against a table to get a confession. "Starkey had it coming," Gavin said when Kirk had expressed shock. "Believe me, this is a guy who shouldn't be out on the street."

"But what if he didn't actually kill his girlfriend?" Kirk had asked. "What if he was innocent?"

Gavin had scoffed. "The guy had a list of priors as long as my arm. And he did confess, don't forget that part."

Now he was asking what Kirk wanted, when the answer was perfectly clear. He said, "I know she's not technically missing, but could you treat this like a missing person case? See if you can find her?" There was a long empty pause. Kirk said, "Are you still there?"

"Still here." He sighed. "Everything I can do, you can do yourself, and more easily. Check her credit card activity and cell phone records, and see what you come up with. If the car has GPS tracking capability, check and see where she went."

"She isn't driving yet and she didn't take her phone or her debit card. She doesn't have a credit card."

Gavin laughed. "Then what exactly did you think I could do? Walk around town yelling her name? Use your brain, Kirk. Call her friends."

"I already did that."

"Then find out if she had any odd charges on her debit card recently. She might have made reservations at a hotel. Then after you do that, go online and see what calls or text messages she's made in the last few weeks. You might get a clue. She's been home a lot. She might have a new friend."

Kirk could imagine him making air quotes around the word "friend" and he knew what that implied. He said, "She's not cheating on me, if that's what you're thinking."

"I never said she was."

"So you're not going to help me?"

Gavin let out an exasperated sigh. "My God, I've never seen a man more obsessed with his wife. Could you give the woman some space?"

"She can have all the space she wants. I just need to know where she is."

After a long pause, Gavin said, "I'll tell you what. Make up a flyer with a good photo of her, and list her physical characteristics—weight, height, hair color, and all that. Put a paragraph about why you're concerned about her well-being. I'd lean heavy on the head injury if I were you. Email it to me and I'll print out a few copies to give to my people, tell them to keep an eye out for her."

"That's it?"

"That's more than you'd get from anyone else, my friend. Just make up the flyer and try to get a good night's sleep. She'll be back and it will be fine. You'll see."

Typical. In the history of their friendship, Kirk had been the worrier, while Gavin had been the one to downplay any concerns. This time, though, he hoped Gavin was right.

TWENTY-THREE

By the time nightfall arrived, Maggie was gone and Sarah was ready. In anticipation of tromping through dirt, she laced up her hiking boots, clipped a small flashlight onto her belt, and went to get the pickax and shovel out of the garage, carrying them through the house rather than circling around outside. The neighborhood was quiet. Another plus? The backyard was lined with tall, closely spaced lilac bushes, creating a green wall on each side. Bordering the rear lot line was Dallman State Park. Nothing back there but hiking trails, trees, bushes, and squirrels.

Sarah stood on the back porch, her hand grasping the handle of the pickax, and assessed her surroundings. With Maggie absent on one side and the house on the other side empty and currently for sale, Sarah felt secure. Luckily for her, the other houses in close proximity were all one-story. No one could peer down from a second-story window and observe what she was doing in the yard.

She rested a toe on the wide blade of the ax and leaned on the handle, surveying Josh and Cady's backyard, uneven piles of dirt still imprinted with the tire treads from a professional excavator. If only she had that Bobcat now. It would make the job easier, but truthfully, she wouldn't have used it anyway, since the noise would have attracted too much attention.

She'd seen overhead photos of the backyard on the county website and close-up photos of the landscape crew at work on Cady's Facebook page, so she thought she had an idea of the size of the property. In person, though, it looked much bigger and she began to doubt herself. What if she went to all this trouble and found nothing inside the bomb shelter? Even more horrible, what if she were arrested for breaking and entering, or trespassing? There would be no explaining what she'd done or why she'd done it. Who would believe such a crazy story? Would they blame the brain damage? It wasn't too late to turn back, but if she did, then what? Could she sit across the dinner table from Kirk wondering if he and his friends were murderers?

She thought about a documentary she'd seen recently about serial killers. All the men's wives said they'd had no idea their husbands were capable of murder. One of them said she hadn't believed it initially until he apologized to her, saying he couldn't help himself, that he wasn't able to control his compulsion to kill. "I slept next to him," she'd said, her voice cracking. "He rocked our babies to sleep. Everyone thought he was a great guy." She'd shaken her head.

At the time she'd watched the show, she thought these women were in denial, but now she wondered if there was more to it than that. Obviously, their husbands excelled at living a double life.

Sarah knew her husband, his expressions, the nuances in his voice. She could always tell when something was troubling Kirk or when he was putting on a brave front. In the same way, she'd instinctively known he was lying when he'd said none of them had any idea what had happened to Jeremy.

The lying, that was the sticking point. She had to know, and intuition told her two teenage boys didn't voluntarily lock up a bomb shelter, one that had served as their clubhouse, unless they had a damn good reason.

She had to know.

Well, there was nothing to it, but to do it.

To get her bearings, she mentally divided the back property into thirds, knowing that she needed to dig in the back third of the lot line, where unfortunately the landscapers had piled mounds of scraped-off sod. Still, she wouldn't have to go too deep to find what she was looking for. She imagined the solid sound of the shovel hitting the concrete blocks or the metallic ring of the shovel hitting against the door. Once that happened, it wouldn't take too much more digging.

Sarah crossed the yard, taking careful steps on the uneven surface, wary of twisting an ankle. The moon was in full view tonight and bright, which helped, since she preferred not to use the flashlight.

Starting in the center of the yard was her best bet. She found the back lot line, walked to the center, and moved forward six feet before digging. She used the pickax to flip some sections of sod to one side, then pushed the shovel into the ground. The soil was more packed in than she anticipated, so after each thrust, she stood on the shovel to get extra leverage.

After fifteen minutes, she'd only uncovered enough soil to insert a child's wading pool. With the back of her hand she wiped beads of perspiration off her forehead, then paused for a moment to look longingly at the house, the small light over the stove in the kitchen providing a warm glow through the patio door. Should she go back inside and regroup? No, she answered her own question with a shake of her head. She knew that once she unlaced her boots and went inside the house, she'd be tempted to stay. Call it a night.

Better to just keep going.

With each thrust of the shovel she hoped to hit concrete, but was disappointed each time. When the ground was too hard, she used the pickax to break it up. She'd read once that the Erie

Canal, which went from New York State to the Great Lakes, had been dug almost entirely by hand. At the time this factoid seemed like a fun bit of trivia; now she had a new appreciation for what it had taken to do such a thing. Good lord, digging was backbreaking work. How had they done such a thing day in and day out, mile after mile? Her body was ready to give up after less than an hour. Her muscles would ache tomorrow, that was a certainty.

Sarah kept going, feeling the widening stain of sweat under each arm despite having applied antiperspirant earlier in the day. The mosquitoes knew she was here, making her glad she'd worn jeans and a thicker crew-necked T-shirt. She waved them away and let her hair fall forward as she dug, which shielded her face. Her arms weren't as lucky.

She was hoisting a shovel of dirt when she heard the rustle of movement in the lilac bushes that defined the border. Glancing up, she spotted a large person stepping out from between the bushes only ten feet from where she stood. She froze, her heartbeat accelerating in fear. Flight or fight? She couldn't be caught here, but if she fled now, what would happen to her things inside the house? Mentally she berated herself for not leaving her backpack on the rear porch where it could be easily grabbed in case of an emergency. She considered running out the back of the property, into the state park, and hiding. She dropped the shovel, ready to flee, when the person whispered, "Sarah?"

Her hand went to her forehead. "Phil?" Oh, thank God. The only person in the world she trusted to be here. He walked around a large mound of soil, and when he went to hug her, she held out a hand. "You don't want to touch me. I stink."

"Yeah, you do." He chuckled.

"You shouldn't be here." It came out in a quiet hiss. "Someone could have seen you."

"I know, I know," he said. "But I was careful. I parked down the block and came in on Maggie's side."

Still, one of the neighbors could have noticed him walking down the street. Well, he was here now. There was no point in worrying about it. "Speaking of Maggie, how did that go?"

"Piece of cake. She's now happily spending four days and three nights at an all-inclusive spa getaway in Madison. She didn't even question how she won the contest."

Didn't even question it. Just got in the van and off she went. Sarah used to be that trusting. She remembered those days in a rosy haze. Always expecting the best of others. Never doubting what others had to say. Not overthinking it when good things came her way. The last year had taught her to be wary. Now she knew that people, even those you loved, lied. Such a shame to have harsh reality intrude on what used to be a happy and satisfied life. In her case, ignorance had been bliss. "I appreciate you doing that."

He waved away a mosquito. "You paid for it. I just set it up."

"Your friend who owns the spa didn't think it was suspicious?"

"An anonymous gift for a deserving old lady? She thought it was sweet." He tapped his chest. "I'm kind of a nice guy, you know."

"I know. Thank you."

"I still think you're crazy for doing this," he said, gesturing to the shovel on the ground. "How's it going?"

"I haven't found anything yet, but I only started an hour ago." She picked up the shovel. "I'm fairly certain I'm in the right spot, though. With a little more work I should be there. I was just about to call it quits for now. I can finish up tomorrow."

"During the day?"

Sarah nodded. "Now that Maggie's gone, I decided I can take the chance. Digging at night is just too hard. The mosquitoes are awful and it's hard to see."

"More chance of someone seeing or hearing you, though."

She leaned in to talk quietly. "If someone in the neighborhood stops by, I'll give them the house-sitter story. I know enough about Josh and Cady to make it sound good."

"Why would the house sitter be digging in the backyard?"

She shrugged. "Maybe I'm a house sitter who also does excavating?"

"Surrrre." He stretched out the word, not sounding convinced. "Even to me, that sounds fishy. Better get your story straight."

"I will."

"I can come and help when I get off work tomorrow. It would go much faster if two of us are digging."

"No," she said, shaking her head, "Even you coming here now was a risk. You've done so much for me already, I couldn't ask you to put yourself in any more danger. Besides, who's going to bail me out if I get caught?"

He looked around the yard. "I can't believe you actually went through with this. Any chance I can talk you out of it? You can leave with me right now, stay at my place as long as you want."

She wiped her forehead with the back of her hand. His offer was tempting. Even with Maggie gone and the house on the other side vacant, there was still a chance she could be found out. The thought of being charged with breaking and entering and having to serve jail time loomed over her, and yet, leaving now meant she'd never know if her theory was correct. She couldn't sleep next to Kirk not knowing if he was involved in a murder. "No, I'm seeing it through."

"You don't think reporting your suspicions to the police would be enough?" He put a hand on her shoulder. "I could go with you."

"We've covered this already, Phil. It's a bad idea." And it would remain a bad idea as long as Gavin Kramer was the chief of police. He and Kirk were too close.

"One more thing," he said, reaching into his pocket. "I believe this is yours." He handed her a thick envelope. "The receipt for the spa getaway is in there. At the coin shop I asked for large bills and this is what they gave me."

"They didn't question the sale?" Phil had sold twenty-six gold Krugerrands at her request. The coins were her half of an inheritance from her father, the only thing left after the funeral costs and other bills were paid.

"Nah." He toed a rock. "I just told him it was passed down in the family. He was pretty happy to get them. Asked if I had any more. You don't, do you?"

She sighed. "No. That's the end of them." She was fortunate to have the ones she had. The coins were her only personal assets aside from her retirement account, which she couldn't touch at this point. Everything else was connected to Kirk. She doubted he'd notice they were gone, but even if he did, there was no paper trail to follow.

"I was thinking . . ."

"Yes?"

"With all that money left over, you could have easily stayed in a hotel."

She exhaled. "We've been over this, Phil. Calling the local hotels is the first thing Kirk would do."

"You could have booked the room under my name."

Sarah said, "Stop worrying. I appreciate your help, but I'm not your problem."

"I know, but it's too late. I'm already involved." He placed a brotherly hand on her shoulder. "I worry about you, Sarah. I'll call tomorrow. Remember, my offer still stands. You can call me anytime and I'll come and pick you up."

"I appreciate it, really I do. But I'm not going anywhere until I find that bomb shelter."

TWENTY-FOUR

An hour after their call, Gavin wasn't surprised to see Kirk's email in his inbox, complete with an attachment. He opened it, scanned the page, and cringed. What Kirk had created was more of a declaration of love than a missing person flyer. The photo he'd chosen of Sarah sitting demurely on a boulder in front of Lake Michigan was extremely flattering and took up half the page. She was laughing in the image, as if the person taking the photo had said something hilarious. Below that was a brief description of her personality—*Always has a smile on her face! Puts others first!*—along with the kind of information found on a driver's license. The rest of it was a lengthy plea for Sarah's return.

It was dated and said:

Sarah Aden is my beloved wife, my reason for living. The minute we met, I knew she was my soul mate. In March, she was attacked in our backyard by an unknown assailant. The road to recovery has been a mixed blessing—over the past months as Sarah has regained her health, we've been able to spend more time together. Now she's done something out of character for her—left our home, only notifying me via a note left on the kitchen counter this morning. The note said she needed a break and would be gone for a few days. Frankly, I don't believe she left of her own accord, and I'm sick with worry because she didn't take her cell phone or say where she was going. I've called friends and family members and no one has heard from her. If you see her, please tell her I love her. I miss her terribly and want her back. Kirk Aden.

At the bottom he'd left his contact information along with the words:

ANY INFORMATION, CALL ME, DAY OR NIGHT!

"Kirk, you're such a moron," Gavin muttered. Giving out a cell phone number like that was an idiotic move. It didn't really matter at this point because the only people who would see this notice would be his officers, but if this had gone out to the public, Kirk would have opened himself up to all kinds of crank calls.

He read it over again, sardonically chuckling. *His reason for living. Sick with worry. My soul mate.* Talk about laying it on thick. Sarah had only been gone a day and Kirk had already worked himself into a meltdown. Not surprising. As long as he'd known Kirk, he'd always been that way. If the guy didn't have something to get worked up about, he wouldn't know what to do with himself.

Kirk had always been a little too sensitive for his own good. Years earlier, when the whole community was searching for

Jeremy, Kirk could barely keep it together. They were all worried, but it hit Kirk the hardest. He'd told Gavin, "I can't sleep. I can't eat. I'm worried sick." Even years later, he still suffered from the loss. One time he'd said to Gavin, "I keep thinking about Jeremy's mom and his sister, and how they're living in limbo, not knowing."

Gavin sighed. At this point he'd been working in law enforcement for years and had seen plenty of tragedies. Sometimes the time-worn platitudes were spot on. It was true: bad things happened to good people and life wasn't fair. "Dwelling on it isn't helping. Try to move on."

"I'm trying."

"Try harder." Gavin spoke bluntly because that's what Kirk needed to hear. With Kirk's history of depression, he couldn't afford to spiral into despair. "You have it made. Great wife, a house in the best neighborhood, your own business. There's nothing to be gained by living in the past."

"You're right," Kirk said, his expression still glum.

Sometimes Gavin and Clarice talked about Kirk and his emotional problems. The three of them had been close in high school, but Kirk had become increasingly cool toward Clarice since then, something that rankled her.

"Kirk and I used to talk on the phone occasionally," Clarice had told him, shortly after Kirk and Sarah had married. "Now he doesn't want anything to do with me. Won't even answer my texts. It's like he's trying to erase me from his life." Gavin was at her apartment at the time, having met her for a tryst. That was her word—tryst. Gavin didn't care what she called it. When Clarice called, Gavin was as good as there. He'd stop what he was doing, put out a call to Natalie saying he had to work late, and he was out the door to meet Clarice. The sex was purely recreational. He didn't really consider it cheating on his wife. He and Clarice had history. He and Natalie had love. There was no conflict of interest. Still, he kept it to himself. Natalie would never understand.

"Why can't Kirk be more like you?" Clarice had asked at the end of their tryst, propped up on one elbow on the bed. "I don't see why we can't all be friends."

Gavin had been standing nearby, buttoning his shirt. He'd shrugged. "I'm not sure why you care, Clarice. You and I are still friends."

"And always will be, right?"

"Sure." He had to agree. "Whatever you want."

And now Kirk had worked himself into a ball of worry because Sarah decided she needed a short vacation and didn't tell him about it. Gavin understood why she didn't give him any notice. The guy was a bit controlling when it came to his wife. If he held Natalie on such a short leash, she'd have left him years ago.

With a sigh he pushed print and made multiple copies of the missing person flyer. Kirk wouldn't be pleased that it wasn't in color, but too bad. When done, he picked up the stack and left his office, heading down the hall to the front desk. These flyers were an embarrassment to his standing as a law enforcement officer, so he'd let Christy give them out. That way his promise to Kirk was fulfilled but it didn't reflect on him.

When he reached Christy's desk, he found she wasn't alone. Heidi, a gray-haired woman who worked as an assistant in the town hall, was leaning over Christy's desk blathering on about something. As she spoke, the reading glasses hanging on a chain around her neck swayed back and forth.

When he approached, the conversation stopped, and Heidi straightened up, but she didn't leave. Instead, she offered an excuse for her presence. "We're talking about the recipe booklet I'm putting together for the police department fundraiser." She gave him a wide smile.

Probably wanted him to gush about her efforts. Gavin was capable of being complimentary, but he wasn't going to make the effort for this woman. "I'll only be a minute," he said.

"We can talk later," Christy said hurriedly to Heidi, but the woman didn't move.

"Christy, I was hoping you can do me a favor," he said. "A friend's wife decided to take an impromptu getaway. She took off for a few days of R&R on her own and he's not dealing with it well. Having a bit of a breakdown, actually." He rolled his eyes. "Can you hand these out to everyone in the office? I imagine she'll be back any time now, but I promised I'd get the word out."

"Of course, Chief Kramer. I'd be happy to."

One of his favorite things about Christy was how often she called him by his full title. He said, "Very good then." He gave a small salute. "Carry on."

Gavin had just begun to walk away when he heard Heidi say, "I know this woman! She came in a few days ago asking about a property."

He turned. "I'm sorry. What?"

"She came into the town hall a few days ago." Heidi shook her head. "Something about her seemed off to me." She lifted her glasses and set them on her nose, then stared straight at him.

"How so?"

"Just shifty. Didn't tell me her name, but wanted some information about a house on Palmer Street. Said she was going to buy it and wanted to know if there were any outbuildings." Heidi tapped on Christy's desk. "She seemed kind of nervous."

Gavin felt his heart constrict in his chest. "Two-fourteen Palmer Street?"

Heidi tilted her head in thought. "Maybe. Sounds about right. She said she wanted to know about any structures on the property besides the main house. I went to ask Gwen about it, and when I came back, the woman was gone." Her eyes widened. "I found it *very* suspicious."

"How long ago was this?"

"The end of last week? I can't remember the exact day. Thursday?" Her face brightened. "Did I help solve the case?"

"You might have." Gavin's smile stretched tightly. "All of us need to get back to work now. Thanks for stopping by, Heidi."

Heidi's smile faded and she nodded. "Talk to you later, Christy."

After the door closed behind her, Christy said, "Thanks, Chief. She's such a pest. I told her I was busy, but she just wouldn't go."

"I understand," Gavin said. "Some people are hard to get rid of."

TWENTY-FIVE

After Phil left, Sarah went inside. She hadn't accomplished what she set out to do, but tomorrow was another day and it would be easier in the morning when there would be more light and fewer mosquitoes. After taking a shower, Sarah settled down with her laptop to check on Cady and Maggie.

Several months earlier when she'd discovered who owned Kirk's childhood home, she'd tried to find information online. Maggie Scott, who lived next door, was one of the few people who still lived in the neighborhood. As an added bonus, Maggie had a public Facebook page. She only updated it sporadically but gave out helpful information when she did. One of her posts was a photo of herself holding a plastic gnome. The caption said: *My neighbor Cady showed me this thing she got on Amazon. I liked it so much I got one for myself. The bottom has a secret compartment for holding house keys! Very cool!* That post was only up for a few hours. Presumably someone had cautioned her about the wisdom of letting people know where you hide your key. In general, Maggie seemed unclear on the concept of social media. She liked to cut and paste her Yelp reviews, as well as posting random pictures of each room in her house from every angle. Sarah could have drawn a floor plan based on the photos.

Cady was more of a challenge. Her account was private, so initially that was a roadblock. Sarah did come across an article on a blog which featured a photo of Josh and Cady among a group of eight Peace Corps volunteers, arms around one another, all of them smiling, bandannas either hanging around their necks or tied around their foreheads. The picture was taken in Guatemala years earlier. The post was written by one of the other volunteers, a woman named Lauren Trumble. In the comments, Cady had written, *You nailed it, my friend! I loved your take on our time there. Glad to see your photo included Alexa Glemboski. She wasn't in any of my pictures. Do you have her contact info?*

Lauren Trumble answered: *Sorry, no. I never really got to know her.*

Another woman added, *I searched for her online and couldn't find anything. Alexa, if you come across this, contact me! I have photos to share.*

Alexa never responded.

As she read this, something stirred inside Sarah. Her curiosity about the house and its past had become amplified. She needed to know more. She sensed that the only way she'd find out what was inside the bomb shelter was to insert herself into the life of the new owners of the property. She didn't have a plan beyond that, but it was a start.

With shaking hands, she created a fake Facebook account under the name Alexa Glemboski and created an avatar to match Alexa's appearance in the photo. Over the next few days, she filled the page with scenery and positive memes, and acquired a few Facebook friends, making a point to target those with the same last name.

When the page looked sufficiently full, she put in a friend

request to Cady Caldwell. It worked. Cady accepted her request the next morning, along with a quick message: *Yes! I'm so happy you found me. I've been thinking about you lately and hoping all is well.*

A wave of guilt washed over Sarah, and she almost deleted the account right then and there. Taking a deep breath, she mulled over how she could justify this deception, and it came down to this: she had to know the truth about her husband. It was an odd juxtaposition thinking of Kirk, the man who rubbed her feet and wrote her adoring notes, as someone capable of killing another human being. At one time they'd talked about starting a family. She'd always wanted to be a mother and knew Kirk, who was endlessly patient, would be a good father. But everything that had happened since she came home from the hospital made her wonder if she'd ever really known him. She closed her eyes and exhaled, bringing to mind all of the events that clouded her certainty of her marriage: Kirk's missing childhood friend, Jeremy, and the machete at Gavin's house. Kirk had ready explanations, but she hadn't found them at all satisfying. She could tell by the look on his face and the sound of his voice that he was keeping something from her, something serious, and she suspected that the answer was in the backyard of his old house.

And then there was the matter of her head injury. Had someone tried to kill her, but been interrupted by Buster's barking? Between the menacing notes and her life-threatening attack, it seemed likely, but why would anyone want her dead?

It wasn't lost on her that this snooping around online and creating a fake account was like something a crazy person would do. A sane person would call the FBI with their suspicions or file a police report. It's not that she didn't want to follow the sensible path. Oh, how she'd love to hand this over to someone else and let them do the investigation. If only her husband's best friend wasn't the chief of police, someone who could easily discredit her. What was it he said? She thought hard, replaying the conversation in her mind. He called it cognitive impairment, and then said: *False memories, memory loss, feeling like you're losing your mind—that must be terrible.* Gavin could portray her as a woman on the edge, one who'd lost her grasp of reality. He had friends in law enforcement in the surrounding communities, so it wasn't as if she could venture outside of town and report it to another municipality.

No, she decided, proof was needed.

After Cady had contacted her, she thought long and hard before she responded. Finally, she'd typed in: *Doing fine. Not on Facebook much, but thought I'd say hello.* Apparently, this sounded like something Alexa would say, because Cady replied by telling her about the move to Wisconsin and their new jobs. Alexa, as written by Sarah, was sufficiently happy to hear how well things were going for the Caldwells, replying with enthusiasm. When it came time for Alexa to share, Sarah begged off, saying she had to go, but that they'd catch up later. Cady answered with the heart emoji.

And that was it.

The only message she got from the other end came from Josh, wanting her to contribute a video clip for Cady's birthday montage. She'd declined, of course, and he was disappointed, but accepted her excuse. She never commented on any of Cady's posts, and because her name never came up, Alexa Glemboski became virtually out of sight and out of mind. Sarah's initial thought had been that in learning more about Cady, she could make some kind of connection with her in real life. Once she knew her interests and routine, it would be easy enough to join the same yoga class or shop at the same places. From there she imagined they'd build a friendship, which would lead to an offer on her part to do some gardening in the back of their yard, or watch their dog when they were out of town. The dog turned out to be temporary—a service dog they'd volunteered to train. And Cady gave up yoga at the studio to do it at home. *Easier with our schedules*, she'd told a friend in response to a comment saying she was missed in class. Even though Sarah was an online interloper, keeping an eye on Cady under false pretenses, she found herself drawn into Cady and Josh's world and struck by their likability. Under different circumstances, she might have become friends with Cady. The trouble was that, in this lifetime, there didn't seem to be a plausible way for Sarah to accidentally meet this woman.

Sarah was ready to give up on the whole idea when Cady announced the big landscape project. *Our whole backyard is going to be torn up, but when it's done, we'll have the garden of my dreams*, Cady had exclaimed, then went on to talk about the new planting beds, fire pit, statuary, fountain, and seating area. They hadn't hired the company Sarah worked for, but she was impressed with the renderings Cady had posted online.

With all they had planned, Sarah had hoped their landscaper would stumble onto the bomb shelter himself, saving her the trouble, but she wasn't that lucky. As the days went on, Cady posted photos of their progress, showing that most of their work was being done closer to the house. It seemed likely that the back of the lot would only get fresh sod.

And then, of course, the Caldwells had the opportunity to go on a month-long research trip. At the time Sarah read that post, it seemed to be a good omen. The universe giving her an opportunity. Now she scanned Cady's Facebook page, only to find her last post from a few days ago, a photo of the ship, accompanied by the words: *Wish us luck!*

She looked over the comments and was glad to see no one mentioned keeping an eye on the house. Most of Cady's friends wished her bon voyage and said they couldn't wait to hear all about the trip after her return. *We have to do a girls' night and go out for margaritas when you get back,* her friend Jocelyn said. Sarah had noticed Jocelyn's comments often mentioned alcohol and getting away from the husbands. There was a story there, not that she'd ever hear it.

Now, ensconced in the Caldwells' house, she checked Maggie's Facebook page, relieved to see that the older lady hadn't made any updates in the last week, not even to announce that she'd won a spa getaway in a contest. Right now Maggie Scott was probably in the midst of getting seaweed wrapped or whatever other treatments Sarah's money had purchased for her.

While she was on Facebook, she switched over to her own profile and checked her messages. There were three. One from her mother-in-law:

Darling Sarah, I hope this finds you well. When you get a chance, could you give Kirk or me a call? We're worried about you. Love, Judy.

Judy always composed messages as if they were letters, which Sarah found to be sweet.

Kirk, too, had left her a message:

Sarah, I'm not sure what prompted your getaway. I'm confused and I miss you. Did I say or do something to upset you? If so, let's talk it out. I love you. Call me, please.

She could picture his voice saying the words and knew that he was sincere. She had concerns about the man she'd married, but had never doubted his love. Her fingertips hovered over the keyboard, considering a response, but then thought better of it.

The last message was from Clarice:

Girlfriend, you're on fire! Good for you, making Kirk sweat. Hope you're having fun!

Hmm. Sarah twisted her lips in thought. It was interesting how much someone could convey in a few lines of text. Her mother-in-law loved her and was worried. Kirk was concerned that he'd offended her and wanted to make it right. And, of course, he'd said he loved her.

And clearly Clarice enjoyed having her gone.

Clarice.

Clarice's Facebook posts matched her personality. Hyperbolic and confident. Even her words on the page were loud. *This book has changed my life! Girlfriend, if you haven't tried this skin serum, you're missing out! Had the best dinner of my life at Golden last night!* And every single photo featured Clarice, looking like the social influencer she clearly wanted to be. So obnoxious and full of herself.

Sarah couldn't believe she'd actually considered the woman a good friend. When Clarice had started working at Garden Design Landscaping, they'd connected easily. Clarice was fun, charming, vivacious. Who knew that she was capable of secretly meeting Sarah's husband for lunch? Not Sarah, who tended to take people at their word. In retrospect, she'd been too trusting and very naïve. Always taking people at face value, was how Phil put it, adding, "I think that's an admirable trait, frankly."

This conversation took place after he'd stopped at the house to show her photos of Clarice and Kirk sitting together in a restaurant, and a few more pictures of Clarice alone, after Kirk had walked out. In a huff, was how Phil had described it. "After he left the table, she yelled after him, 'You can't get rid of me that easily, Kirk Aden. I'll tell Sarah.'"

"Oh." Sarah looked at the photos, feeling like she'd been smacked in the face. In one moment she'd gone from happily married, to questioning everything she knew about her husband. Previously, she'd been disappointed each month when her period had arrived. Now she was grateful not to be pregnant.

"I'm sorry, Sarah." Phil's face was creased with concern. "I know this is none of my business, but as your friend, I thought you should know. Maybe there's a good explanation?"

"Maybe," she'd said, but they both knew that was unlikely.

Of course she'd confronted Kirk when he'd gotten home that night. Over dinner she'd casually asked about his day. He mentioned a few problems with car deliveries, and told her one of the saleswomen had gotten roses delivered for her birthday. Foolishly, she'd secretly hoped he'd bring up seeing Clarice and offer a story that explained both their meeting and her outburst. As he kept talking, she realized it wasn't going to happen. When he paused to take a bite, she asked, "What did you do for lunch today?"

She saw a flash of emotion cross his face—guilt perhaps? There was something there, but only for a moment. He recovered quickly and gave her a charming smile. "I imagine you heard about my running into Clarice?" Kirk shook his head as if the situation was comical, and she felt her breath catch in her chest. He took a sip of wine, a casual gesture. "I know she's your friend, but good Lord, that woman is not my favorite. I ran into her when I stopped for lunch. She insisted on eating with me, even though I told her I was in a hurry. Then, when I had to rush out because there was an emergency at work, she became angry and created a scene. Frankly, she sounded unbalanced." Sarah felt her muscles tense. "I saw your P.T. guy sitting at the counter on the way out.

I had a feeling he'd tell you. I just didn't think he'd be so quick about it. Some people have nothing better to do."

The overexplaining, the false frivolity, the directional shift to Phil—all of it added up to one conclusion. *He was lying.*

"Yes, Phil did tell me about it," she said, keeping her voice even. She took a sip of wine. "Clarice does have a flair for the dramatic."

"I'll say."

"Funny how both of you were there at the same time, alone."

He couldn't meet her eyes, instead gazing down at the table. There was a pause and then he looked up and said, "I thought the same thing. Highly suspicious. I'm not sure what to make of it."

"So if I checked your phone, there wouldn't be messages between the two of you?" A bluff on her part. She'd never looked at his phone and didn't know the password. It hadn't occurred to her that she'd even care who he was calling or texting. Too trusting.

He gave her a look of reproach. "Come on, Sarah. You don't really think I'm having an affair with Clarice Carter, do you? You know me. I am one hundred percent devoted to you and our marriage. Clarice is just someone I went to high school with. She was a drama queen back then and she hasn't changed since."

She took another bite of her salmon, gave him a small smile, and nodded. Everything he said was true, but she sensed a lie hidden somewhere in the words. She blinked away tears and tried to hold back all the other questions that came to mind. If he wasn't going to be honest, there was no point in asking them.

He reached over and put his hand on hers. "Sarah," he said in a quiet voice, "I'm not sure what Phil thought he saw or heard, but I assure you there is nothing going on with me and Clarice. You're the only woman I've ever loved."

That last sentence was the only one that rang true to her. "Let's just drop it," she said.

Relieved, he launched into a story about a woman who came

into the showroom frustrated because she couldn't understand her car's navigational system. "Luis spent the whole afternoon teaching her how it works. I hope she leaves us a good review online."

"I'm sure she will," Sarah answered politely, her attention still on Clarice's outburst at the restaurant. *I'll tell Sarah.* What exactly did she mean by that? She was determined to find out.

TWENTY-SIX

HER

After my visit with Maggie Scott, I returned home, but the thought of Sarah Aden going into Kirk's childhood home never left my mind. I'd spent so much time in that house so many years before. I remembered Kirk's mother, Judy, hovering around us, offering snacks and making pleasant small talk. She had an incredible, loud, happy laugh, something that embarrassed Kirk, but delighted me. No one laughed at my house. Kirk's dad, Bert, was one of those lovable curmudgeons, the kind who would order pizzas for us teenagers and as we sat down to eat, he'd bark, "You kids better clean up after yourselves when you're done," with a wry smile. Kirk didn't know how lucky he was to have those two in his corner. He'd won the parent lottery and didn't even appreciate it.

I spent hours at their house—hanging out in the family room to watch movies or play games, eating in their sunny kitchen, going down into the bomb shelter. Being down below had an otherworldly feeling, like there'd been a catastrophic event and the five of us were the last people on the planet. So much talking and laughing went on below the surface. I loved being included in that circle of friendship. I felt like I mattered.

And then the unthinkable happened, and just like that, all of my memories were tainted.

Knowing what I did about that property, and what I suspected Sarah was doing, it was a certainty I'd be returning. It would have been impossible to stay away.

The next morning, I called in sick to work. When I was done, I took a deep breath, ready to lie to a complete stranger. I dialed *67 for anonymity and called the company where Sarah had been employed. When a woman answered in one long rush of words, saying, "Garden Design Landscaping, Britney speaking, how can I help you?" I was ready.

"Hi, my name is Kerry Jakubowski. Could I speak to Sarah Aden, please?"

Britney hesitated. "Sarah's on leave right now, but I can connect you with the lady who's handling her job during her absence."

I sensed her finger on the button, so I hurriedly said, "Oh no, that won't work. This isn't business. I'm a good friend of Sarah Aden's. We grew up in the same neighborhood and I'm passing through town. I was hoping to get together with her while I'm here, but I don't have her phone number."

Again, she paused, this time longer. "You're a friend of Sarah's?"

I laughed lightly. "When we were kids, we were best friends. Nothing could keep us apart. After finishing college, we only stayed in touch online. You know how that goes. I did know she worked at your company, but for some reason I never got her new number. I'm so mad at myself for not having it. I tried messaging her but haven't heard back. I figured it would be easiest to just give her a call. Can you help me out with the number?"

And just like that, Britney gave me Sarah's cell phone number. She even repeated it to make sure I got it right. "Tell her the gang from the office misses her," she said, before ending the conversation.

"I will," I promised as I entered Sarah's number into my list of contacts. When I was finished, I tucked my phone into my bag and smiled. I'm sure Gavin and Kirk would not have thought me capable of such deception.

After that, I climbed into my car and headed back to the old neighborhood, driving down the street just in time to see movement over at Maggie's house. A white business van was parked in the driveway. Leaving the house and going down the walkway was a young woman pulling a suitcase alongside Maggie, who carried an overnight bag. They chatted in a friendly manner, Maggie with a big smile on her face. While I watched, they loaded up the luggage and got into a white commercial van. Letters on the side of the vehicle said, *Royal Transport—Let us take you there in style!* Odd. Maggie hadn't mentioned going anywhere the day before. In fact, she made it sound like she didn't have much of anything going on. You'd think she'd have mentioned an upcoming trip.

I went to the end of the block and circled back, passing the white van, which had just backed out of the driveway. I turned at the end of the street and made another pass, slowing in front of the Adens' old house. It didn't look that different from my childhood days: neat front lawn, white siding, and black shutters. The blinds were down, and the front porch light on, the illumination barely distinguishable in daylight, unless you were looking for it, as I was. I didn't spot any signs of life inside. No movement at all. Perhaps Sarah Aden knew the new owners and had a legitimate excuse for going inside when they were out of town and only stopped in for a bit? Maybe she was watering their plants or checking on a cat? Possible, but I doubted it. I'd noticed the way she glanced around nervously before disemboweling the garden gnome, freeing the key from inside.

So I ruled out the idea that she had a legitimate reason for being in that particular house when the occupants were away. She was there on the sly and her deliberate proximity to the scene of what I was certain was a crime made me sure she was investigating.

Halfway down the block, I pulled over to the curb and watched the house. After an hour with nothing to show for it, I wondered—should I just knock on the door? No. I wasn't that willing to play my hand just yet.

Instead, I fished my cell phone out of my bag, pushed *67, then called Sarah's number. It rang twice. When it was answered, it was Kirk. His words came out in a rush. "Sarah, is that you?"

"Excuse me?"

"Oh, I'm sorry." He was clearly disappointed. "Who is this?"

I changed the pitch of my voice and said, "I'd like to speak to Sarah Aden."

"This is Kirk Aden—Sarah's my wife." A pause. "I'm actually trying to find her myself. Are you a friend?"

I clicked on the button, disconnecting the call. *Goodbye, Kirk Aden. That's all you're going to get from me.* I felt a slight triumph in knowing the location of his wife, while he was still in the dark. And I found it interesting that he'd said Sarah was his wife. Most men would have identified themselves as the husband. A small distinction, but notable for its possessiveness. His wife. As in, she belonged to him.

How much easier would it have been to ignore her suspicions, and just live her life? She had the big house and plenty of money. For most women it would have been more than enough. They'd have left the past alone and carried on with their vacations and dinners out, worrying about the kitchen remodel and what to wear to formal charity functions. But not Sarah.

I'd underestimated her.

Well, if Sarah was going to keep pursuing this, I wanted to keep an eye on the proceedings.

That night, just after dark, I returned. I parked down the block and cavalierly walked down the street, hands in my pockets as if just taking a stroll. For those who had security cameras, I didn't want anything to show up that might arouse suspicion. When I reached Maggie's house, I went up to the front door and knocked twice, waited a bit, then rang the doorbell. While I was biding my time, I glanced down to see a plastic garden gnome, identical to the one next door. I picked it up and turned it over, wiping off the remnants of mulch clinging to the bottom. Sure enough, there was an opening with a small tab, which I pushed with my fingernail. It popped open, revealing a house key on a metal ring. I shook my head in dismay. *Oh, Maggie, this was not your smartest move.* At the very least she could have hidden the gnome behind a bush to make it less noticeable.

She was lucky I had no interest in going inside her house.

I waited long enough to make sure no one was home at Maggie's, then circled around the side of the house, coming to a stop to look at the house next door. I crossed my arms and took it in. When I'd lived in the neighborhood, the Johnson family had lived there, but that was a long time ago and I'd heard they'd moved somewhere warmer. Florida, maybe? Their kids were all much older than me, and I had no idea what had happened to any of them. Standing in the dark, I had no fear of being spotted. The lights were on in several rooms. Through one window, I saw a woman sitting at a computer, her back to the window. In the kitchen, a man wiped off the counters, oblivious to my presence. I watched for a few minutes, amazed at how much I could see without being seen.

When a mosquito buzzed around my ear, it took me out of my thoughts. I waved it away and continued to the backyard. When I started to round the corner, I nearly jumped, startled to see someone else on the property. I took a step back and peered around the side of the house, watching as an adult man walked slowly along the row of bushes dividing Maggie's property from the Adens'. He slowed toward the back, then pushed his way through the shrubs to the other side, disappearing from sight.

I darted out from my hiding place, following him all the way to the back of the lot. When I got to the point where he'd vanished, I peered through the branches. I couldn't see much, but I heard Sarah say, "You shouldn't be here. Someone could have seen you." Then came the clink of a metal tool against a rock. It sounded as if she was digging.

He answered something about parking down the street, and after that, they lowered their voices, so I couldn't quite make out what they were saying. At one point I caught the name Phil, so I knew it was her physical therapist friend. Like me, he'd used Maggie's yard to access the Adens' former property. From the overheard conversation, it sounded like he had gotten some money for her. His voice was concerned, beseeching. He was worried about Sarah.

It was sticky hot and the mosquitoes were out in full force, making concentration difficult. I could tell by their voices when they were wrapping up the conversation, and then I clearly heard Sarah say, "I'm not going anywhere until I find that bomb shelter." So I was right. She *was* trying to uncover the bomb shelter. I wondered what had made her suspicious. When they exchanged parting words, I heard her saying something about quitting for the night and continuing tomorrow. When I sensed Phil's movement, I vacated my spot, crossed the lot, and returned to the side of the house. I kept an eye on the yard, and just as I'd thought, Phil came out through the same spot in the bushes and walked along the property line until he was past the house and out of sight. I moved closer to the front, and peered around the corner, watching as he walked down the street. Just as I had, he played it cool, acting as if he was out on an evening stroll, his arms swinging only slightly, his pace relaxed. I waited until he was long gone, and then decided it was time for me to go home.

Later that evening, watching a Lifetime movie with my mother, I mulled over my options. I could do nothing, stay at home, mind my own business, and keep an eye on the local news to see how this played out on its own.

Or, I could continue sneaking over there, watching to see what she found. In my heart, I knew I couldn't stay away. My years of waiting were over.

TWENTY-SEVEN

Sarah had intended to put the shovel down and quit for the night, but after Phil left, a breeze picked up, driving away the mosquitoes, so she kept going. She shoveled until her back and shoulders ached, scooping up dirt and tossing it to the side. Periodically she stopped to stretch, then continued. She was getting close. When the shovel at last contacted metal, she felt the reverberation go up her arms.

Her reaction was not jubilation. Instead, a knot twisted in her stomach followed by a sense of dread. Part of her didn't think she'd actually accomplish the task, and now she wondered if she'd made the biggest mistake of her life. There were only two possible outcomes to opening up the shelter and neither one was appealing. Discovering a body would point the finger at Kirk as a murderer, while finding it empty would prove nothing and she'd still be left wondering.

"Now what?" she muttered under her breath. It wasn't too late to take a shower, pack her stuff, and call an Uber to take her home. She could tell Kirk she'd had a mild breakdown. He'd be hurt, but glad she was back. Later, they'd laugh about it. Absolutely she could depart right now, but in her heart she knew leaving at this point didn't make sense. She was so close. She needed to see this through.

Using the long edge of the shovel, she scraped dirt off the shelter doors, working around the handles in the middle. Finally, she knelt down. Brushing away the last of the soil as best she could, her hands encountered a thick padlock, the U-shaped shaft enclosing the two handles. Yanking on them only raised the doors slightly.

Sarah vaguely remembered her mother-in-law mentioning how Bert had locked up the bomb shelter, but she hadn't envisioned it like this. She took the pickax and hit the lock, then recoiled at the sound and stopped. Anyone on the block could have heard that noise. She couldn't keep banging on it like that. It would be best to cut it off. Getting up to a stand, she brushed the dirt off the front of her jeans, then went into the house, leaving her boots on the back porch.

Inside the garage, she pulled the toolbox off the shelf and her heart rose on finding a set of bolt cutters. Once she was back in the yard, she knelt down to cut through the lock. After ten laborious, frustrating minutes, she only succeeded in making notches in the metal. Wiping the sweat off her forehead, she sighed. Tomorrow would be better; she needed to give her arms a rest.

If it came to it, she could always ask Phil to come back and cut open the lock. She hated to involve him, but he *did* offer. It was a shame to quit when she was so close, but it wasn't like she was going to go down below when it was dark anyway.

Decision made, she set the shovel and pickax off to one side and set the bolt cutters on top of the door. Time to go inside and take a shower. Hopefully she'd be able to get some sleep because tomorrow was going to be a momentous day.

TWENTY-EIGHT

Gavin made the usual call home to let Natalie know he'd be working that night. "Again?" she said. "Oh, babe, you're way too dedicated. You need to learn to delegate."

Delegate. If she only knew. "It's not a matter of delegating." Gavin glanced at the framed photo of the two of them on his desk. Taken during their honeymoon in the Bahamas, it was one of his favorites, chosen for the beachfront in the background and the admiring way she looked up at him. He continued, "You know we're shorthanded. Chuck is still on vacation and Kalisha is on maternity leave until the end of the month. The rest of us are covering until they get back."

"I know," she said with a sigh. "Just come home as soon as you can."

"I will," he promised. "But don't wait up. It might be late."

After he'd hung up, he went to his gun safe and pulled out his personal handgun, along with his silencer, then locked up the safe. Unauthorized, but still deadly. He hoped he wouldn't need the gun, but being prepared never hurt. He'd been in law enforcement long enough to know anything could happen. He tucked both into a canvas bag, then shut down his computer, turned off the lights, and left his office, taking the bag and locking the door behind him.

From the car, he called Clarice. "We need to talk," he said.

"About what?"

"Your friend Kirk and his wife."

She let out an aggravated sigh. "This will have to wait, Gavin. I've got company right now." In the background, he heard a man's voice, but he couldn't make out the words.

"Tell lover boy to go home. This is important."

"You're becoming very needy," she said in a lighthearted flirtatious tone. "You're going to have to get in line. I'm very popular." He imagined her in some flimsy lingerie, sprawled seductively across her bed.

"Look, Clarice, I'm not kidding around here. I'm coming over." Another squad car pulled into the adjacent parking space. He gave a nod to the officer, who nodded back before exiting the vehicle and heading into the building. "So you better tell your friend to leave or I'll find an excuse to arrest you. I'm sure your neighbors would enjoy seeing you hauled out in handcuffs."

"Okay, look." She lowered her voice to a whisper. "I need some time, so how about a compromise? Come over at eight thirty and I'll be all yours."

Grudgingly, he agreed. Typical of Clarice that she wasn't even curious about why he needed to talk to her about Kirk and Sarah. Her world was very Clarice-centric. Everything else was unimportant. To pass the time, he stopped for dinner at a local Greek restaurant, then drove around, taking a few passes at Palmer Street. The Adens' old house was quiet: garage door down, no packages on the porch, no signs anyone was home, but, of course, it was hard to tell just from doing a drive-by.

He arrived at Clarice's at exactly eight thirty and parked at the curb. Taking the gun with the attached silencer out of the bag, he tucked it under the seat. A young woman jogging in what looked like a diving suit gave him a curious look as she approached. He waited until she'd gone past before getting out of the vehicle. When he made it to Clarice's apartment door, she answered his knock by flinging the door wide open. Thankfully, she was fully clothed.

"Well, look at you," she said. "I do love a man in a uniform." She gave him a lascivious wink.

Under other circumstances, he might have been charmed. Not now. "This isn't that kind of visit. We need to talk."

"Ooh," she said. "Using your official voice. Of course, Chief Kramer, come right in." As he followed her into her apartment, she said, "If this is about the rock, I can tell you that finding my DNA on it is circumstantial. You can't prove anything."

He met her gaze. "You *were* the one who attacked Sarah?"

She stood facing him now, so close he could see the veins in her eyes. "You didn't figure it out? I thought that's why you were here." She sounded almost disappointed. "You actually believed my story about being in their backyard to see their new patio set? Oh, Gavin, what happened to your powers of deduction? Seems like you're slipping."

"Why would you do such a thing?"

Just when he thought she wasn't going to address the question, she said, "It's that damn Kirk. Ever since he's been with Sarah, he acts like I have leprosy. That's no way to treat an old friend." She leaned toward him, making eye contact. "No one casts me aside, Gavin! Did you know that I've never even been invited over to their house? It's like they think I'm no one." Her hurt feelings came out sounding like anger. "Even Sarah, who is a total pushover, wouldn't go for it. Says she prefers to go out to lunch, that she's not much for entertaining at home." She exhaled loudly. "That day I did pick her up, but I didn't even have a minute to get out of the car when she came running out.

I could see what that was all about. I'm not welcome in their home."

"How did you get from hurt feelings to hitting her with a rock?"

"I wasn't planning on smashing her head with a rock, if you want to know the truth. It was supposed to be an impromptu visit. Thought I'd drop in, say I was just in the neighborhood." A smile spread across her lips. "I was looking forward to seeing the look on Kirk's face, if you must know. But they didn't answer their doorbell and I knew someone was home. *Deliberately ignoring me.*" She spat out the words. "I walked around back and who comes flying out the door, but Sarah! She didn't even see me, she's so busy struggling to close the patio umbrella. It made me so damn mad." Her voice quavered. "I couldn't help myself. I was so upset I picked up a rock from one of their flower beds. I wasn't even planning on doing much more than throwing it in her direction, and giving her a scare, but you know what? As I got closer and closer, and she still didn't acknowledge me, it just infuriated me." Tears filled her eyes. "It's not my fault. It just happened. The way she was treating me. She was so *rude*."

"So you think that justifies knocking her unconscious?"

"Anyone would have done it," she insisted. "Even you, Gavin. Some things are unforgivable. I mean, she acted like I wasn't even there. I'm not *nothing*."

"You know you could have killed her."

"Oh, please," she said dismissively. "I didn't hit her that hard. Besides, it was a rock, not a bullet. I've had worse injuries myself and bounced right back."

"And then you left her there?"

"Well, I wasn't about to take her with me!" She smiled and gave his shoulder a squeeze. "What else could I do?"

"You do realize you could go to prison for this?"

She gave him a sultry smile. "Luckily, I look fabulous in

orange, and can fit in anywhere. I'd be the most popular girl in jail. The guards would love me, the other prisoners would aspire to be like me, and I'd pull my attorney around by his tongue. No one would believe I could commit such a crime and they'd eventually let me off with an apology for wasting my time. Admit it, you know I'm right."

"You're unbelievable," he said.

"Right?" She grinned.

Even though he'd initially suspected her, it still came as a shock. All these years he'd made excuses for Clarice. She was a free spirit, a trait he'd admired. Yes, she was selfish, but her fun personality made up for it. All of those things were true, but now he saw her from a different angle. She'd gone out of bounds so easily and not thought twice about it. Her lack of shame took his breath away. He couldn't waste time thinking about that right now. Shaking it off, he got right to the business at hand. "The reason I'm here is that I got a call from Kirk that Sarah took off, without notice, only leaving a note on the kitchen counter."

"I know." Clarice walked into the living room, sat down on the couch, and crossed her legs. "Sarah sent me a text saying she needed some time away. And then Kirk called me all frantic, wanting to know where she is." She exhaled loudly. "You know Kirk, always needing a security blanket. Sarah is apparently his go-to for that right now. The boy is so insecure."

Taking a seat next to her, he asked, "You know where she went?"

"I haven't a clue. I don't care either. You sure you don't want a drink? Oh wait," she added with a laugh. "You can't drink while you're on duty, can you?"

"I'm not technically on duty," he said.

"So the uniform's just for me?"

"Look, Clarice, we've got a big problem. A woman at the town hall recognized Sarah's picture on Kirk's missing person flyer—"

She hooted. "He made up a missing person flyer? After she left him a note? That's hilarious. Kirk is too much."

"Focus, Clarice. You're missing the point." He gripped his knees with both hands. "This woman said Sarah came into the town hall sometime in the last week, asking about 214 Palmer Street. The bomb shelter. Not only that, but Sarah knows about Jeremy's disappearance and was asking questions. It sounds like some red flags were raised for her. I have a bad feeling about this."

"You think she knows what happened?"

"Not knows, but suspects. It wouldn't take too much to put it together."

"What do you want from me, Chief Kramer?"

"What I'd really like to do is find Sarah. You have any idea where she might have gone?"

Clarice shook her head. "I can text her if you want."

"That wouldn't help. She left her cell phone behind."

Her brow furrowed. "That's odd. Why wouldn't she take it? I don't go anywhere without my phone."

"Well, she's not you. It appears she doesn't want to be found." Despite his worries, Gavin was impressed with Sarah. She hadn't taken a car or her cell phone, and she'd also managed a disappearing act without using a credit or debit card. Since she wasn't shown leaving out the front of the house, she must have circled around the back. She'd thought of everything.

"Sorry I can't help." She sidled over closer, pressing herself up against him. "But since you're here . . ."

He stood up and held out a hand. "But I think you can help. Let's go for a ride."

"I don't understand," she said when they were nearly there. "Why are we going to the state park?"

Gavin tried to remain calm, even though she was aggravating the hell out of him. He realized he'd never fully appreciated his wife Natalie's gentle voice and agreeable demeanor, until now. "Because we can access the old Aden property through the park. I want to make sure the ground over the bomb shelter hasn't been disturbed."

"I get *that*," she said, impatient. "But why? Why not drive to the house and walk around back? You're a cop. Can't you just say you're checking things out? That you got a call or something?"

Clearly, she had no idea how his job worked. "No. That's not how it's done. We're trying to avoid attention, remember?"

"I'm not even sure what we're doing." She tapped the dashboard. "Driving around in a squad car is not as much fun as I would have thought."

When they arrived at the park entrance, he ignored the signs saying it closed at sundown and continued down the road, slowly following the twists and turns. When he came to the right spot, he pulled over and shut off the engine.

"Now what?"

"Now we get out and walk through the trees to the Adens' house."

"I'll wait here," she announced.

"You're not getting off that easily." He forced a smile and beckoned. "You were here at the beginning. Time to see how the story ends."

"Such drama, Gavin. You've been spending too much time with Kirk." She laughed while unbuckling her seat belt. "Okay. Have it your way."

As she left the vehicle, he reached under his seat for the gun, and grabbed a small flashlight. Getting out of the car, he found Clarice waiting on her side of the vehicle. "So dark," she said.

"That's why I have this." He clicked on the pen light and led the way through the trees, hearing her shuffled steps behind him.

"You really need the gun?"

"I always carry a gun." There was more distance between the edge of the park and the residential section than he'd remembered.

For a minute or so, he wondered if his estimate was off, but no, now he saw lights glinting through the trees, leading them to the houses in the subdivision. He stopped at the edge of the tree line, shutting off the light, and tucking it into his pocket.

Clarice came up behind him and patted his backside. "Now what?"

From the safety of the park, he surveyed the yard in disbelief. "What the hell?"

The whole thing was torn up. The grass had been scraped off; piles of dirt were scattered around the perimeter. Tread from an excavator's tires crisscrossed the ground, and in front of him, the dirt that had covered the bomb shelter was gone. He walked out of the park and into the Adens' yard, then looked down at the partially exposed metal doors. "Damn." Looking around, he saw a shovel and a pickax neatly lined up on one side. The padlock Kirk's dad had used to secure the handles was still in place, but a bolt cutter lay alongside it. He started to doubt it was Sarah who'd done this. Would she have trespassed and physically dug out the bomb shelter on a shaky supposition? Unlikely, he thought. Sarah was delicate, ladylike. Whoever had done this was physically strong.

Clarice, always the clever one, came up behind him, pointed to the yard, and said, "What happened?"

Earlier in the evening when driving down the street, checking out the house, he took note of the ones on either side. The house to the south was for sale and currently empty. On the other side, the Scott house looked unoccupied. An Amazon package on the porch sat next to an uncollected newspaper. The Adens' old house was also dark. Clearly, no one was home in this section of the neighborhood. There would never be a better time to fix this.

He caught Clarice's gaze. *"What happened?"* he repeated. "What do you think happened? We're screwed."

He tucked the gun under his left arm and picked up the bolt cutters. Crouching down, he positioned the blades around the shackle, gripping hard. It took four tries to get through the metal, but eventually it snapped. He pulled a tissue out of his pocket and used it to maneuver the lock off the handles. Once he'd yanked it free, he set it off to one side.

"What are you doing?" She crouched down next to him.

"What do you think? We're going down and moving the body."

"No," Clarice said, horrified. She stood up abruptly. "I'm not moving a corpse."

"You don't have to worry about that. It's probably a skeleton by now."

"Gross."

"Pretend it's a Halloween decoration," he said firmly.

She exhaled dramatically. "I seriously hope you're kidding."

"I've never been more serious. Come on, Clarice. An hour of work is a fair trade for staying out of prison." She folded her arms, but didn't say no, so he continued. "It's wrapped in plastic. The two of us can easily carry it."

"And do what with it?" she hissed.

"We've got a whole state park behind us. We'll find a spot."

"This is crazy. You didn't say anything about moving a body."

"I'm saying it now."

"If someone finds the body, it will lead back to Kirk, so who cares? It's not our problem."

He set the bolt cutters on the ground. "Clarice, you've known me how long? Do you think I'd do this if we had any other choice?" He gingerly opened the double doors, revealing the stairs below. "Kirk will crack under questioning. There's no way he'd hold up." He took the flashlight out of his pocket and aimed the beam down, seeing the same concrete steps he remembered from so many years before.

"I'll go first," he said, "and make sure it's safe. Wouldn't want you to get hurt." He grinned at her and was relieved to see a playful smile twitch across her lips. Despite her protestations, he knew she'd follow. The curiosity would kill her. Besides, he had the car keys. She wasn't going anywhere.

TWENTY-NINE

The smell hit him before he even reached the bottom of the stairs, making him want to heave, but Gavin pushed on, shining his light ahead of him. The shelter was smaller than he remembered. The metal shelves along the back were still there, but the fabric covering of the camping cot where he and Clarice had sex was now in shreds. The single sheet of plywood Kirk's dad had put in place to cover the sand layer on the bottom had also deteriorated. He toed what was left of the plywood and pushed it up against the wall. In the spot where they'd buried Jeremy, the blue plastic sheeting had started to work its way to the surface of the sand, the length of his form rising like a ridge across the center of the floor.

Poor bastard. Couldn't even stay buried.

He stuck the gun into his belt, took a step back to the stairs, and called up to Clarice. "Everything's good. Grab the shovel and come on down."

"You sure?"

"Just get down here."

Clarice came down slowly, the shovel clanking against the

concrete stairs. "My God, the smell! I'm going to throw up." She made a gagging noise.

"It's the rotten wood and the mildew. It's not that bad."

"Not that bad?"

"Let's just get this done. I don't want to be here either." Handing her the flashlight, he took the shovel and began digging around the plastic.

"Maybe if we just bury it deeper in here, we wouldn't have to move it."

He shook his head and kept going. Typical Clarice, always the queen of bad ideas. Kirk had been the one who invited her to hang out with them to begin with, but Gavin could have put his foot down and put a stop to it. Kirk would have listened to him. If only he'd trusted his instincts as a teenager. Clarice was always going to stir up trouble. She was the reason Kirk was a blithering mess, and now, because of her, he was digging up a corpse in the dead of night when he'd rather be home with his wife.

Take Clarice out of his teenage history and it would have been just the three guys way back when. And Stephanie too, but she was never a problem. Just sat in the corner, reading a book. Sometimes he only remembered she was there when Jeremy shushed him after he or Kirk said something particularly raunchy. After Jeremy was gone, he'd thought Stephanie would be a problem, but she hadn't made a peep in years.

Clarice, who now was pinching her nose, was another matter. Light her fuse and he knew she'd betray all of them and not think anything of it. Trouble was, he had no idea what her fuse might be at any given moment. The woman was unpredictable. The same thing that made her exciting also made her dangerous.

When he'd made some progress, he crouched down and pulled at the plastic, working it loose. Finally, he looked up at Clarice in annoyance. "A little help?"

Wordlessly, she knelt opposite him, set the flashlight on the ground, and pinched at the piece of exposed plastic on her side. She gave it a small tug before wrinkling up her nose. "No way." She shook her head. "No way in hell, Gavin. I can't do this." She stood up. "This is disgusting. Leave the damn body here. Who cares if someone finds it? I want to go home."

Who cares if someone finds it? Clarice navigated through the world, taking what she wanted without worrying about the consequences and refusing to take responsibility for her own actions. Anything she didn't want to do became other people's problems. Well, this was one problem he wasn't taking on by himself.

"Come on, Clarice. An hour from now, we'll be done with this forever." Even as he spoke, he knew it was pointless. When Clarice took that tone of voice, there was no persuading her otherwise.

"No. Not an hour. Not even another minute. I'm done here. Time to go." She snapped her fingers.

"You're not going anywhere. I have the car keys. We're going to see this through."

"Not a chance. Get Kirk to help."

"You're here and he's not."

"I'm not kidding around, Gavin. I'm going. If you're smart, you'll leave with me."

She obviously didn't understand what was at stake here—either that or she didn't care. He stood up and pulled the gun out of his belt, then pointed it at her.

"You're not going anywhere until we move this body. Pick up your end. Now."

Clarice tilted her head back and laughed. "Or else what? You're going to shoot me? Stop being so stupid, Gavin."

Stupid? With a steady hand he kept the gun aimed right at her head. "Don't push me, Clarice. I *will* shoot you." Once again, her challenging expression reminded him of Blake Starkey right before he got the pissant to confess. Fury boiled up inside Gavin.

"No, you won't," she taunted. "You need me like an addict

needs his fix. Be a nice boy or I'll tell Natalie all about her husband's extracurricular activities." She walked over to the stairs, but stopped short of the first step, saying, "Hell, I might tell her anyway. Just for fun."

Now she'd gone too far.

He pulled the trigger.

THIRTY

I came back after spying on Sarah at the Adens' old house to find Mom asleep in her recliner. With her face relaxed—eyes closed and mouth slightly open—her worry lines had softened and time erased. Except for the gray in her hair, she looked exactly like the mother who had raised me, the one who listened sympathetically when I'd had a bad day and bought me the expensive jeans I was dying to have even though we couldn't really afford them, and I probably didn't deserve them. I knew she'd done everything she could to make up for my dad. On his good days he was pleasant enough, but those days became fewer as Jeremy and I reached our high school years.

For the most part, I remember the rages, the way he'd blow up over nothing. Shoes left in the front hall. A bad grade on a math test. The wrong look on my face. Sometimes just our existence seemed to enrage him. We always trod cautiously, never knowing when we'd step on one of his emotional land mines. I didn't even know how much stress he'd caused our family until he was gone. Then it was like someone had lifted an anvil off my back.

Jeremy had vowed to go away to college and said he'd make sure I could join him when I turned eighteen. At the time we planned it, I secretly felt guilty for planning to leave Mom behind, but as Jeremy pointed out, she'd be free to leave then too. When I was a kid, it didn't occur to me that she could have taken us kids and left at any time, sparing all of us so much of the pain. I don't fault her for staying. For some reason she couldn't make the break.

For Jeremy, escape was on the horizon, and while we waited for time to pass, we spent as much of it away from our house as possible. Kirk's mother welcomed us with open arms, giving us snacks, laughing at Jeremy's jokes, inviting us to stay for dinner. Kirk had lucked out having a warm and inviting home life. And then there was the bomb shelter, our private teenage enclave. The three guys played Risk down there and told ghost stories and argued about sports. I was always in the background. They barely noticed me, which was fine. I had my nose in a book, peacefully reading. No one was criticizing me or slamming me against a wall because I hadn't pushed my chair back to the kitchen table when getting up after a meal.

Everything was perfect until Clarice Carter showed up. Jeremy adored her and she reveled in being the center of his world. She strung all of them along, soaking in their adoration like it was nectar from the gods. She blatantly made the move on each one of them, not even caring who was watching. Resting her hand briefly on a thigh. Making comments about their strength. Licking at the ice cream cone supplied by Mrs. Aden in a provocative way. Jeremy, who'd never had a girlfriend, or even a date to a school dance, was smitten. One time he'd asked me to leave the bomb shelter for a few minutes after Kirk and Gavin had gone to pick up a pizza. Dutifully, I took my book and read under a tree in the backyard for half an hour until they'd returned, crossing the yard, pizza box in hand.

"What are you doing out here?" Gavin had asked.

"Just getting some fresh air," I'd said, closing the book and following them down.

Jeremy never told me what happened during that time, but I could guess. He'd fallen hard for Clarice. "I love her," he'd told me. "And she feels the same way about me." He was such a boy then, but because I was younger, he seemed like an adult. Still, I knew he was wrong about Clarice.

I tried to tell him she was playing all three of them, one against the other, but he refused to listen. "She's nice to everyone," he'd said. "Because she doesn't want the other guys to feel left out."

After Jeremy was gone, my dad died, and Mom had a stroke. There were four of us to begin with, and then it came down to one fully functioning family member, and it was me. I couldn't leave my mother. She needed me and, in a way, I needed her too. We were a family of two, bonded by blood and shared experience. No one else knew the void left by a missing loved one the way we did. People thought that after so many years we'd be accepting of our loss, but they were wrong. My anger at the injustice of it all gnawed at me and grew over time. I thought of my brother and missed him every single day. He'd been ripped away from us, but we still held him in our hearts.

I never once believed he'd run away. I knew something had happened to him, something terrible, and it had to do with his friends. I didn't trust any of them, but I could read the guilt on Kirk's face as easily as if it was a billboard.

When I heard that they'd sealed up the bomb shelter, I was sure they did it to cover up something they'd done, but no one would listen to me. Gavin's dad, the original Chief Kramer, told me he'd inspected it himself. "It was empty, Stephanie," he'd said. "Trust me, Jeremy was not hiding down there. Nothing was inside but a cot and some empty shelves." He put a fatherly hand on my shoulder and I flinched because having a man touch me never ended well. "I know how it is when someone takes off and you don't know where they are. Imaginations go wild. For what it's worth, I've seen good outcomes in cases like this. Usually, once the individual cools off, they come back. You'll hear from Jeremy soon. Just give it time."

Time. I'd given it time and what had it gotten me? More sorrow than one person should have to carry, the agony doubled because I shared it with my mother, who'd been burdened with her own version of the pain. Now I saw her sleeping peacefully and the sight made me smile. I took the crocheted throw off the back of the couch and covered her, tucking the sides in around her.

She stirred, her eyes fluttering. "Oh, Stephanie," she said. "I was just having the loveliest dream. Jeremy was in it and he was telling me he'd be home soon."

"That is a lovely dream," I said with a twinge of jealousy. I had never dreamed of my brother despite having desperately yearned for that kind of visitation. I was glad my mother had gotten the comfort of seeing my brother again, even if I hadn't.

My schedule for my janitorial job changed from week to week, allowing me the freedom to come and go as I wished, but my mother still wanted an accounting of my whereabouts. Earlier, I'd told her I was helping a friend from work who'd just had surgery and now I came up with another excuse.

"Mom, I'm going to go out for a bit, meet a friend for a drink. Will you be okay while I'm gone?"

"Of course," she murmured.

"I know I just got home, so I hate leaving you again. It's just, something came up."

"No worries, my darling. I'm glad you're going out. You should be doing more with friends."

"You want help going up to bed?"

"No. I just want to rest here for a while. I'll go up in a bit."

"I won't be too late." I kissed her forehead. "Home by midnight for sure. Call me if you need me." I stroked her hair as if she were the child and I were the adult.

"I'll be fine, Stephanie," she said, closing her eyes. "You don't need to worry about me."

THIRTY-ONE

Someone was in the yard. Sarah was sure of it. After digging for hours, she'd come in soaked with sweat and covered in dirt. Her first course of action had been to turn on the outdoor faucet to wash off her boots. After that, she'd headed inside to take a shower in the darkened bathroom upstairs. While toweling off afterward, she'd glanced out the window and saw movement in the backyard. Alarmed, she stepped closer to the glass and squinted, trying to make out what she'd seen in the darkness.

No. She'd been mistaken. Nothing was out there. She was on edge, imagining things. Staying in the Caldwells' house had rattled her and knowing how close she was to opening the bomb shelter had shredded her nerves. For the first time since she'd left home, she missed Kirk, his steadiness and the calm way he reassured her during her darkest moments. She could almost feel his arms lovingly embracing her. Doubts swirled around her. Would it have been so hard to ignore the thought that Kirk had been responsible for his best friend's disappearance? To put her doubt behind her and go on with her life? Her mind had been so muddled lately. Had she gotten it all wrong?

She dried off her hair and pulled on her clothes, ready to go to sleep for the night, but something nagged at her. Why would anyone be out there at all, much less at this time of night? Kids, maybe, wandering in from the state park?

Downstairs, she peered through the window of the back door and her breath caught in her chest. Someone *was* out there. She saw the outline of a large figure, a man, as he rose up out of the bomb shelter. She opened the inside door and heard a heavy clang of something metal coming from the backyard. Without thinking, she yelled, "Hey!"

The man's head rose like a deer sensing a predator, and quickly he turned and ran into the woods before she could get a good look. Even though she was safely inside, her heart pounded in her chest. She'd heard the sound of the door leading into the underground shelter clang shut, hadn't she? Had someone gotten wise to her mission and gotten there first? Or was it just teenagers, out in the neighborhood creating havoc? She remembered the days of TPing friends' houses or sneaking into backyard pools. It could very well be something innocent, couldn't it?

But deep down inside she felt that something was very wrong, that it wasn't kids at all. The figure had looked like a man. From what she saw, he was a big guy, larger than Kirk, and he'd moved quickly too, as if he'd been caught in the act of doing something serious. If nothing else, she'd called out to him and now he knew she was in the house. This thought made her uneasy. She'd known from the start she was breaking the law, but had justified it by thinking she'd leave the house exactly as she'd found it. No one would know. If there were one or two meals taken from the freezer or the level of shampoo was a bit lower, who'd be the wiser? After a month away, Josh and Cady would probably dismiss these inconsistencies as lapses in memory. Now she'd possibly outed herself as an intruder. A shiver of fear came over her.

THIRTY-TWO

He'd been trained and knew what he was doing. Discharging the weapon—while done impulsively—was no accident. Still, after it was over, the possible repercussions were not lost on him. When Gavin trotted up the shelter stairs, his heart raced while his mind shuffled through all the ways he could cover up this latest transgression. In the eyes of the law, he'd committed a crime, but was it really a crime when he'd been pushed to his limit? He thought not. He'd given her plenty of opportunities to cooperate. It was like she picked out the bullet herself.

Damn Clarice. She'd made him do this and now he was left to pick up the pieces.

As he closed the doors of the bomb shelter, the back door squeaked open and a woman called out, "Hey!" He recognized the voice.

Instinctively, he turned and ran, disappearing into the thicket of trees, thankful for the protection of the dark and for the foresight to have left the car in the park. He crashed through the underbrush, not taking care to be quiet. His only objective was to get back to his vehicle. From there, anyone seeing him drive away would assume he was on patrol.

Once he'd made it back and was safely inside the squad car, doors closed and locked, he called Kirk. "I found your wife."

"You did?" The relief in his voice was palpable. "Put her on, I want to talk to her."

"She's not with me, but I know where she is. I'm in the car and coming to pick you up."

"To take me to her?" Kirk's voice rose in excitement.

"Absolutely," he said. "Time for you two lovebirds to be reunited."

"Where is she? What did she say?" When he got excited, his voice rose an octave. Kirk was so easy to manipulate. He loved Sarah, that much was clear, and Gavin knew he could use that to his advantage.

"I'll be in your driveway in ten." He hung up before Kirk could say anything else. Besides hating to wait, he also hated being peppered with questions he had no intention of answering.

Gavin sighed in aggravation. He knew it was time to take control. He was tired of covering for everyone else, but there was no way around it. Clarice had forced his hand and made him pull the trigger. Too bad because they'd been friends for a long time and it had been beneficial for both of them, but that was life. You win some, you lose some.

And now it was clean-up time. He came up with a plan in short order, something that would end all of this once and for all.

It wasn't going to be easy to pull off, but it was necessary. He started up the car, and pulled onto the roadway, headlights leading the way. Soon it would all be over.

THIRTY-THREE

Sarah went into the living room and sat on the couch, weighing her options. Five minutes later, she got her backpack and riffled through the compartments, double-checking the contents. It wasn't too late to pack up and go home. Call for an Uber, ask Kirk for forgiveness, and resume her normal, lovely life. At her core, she was an honest person who always thought the best of people. She didn't want to believe that her husband and his friend were murderers. Wasn't it possible that Jeremy ran away, and that sometime after he'd left, he'd come across the wrong person and was murdered by a stranger while on the road?

Or maybe he'd taken up a new identity and was now living happily in Montana with a wife, three kids, and an adorable, fluffy dog. She fervently hoped this was the case.

Yes, she decided, she would leave tonight. She hefted the backpack onto her shoulder and headed to the front door, but once her hand was on the knob, something stopped her. She sighed, knowing that as much as she wanted to go, there'd be no rest until she knew for certain what was inside the bomb shelter.

She went out the back door, leaving her bag on the stoop. With the porch light on, navigating the property was much easier. She made her way across the yard, carrying a flashlight and a crowbar she'd found in the garage. She shone the cone of light onto the ground. The earth around the shelter had been disturbed, with footprints from an adult man clearly imprinted. The lock, which had been severed, now sat off to one side. Holding it up, she saw it was a clean break, probably done by the bolt cutters she'd used earlier, which now had seemingly disappeared.

She heaved open the door. "Hello?" Taking a step backward, she turned on the flashlight, tucking the crowbar under one arm. Returning her attention to the opening, she checked again, first calling out once more, and then dropping a pebble. "Is anyone down there?" She sucked in a deep breath, and talked herself through her fear.

Nothing to it, but to do it.

Sarah slowly made her way down the narrow stairs, her heart pounding. With every step the air became thicker, the odor nothing she'd ever experienced. She choked back bile and tried not to think about it. "Hello?" she called out.

When she got to the bottom, she saw a woman crumpled on the ground. "Oh my God." She dropped the crowbar, rushed over, and dropped into a crouch. Touching the woman's shoulder, she became aware of the blood pooled beneath her head and a gaping, raw hole in the middle of her forehead. She gasped in recognition. It was Clarice and she was dead. The stench suddenly became overwhelming.

Sarah jolted to her feet, her stomach churning. Clarice was dead. What the hell was going on? Was this because of her?

Her mind blurred trying to make sense of it and her heart beat in double time, pounding so quickly, she thought she might faint. "Think, think, think," she said aloud, clutching her hand to her chest. "I need to call the police." There was no getting around it. This was no hypothetical murder from two decades before. This horror had happened recently and she was right on top of it. Who could have done such a thing? She knew Clarice, and although their friendship had faded, she'd never wished her harm.

It had been at least forty-five minutes since she'd spotted the man in the yard—the man who surely was the murderer. Chances were good he was long gone. Still, he could be nearby, maybe even waiting in the woods. For all she knew, he'd watched her come out of the house and was coming to kill her too.

She thought about her burner cell, tucked away in her backpack on the porch. *Damn.* So stupid of her to leave it behind. Thinking quickly, she made a plan. Get to the house. Get the phone. Call the police and then call Phil and ask him to come right away. He was the only one who could vouch for her.

Yes, that's what she'd do.

THIRTY-FOUR

This time around I was better prepared, having doused myself with bug repellant and grabbed a small flashlight, which I'd then tucked into my bag. I drove without effort, as if pulled by a string. When I arrived in the neighborhood, it came almost as a surprise. Turned out that my muscle memory had a strong knack for going back to the house I'd once thought of as a second home.

Just as I had earlier, I parked down the street and made my way through Maggie's yard. Sneaking around on someone else's property was not something I commonly did. So why was I doing this? It was simple. I had no choice. I had to see if Sarah found my brother's body. My mother's dream of my brother giving her words of reassurance seemed to be a sign. We were going to get answers soon.

When I got to the rear of the property, I peeked through the gap in the hedge that Sarah's friend had used as an entry into the Adens' yard. Someone had turned on the back porch light, and now I could see the mounds of dirt more clearly. The silence of the night was punctuated by the soft chirping of crickets. A slight breeze offset the humidity.

I was about to step through to the other side of the bushes

when I heard the back door open. While I watched, Sarah Aden came out, letting the door close behind her, then walked tentatively toward the back. She had a crowbar in one hand, held aloft as if ready to confront an intruder. In the other hand, she had a flashlight.

When she got to the doors of the bomb shelter, she picked up the broken lock and inspected it. A moment later, she set it on the ground and lifted one of the handles. After the door fell to the side with a loud clank, she tentatively went to the edge of the opening and peered down into the hole. "Hello?" she called down. To my ears, she sounded afraid.

I knew the feeling. I was frightened for her. When I'd been there earlier, she hadn't even uncovered the bomb shelter yet. While I was gone, someone had uncovered it and broken the lock as well, all of which appeared to be news to Sarah. If it wasn't her, who was it? I would have loved to have stepped out of my hiding spot and helped, but I found myself frozen in place, unable to think of how I would explain my presence. So I stayed there, rooted to the ground, and quietly got my cell phone out of my pocket.

She took a step back, switched on the flashlight, and tucked the crowbar under one arm. Combined with the back porch light, the yard was now as well-lit as the break of day. Now she returned to the opening and shone the light down the stairs. "Hello!" She spoke more forcefully this time. It seemed to me that in a short time she'd mustered up some courage. She pulled on the other door and flung it open, then cast her light down the concrete steps. She wouldn't be able to see much of the rest of the shelter from outside, I knew. There was no way around it. If someone wanted to know what was inside, they had to go down those steps and take a look.

Sarah picked up a pebble and tossed it into the hole, like someone testing for depth. Finally, she called out, "Is anyone down there?" Not even an echo.

I aimed my phone in her direction and took a few pictures, wanting to document what I was seeing. She paused for so long I wondered if she'd heard the almost imperceptible click coming from my direction, but her attention never veered from the bomb shelter.

Just when I thought she'd lost her nerve and was going to turn back, she headed slowly down the stairs. I watched as she got lower and lower, finally getting swallowed up into the void.

Through the lens, I followed her movement.

Click.

Click.

Click.

THIRTY-FIVE

Luckily, Kirk was ready and waiting when the squad car pulled into the driveway. Gavin rolled down the window as he came to a stop and stuck out his head. "Do you have your cell phone with you?"

"Yes, of course." Kirk fished it out of his pocket and held it up. "Always have it on me."

Gavin shook his head. "Not tonight you don't. Leave it here."

"Why?"

"A request from your wife. She doesn't want you bringing your cell phone."

"You're kidding, right?"

"Do I look like I'm kidding?"

"It's just . . . I don't understand why she'd ask that. It doesn't make sense to me." Kirk's eyebrows furrowed as he ran his fingers through his hair.

"Maybe she wants your full attention for once?"

Kirk looked down at his phone, his forehead creased in thought. "Maybe."

A wave of urgency came over Gavin; it was all he could do not to rip the phone out of his hand and throw it across the yard.

"Look, Kirk, it's late, and frankly, I'd rather not be doing this at all. I've been killing myself looking for your wife, and having finally found her, I've gone out of my way to bring you two together. Leave the cell phone here or I'm not taking you to see Sarah."

"Okay, okay." Obediently, Kirk trotted back to the house, disappeared inside, and came out a minute later, keys in hand. He slid into the passenger seat and clicked on his seat belt. "Tell me about Sarah. Where did you find her? Is she okay? Is she angry with me?"

Kirk's neediness was off the charts. He had a habit of attaching himself to people, making them his sole focus. Jeremy had been the first recipient of his undying loyalty. Those two had been inseparable. They were going to be roommates in college and then start a business. Everything was going to be done in conjunction with the other one. Gavin had imagined them marrying twins, buying houses next door to each other, and raising their children together. So many plans and none of them included Gavin. Things changed once Jeremy was out of the picture. Kirk was adrift. And he remained that way until he met Sarah, his new addiction. It was like the guy couldn't function on his own. Gavin didn't answer until they were off the driveway and on the road. "She's taking a trip down memory lane. And if she's not angry with you now, she will be. Soon enough that will be the least of your worries." He smoothly accelerated. The more quickly this was over the better.

"Why aren't you giving me a straight answer?" Kirk drummed his fingers against the base of the window.

"We'll be there in ten minutes."

They drove in silence, not even a peep from the police radio. Gavin felt a surge of hope. As if the universe was looking out for him, all the pieces were falling into place. Maybe he'd be able to ease his way out of this after all. When they turned in to the state park entrance, Kirk sat up. "This can't be right. She's here?" He turned to Gavin and gave him a quizzical look.

The headlights led the way, following the curving road. When they got to his earlier stopping point, he pulled off the road and parked, then shut off the lights and stilled the engine.

"Why are we here?" Kirk wondered.

"We're here because your lovely wife was last seen at your childhood home." He glanced over at Kirk, who was staring at him slack-jawed.

Finally, he spoke. "No."

"Yes. It seems she's taken an interest in the old bomb shelter. Your job is to talk her out of getting all of us charged with murder."

THIRTY-SIX

"What the hell are you talking about?" Kirk asked. Gavin had pulled a lot of crap over the years, but this was taking it to new heights. Was this some kind of sick joke? If he discovered Gavin was mocking him about Sarah's disappearance and tying it to what happened to Jeremy, they were through. He didn't care about their past history. The friendship was over.

"Your wife is camped out at your old house and has been trying to dig out the bomb shelter." From the way he said it, Gavin was offended that Kirk was questioning him.

"My wife has been *digging* in my old backyard?"

"Is there an echo in here? Yes, that's what I said."

Kirk gave him a look of disbelief. "You're out of your mind. That doesn't sound like Sarah. Why would she do that?" He knew Sarah as well as he knew himself. Her level of empathy was beyond measure. She thought carefully before she told someone they had spinach between their teeth. Besides, she was delicate, and still needed him for so many things. Just the other day he'd opened a jar for her. The idea that she'd leave him to dig up a stranger's backyard was unthinkable. "No way."

Gavin folded his arms. "You're wrong."

Such a Gavin answer. There was nothing he loved better than knowing he had something on Kirk. Truthfully, as adults they had nothing in common. Kirk knew their friendship would have run its course a long time ago if not for the shared history of what happened that night in the bomb shelter. On occasion he'd thought of distancing himself from Gavin, but reminders of the past always pulled him right back. They were friends because he couldn't afford not to be Gavin's friend. If Gavin became alienated, who knew what he might do or say? One fateful night had changed everything, the repercussions hanging over his head forever.

It had started so innocently. Just a group of friends spending time together in what they'd thought was the coolest hangout in town. Kirk's mom, Judy, had supplied them with a blanket and a cache of food, plastic containers of snacks and cans of soda, which they kept on the shelves stretched against the back wall. The guys had supplemented those supplies with other necessities. Clarice brought a battery-powered lantern. "It's for camping," she'd said, pulling a face. "But my family never goes camping." Kirk had brought his Risk game from the house. Jeremy had a notebook for jotting down their ideas for movie scripts. And Gavin brought weed and liquor, which they hid in a box under the cot.

That day Kirk had brought his dad's machete, just to show the guys. Gavin called him a show-off, but Kirk could tell he was impressed. Jeremy held it and turned it from side to side, watching the glint as the light caught the metal. "Cool!" he'd said. Jeremy could always be counted on for a show of enthusiasm.

Kirk had said, "Made of Damascus steel." They all admired it while Kirk described how his dad had bought it from a collector. "It's one of a kind. The guy didn't want to part with it, but eventually my dad wore him down." After they'd all had a good look, he set it on the lower shelf, blade inward, to keep it safe. A hundred times, no, a thousand times since then, he'd asked himself why he didn't take it back into the house.

And now Gavin was yanking his chain, telling him that Sarah was there, digging up what they'd buried so long ago? Impossible. "I don't know what you think you saw, but it wasn't my wife digging up my old backyard."

"You don't believe me? See for yourself."

"I think I will."

Kirk got out of the car first and headed into the woods, not waiting for Gavin. He heard footsteps behind him and knew Gavin was close to catching up when he saw the beam of light from a flashlight, pointing the way ahead.

Gavin called out, "Slow down or you'll trip on something and break a leg."

Kirk paused and looked back. "She better be there."

"I'm telling you, she is."

Kirk kept going, pushing branches aside, leading the way. A symphony of crickets chirped all around them, while off in the distance an owl hooted. On the ground, there was only the sound of their footsteps. When they saw the residential light through the trees, Kirk upped his pace, forcing Gavin to break into a jog. Again, he called out, saying, "Wait up, Aden." Not that it did any good. Kirk wasn't going to stop until he saw what this was all about. Gavin may have started this, but Kirk was going to finish it.

When they got to the place where the park ended and the property began, Kirk finally came to a halt and surveyed the piles of dirt. "What the hell happened here?"

Gavin came up next to him, clicked off the light, and stuck it in his pocket. "What do you think?"

"Are you telling me Sarah did all this?"

Gavin pointed to the bomb shelter doors, which were wide open now. "She did at least some of it. I think she's down there now." He pointed, then swatted at an insect buzzing close to his ear. "Why don't you take a look?"

Kirk stepped over dirt piles and strode over to the opening. "Sarah?" As he leaned in, he felt a shove from behind, strong enough that it knocked him off his feet, and launched him down the stairs.

THIRTY-SEVEN

Sarah was starting up the steps when she saw her husband's face peering down from above. "Sarah?" he said, an air of surprise in his voice. Before she could respond, he came hurtling toward her. They collided, and she fell to the ground, Kirk on top of her. The impact knocked the breath out of her and slammed her head onto the sand. They landed only a few feet from Clarice's body.

Before either of them could move, Gavin came trotting down the steps, whistling, his flashlight nearly blinding her. When he got to the bottom, he tucked the flashlight in his front pocket, the light aiming upward.

Kirk rolled off of her and asked, "Are you okay?" and when she nodded yes, he picked up his glasses and set them back on his nose before helping her to her feet. He turned to Gavin. "You need to explain what the hell is going on. Right now."

When Gavin raised the gun and pointed it at Kirk, a cold shiver ran down her spine. The truth came to her all at once. Gavin was the one with the machete made of Damascus steel. His father was the chief of police when Jeremy went missing. He was the one who'd killed Clarice. And he was probably the one who'd murdered Jeremy.

And now he had a gun aimed toward her and Kirk.

Gavin's voice was cold. "You always were slow on the uptake, Aden."

"Put the gun down," Kirk said. "Nobody needs to get hurt."

Sarah took his arm, trying to hold him back. She gestured behind where they stood. "He killed Clarice."

Kirk glanced backward and his face registered shock. Clarice lay sprawled on the ground, one arm over her head, her legs bent, her body illuminated by the flashlight that had been knocked out of Sarah's hand when she fell. "Oh no," he said. He turned back to Gavin. "Why the hell would you do that?"

"I'm surprised you care after she hit your wife in the head with a rock. I'd have thought you'd be happy about it."

"Clarice was the one who attacked me?" Sarah asked in disbelief. Her mind reeled. She knew Clarice had her faults, but she'd never seen her as a violent person.

"Yeah, she attacked you. Does that surprise you? She killed Jeremy too. Our friend Clarice was full of tricks."

"No," Sarah said, incredulity in her voice. "Clarice?" She looked to Kirk, who gave a slight nod of affirmation. She felt a rush of relief of knowing her husband wasn't a killer, but the feeling was only momentary. The reality of a gun being pointed in their direction overrode everything else.

Kirk held up his hands and said, "Gavin, put the gun down. You and I, we go way back. We've been friends forever. I know you don't want to do this."

"You're right, I don't—but your wife started it and now I'm going to finish it."

"Gavin, please," Sarah said.

"Please what?" he said, his voice harsh. "You have a lot of nerve asking me for anything. You're nothing but a loose end."

To Sarah he no longer sounded like the Gavin who'd had them over for dinner, telling jokes, complimenting his wife's cooking, and showing them around his man cave. Instead, he sounded completely callous, as if someone had stripped away his humanity leaving a cold-blooded doppelganger in his stead.

She said, "Let's talk this through. I'm sure we can all walk out of here with an understanding. No one else has to die." Even to her, the words sounded strained, like dialogue borrowed from a crime show.

Gavin said, "Kirk, take three steps to your right." He gestured with the gun. "Sarah, kneel on the ground." When they hesitated, he yelled, "Do it! Right now!"

Her heart racing, she knelt on the ground, watching as her husband stepped to one side. In a matter of a few seconds, a flurry of thoughts went through her brain. Gavin was right about one thing: she *had* started this and her curiosity was going to get them killed. The bomb shelter would be their tomb, and if and when their bodies were discovered, Gavin would make it look like a murder-suicide. Or else he'd torch the place, leaving little forensic evidence behind. No one would ever suspect the chief of police.

And even if she screamed, there was no one around to hear her. She'd ensured that by sending Maggie Scott away.

She wondered if it made sense for her to make a break for it, to take Gavin by surprise, pushing past him and dashing up the stairs out of the shelter. She pictured her backpack with the cell phone in the front pocket and mentally calculated how many steps there were between the shelter and the porch. How long would it take to call for help? With a sinking heart, she realized the metrics didn't work. She was tired from digging and unlikely to get by Gavin. And even if she could get away, he would shoot Kirk in the meantime.

And it would be all her fault.

With every beat of her heart, Sarah wished she could undo this. Go back in time and let the past stay in the past. Accept her husband for the good man she knew him to be. Suppress her nagging doubts and move forward with her life.

If only she could.

She didn't want to die, not in this hole in the ground next to a dead woman. And she didn't want Kirk to die, especially now that she knew the truth.

If only there was a way out.

THIRTY-EIGHT

Kirk saw the crazed look in Gavin's eyes and knew this was not going to end well. There was no chance of both of them getting away, but he'd gladly die in this pit if it meant Sarah could make it to safety. He gave her a sideways glance and tilted his head toward the bomb shelter's opening, hoping she'd take the hint. After she'd made her move, he planned to charge at Gavin, hopefully catching him off guard and giving her enough time to escape.

"Gavin," he said evenly. "There's already been too much death. Clarice was a problem, but she's gone now. We can make different choices. Better choices."

His mind flashed back to that evening. It began with a phone call from Jeremy asking if he could spend the night in the bomb shelter. Jeremy had said, "My dad went ballistic. I need to get out of here." Kirk didn't need to hear any more. He knew what that meant.

Jeremy was embarrassed, so Kirk didn't tell his parents that his friend was going to be staying overnight. Instead, the two guys met in the Adens' backyard and headed straight to the bomb shelter. Jeremy went down the stairs first, with Kirk right on his heels.

Both were startled to stumble upon Clarice and Gavin, who'd clearly been interrupted in the middle of something intimate.

"Hey, guys." Gavin apparently decided to play it cool. "Sorry about the mess. We weren't expecting company." He picked his T-shirt up from the plywood floor and pulled it over his head.

Jeremy wasn't going for it. "How could you?" he said, his voice rising with each word. He ran at Gavin and pushed him with both hands. "You knew I liked her! How could you?"

"Hey!" Gavin caught his balance and braced himself. "Stop it."

Kirk, who'd suspected Gavin and Clarice were hooking up, was still shocked speechless to see actual evidence right in front of him.

Jeremy's skinny arms flailed, pounding nonstop on Gavin's chest. While Gavin held him off, he tried to defuse the situation. With a smirk on his face, he said, "This isn't resolving anything, Jeremy. Let's settle down and talk."

Clarice got up from the cot, letting the throw drop, startling all of them into stunned silence. For so long Kirk had wondered what she looked like naked, but seeing her expose herself to all three of them at once seemed indecent. She turned to grab the machete off the shelf, giving them a view of her backside and long legs, then swung it toward them.

"Bad boys," she said with a laugh. "All of you are such bad boys." From her voice, it was clear she'd been drinking. She waved the machete back and forth, swordplay style, putting one hand on her hip. "You'd like a piece of me, wouldn't you?"

"Put that down," Kirk said, "before you hurt someone."

They were mesmerized by her blatant nudity. All three guys stood there, watching her wield the weapon, each one taking a step back when she got too close. Gavin was the first to recover his wits, grabbing his shoes and socks off the floor. "Clarice, it's not funny. Get dressed."

Kirk moved in to take the machete out of her hands. "Hand it over, Clarice. Give it to me."

"Make me," she said and laughed, twirling around. Both Jeremy and Kirk edged closer in order to grab the machete, but her nudity made them hesitant. Over and over again she taunted them, letting them approach and then waving the machete in their direction, forcing them to step back.

All of the attention was aimed her way. It was Clarice's favorite kind of game; she had something they wanted and she wasn't going to give it up too easily.

If only they'd left then, all three of them. If only they'd retreated, walked up the steps and out of the bomb shelter together. Without an audience, Clarice would have been forced to put the machete down, get dressed, and go home.

More importantly, Jeremy would still be alive.

THIRTY-NINE

From my hiding spot behind the shrubbery, I saw it all.

Sarah had been down in the hole for only a few minutes when Kirk came bursting out of the park followed by Gavin, who held a flashlight in one hand. From his other hand, a gun with an attached silencer hung loosely by his side. My mouth dropped open at the sight of the gun. *What in the world?* Gavin had his uniform on, which I found confusing. Was this an official visit? Had someone in the neighborhood made a complaint?

But if that was the case, why would Kirk be accompanying him on official police business? It seemed more likely that this visit was personal.

I lifted my phone, taking picture after picture.

I kept spying, straining to hear their talk. It sounded as if Gavin was in charge, while Kirk seemed unsure of what was going on. I heard Kirk ask about Sarah, and Gavin answered, saying, "I think she's down there now. Why don't you take a look?"

And then, as Kirk peered down into the opening, calling out his wife's name, Gavin tucked the flashlight under his arm, came up behind him, and gave his back a shove, deliberately pushing him down the stairs. I recorded all of it through my phone, picture after picture, and watched, aghast, but also oddly fascinated, like this was a movie with a surprise twist at the end. I'd known both of these men since I was a young teen, but I had the feeling only now was I seeing who they really were. Especially Gavin, who trotted down the steps after he'd committed this act of violence, whistling as he went. I heard some commotion from down below, voices that sounded anguished, and after that, shouts I recognized as Gavin's.

I stopped taking pictures and clicked over to phone mode, tapping out three numbers. The dispatcher, a woman with a strong clear voice, answered, saying, "Nine-one-one, what's your emergency?"

I said, "This is Stephanie Bickley. I'm at 214 Palmer Street. There's a man armed with a gun in the backyard, holding two people hostage. You need to send someone right away. Tell them to hurry!"

FORTY

As Sarah got down on her knees, trying to think of ways to escape, Kirk kept talking. "Gavin, I understand why you're upset, but we can fix this. You know I can keep a secret," he said with a note of gentle reassurance. "And I can vouch for Sarah too." He lowered his hands to take off his glasses, which he wiped with the corner of his shirt. The movement was casual, as if the smudge on a lens was his most immediate concern. "Clarice has always been a problem, so I understand you did what you had to do, but you and me? We've always gotten along. You're the brother I never had."

His strategy seemed to be working. Gavin's stance was more relaxed. "Clarice always was a problem," he repeated, his voice still belligerent, but less angry. "Never knew when to quit."

"Yes, that's true." Kirk sighed. "If it weren't for her killing Jeremy in the first place, none of us would be here." His eyes darted over to his wife. "I wanted to tell you, Sarah, but I didn't want you involved in this. Jeremy was crazy in love with Clarice, so when he and I came down here that night and saw Gavin and Clarice together, he was devastated. Poor guy. He and Gavin got into a fight and Clarice started waving the machete. She'd been drinking and was completely irrational." He took a deep breath. "Wouldn't listen to a word anyone said."

Sarah listened, spellbound. So she'd been right about the machete. "Then what happened?"

Kirk shrugged. "She kept swinging that machete. All three of us tried to take it away from her, but Jeremy got too close and the blade sliced into his abdomen. He bled out before we could get help."

Sarah looked from her husband to Gavin, trying to process the story she'd just heard. "But why didn't you tell anyone?"

Before he could answer, Gavin interrupted. "You were the one who invited her," he said. "This was supposed to be a guys' club and suddenly Clarice is there, embedded in our group, part of everything. If you remember, I objected at the time, but no, Kirk said she was cool." He looked Sarah in the eye. "He isn't the best judge of character."

Kirk nodded. "You're right. This is all on me. Right from the start, I made a mistake. I had no way of knowing how it would go."

"Jeremy was so sure she had a thing for him."

"She played all of us," he continued. "Clarice was the consummate liar, telling all of us what we wanted to hear. I know she fooled me—at least at first."

Gavin said, "I caught on to her right away, but Jeremy never did. He was clueless."

"He was just a kid. I mean, at the time, we all felt like adults, but now in retrospect, we hadn't even started to live." Kirk shifted, his hand going to his pocket, thumb looped over the edge. "Such a tragedy. The way she hit him with that machete was unreal. I still have nightmares about it. So much blood."

Sarah sat in disbelief. Clarice killed Jeremy? The woman she'd spent hours with—chatting over lunches, planning events at work, telling her the story of her parents' deaths, something she rarely mentioned to anyone—had killed an innocent person, a teenage boy? And Kirk and Gavin had witnessed it and covered it up?

All these years Jeremy's family had lived in limbo, yearning for their lost son, when all the while three people knew exactly what had happened to him. A tragedy compounded by a thousand.

Gavin gruffly said, "Just so you know, it's not like I wanted to kill Clarice. She couldn't be reasoned with—said she was going to come clean. I couldn't let her do that. I gave her plenty of chances to cooperate."

"Killing her was the right thing to do," Kirk said approvingly. "You had no choice."

Sarah inched forward as a test, but neither man noticed, so intent were they on what the other was saying. Kirk's method of emotionally disarming Gavin with a trip down memory lane, rephrasing it as Clarice's issue and pointing out their previous solidarity, was shrewd. But was it enough?

"Damn right I had no choice."

"I'm glad we understand each other," Kirk said. Even without looking at his face, Sarah could imagine the smile, well-practiced from years of selling cars. "Put the gun down and let's figure out what to do with Clarice's body." Kirk gestured to Sarah with a slight bob of his head. She thought he was indicating this was her opportunity. *Run!*

She knew it was a bad plan. Gavin physically blocked the only way out. There was no way she'd get past him. He was a head taller, much stronger, and had a gun. She'd be dead in seconds. A distraction was needed. The flashlight she'd been using lay on the floor, beam shining. It was too small to use as a weapon, but turned off, it might cause some momentary confusion, giving them an advantage. She surreptitiously moved slowly in that direction.

"Freeze!"

Her glance went to Gavin's face. He had the gun barrel trained on her.

"Whatever you're thinking of doing, forget about it," he told her.

Her stomach dropped and she felt like crying. She wanted to beg him to let them walk away, but she held back, sensing he'd love to hear her pleading, reveling in the idea that he had the upper hand. She'd made a big mistake, drawing his attention. She should have just gone for it. Now she was going to die here, kneeling in the dirt, covered in sweat. Once he shot her, she'd bleed out like Clarice. Another dead woman in the hole.

Kirk said, "Why don't you let her go? You and me, we can work this out."

Sarah let her fingers trail the floor of the bomb shelter, hoping to scoop up dirt to throw in his direction, but she only came up with small damp clumps. Her fingernails scrabbled at the ground, reaching farther from where she knelt, and when she hit something solid and metal, she immediately knew what it was. The crowbar she'd brought with her earlier. It had been knocked out of her hand when Kirk fell on her, but it hadn't gone far.

"Enough!" Gavin swung the gun toward Kirk. "You always did talk too much. I'm done listening."

Sarah's fingers curled around the crowbar. Adrenaline surging, she leapt to her feet, swinging the tool up and bringing it down with all the force she could muster. She felt the impact when it struck Gavin's head. Her ears registered the muffled noise of the gun as it simultaneously went off. She heard Kirk crying out, "No!" as if from a distance. His wail echoed off the concrete walls. She watched in utter horror as he clutched his chest and toppled to the ground. At the same time Gavin staggered and fell backward onto the stairs. The gun he'd fired bounced to the shelter floor.

Sarah rushed to her husband's side and dropped down next to him. She pressed her palms against the wound in his chest, trying to staunch the bleeding. "Hang in there, Kirk. Don't leave me."

"Sarah," he whispered, his lower lip trembling. "I love you."

"I know, babe, I know. Save your strength." She quickly pulled her T-shirt over her head and flattened it to the gaping hole oozing blood. "Can you hold this here while I go for help?" She set his hand on top of the makeshift compress. "I'll be right back."

Kirk's mouth moved, and he grasped her hair with his free hand, pulling her closer. His words were labored. "Tell Jeremy's mom I'm sorry."

"You can tell her yourself," Sarah said, kissing his forehead. "I'm going to call for help. I'll be right back. Promise."

She reached down to scoop up the gun as she left, veering around Gavin's silent body, and praying that help would get there in time to save her husband.

FORTY-ONE

Initially I was confused. Had Sarah found something in the bomb shelter and called Kirk and Gavin to the site? It seemed like the most likely possibility, but when I saw Gavin's gun and witnessed him pushing Kirk down the stairs, it changed my thinking. Hearing his furious shouting twisted a knot in my stomach. So much anger. Someone was going to die.

Despite my own fears, I ventured out from behind the bushes then, making my way to the opening. I wasn't concerned about Kirk and Gavin. Those two could go to hell for all I cared, but Sarah seemed like a decent human being. I could never go down those steps again, but I thought that if I called out, and they knew someone else was there on the property, it might defuse the situation.

I heard a popping noise and a scuffle, then a muffled thump. No sooner had I gotten to the bomb shelter and opened my mouth than Sarah came frantically running up the stairs, wearing a sports bra and jeans splattered with blood. When she saw me standing there, she squeezed my arm with the fierceness of a drowning victim grabbing hold of a lifeguard.

For me, it was the beginning of the end.

FORTY-TWO

When Sarah caught sight of the woman outside the shelter, her shock was immediately eclipsed by relief. She frantically grasped the woman's arm. "I need help!" she said, the words coming out rapid fire. "My husband's been shot."

"I already called 911." The young woman held up her phone. Her voice was surprisingly calm. "They're on their way." As if on cue, a siren sounded, wailing in the distance.

Sarah dropped Gavin's gun at the woman's feet, then said, "When they get here, send them down right away. Tell them to hurry!"

She rushed back down the stairs, again bypassing Gavin's still form and heading straight to Kirk. Kneeling beside him, she said, "Kirk, I'm here, babe." She pressed down on the blood-soaked T-shirt. "Hang in there. Help is on the way." And even though his eyes were open and unseeing, and he didn't move or respond to her words in any way, she kept talking to him, begging him to stay with her. "We'll get through this. It's going to be fine, you'll see." Her eyes brimmed with tears. "Please, Kirk, say something."

A fleeting thought crossed her mind, one that told her

checking for a pulse would be the true test, but she really didn't want to find out. Not knowing meant there was still hope.

She heard their arrival first, a commotion of voices outside, and then saw a strong light shining down from above, so bright that she had to shield her eyes. When two uniformed cops came down, guns drawn, she held up her hands in surrender and called out to them. "Over here! You have to help my husband. He's been shot!"

And then the tiny bomb shelter, smaller than her entryway at home, was suddenly filled with the buzzing of police followed by EMTs, one of whom gently took her by the elbow and said, "Ma'am, you need to come with me and wait outside. Let them do their job."

Mutely, she let him lead her back up the stairs and into the yard where another EMT draped a blanket around her shoulders and began to assess her. "I'm fine," she said, waving him away. "This isn't my blood. It's my husband's."

A petite woman in a neatly pressed police uniform and a tight bun guided her away from the scene and toward the house. Everything about her said professionalism, but she had the soothing voice of a mother comforting a child. "My name is Hannah. Can you tell me what happened?"

Sarah found herself telling the whole story, frantically spitting out the words, as if making this woman understand would fix everything. She began with her initial descent into the bomb shelter and finding Clarice's body, and what happened soon after.

"I was horrified when I realized who it was—she was my friend. Just so awful. I was about to get my phone and report it when my husband and Gavin Kramer showed up." She choked back a sob, explaining how Gavin had made her kneel on the floor while his gun was aimed at Kirk. "I knew he was going to kill both of us, so I picked up the crowbar and hit him over the head. I had to do it. There was no other way." She stopped and took in a deep breath and then began to weep.

Hannah gave a sympathetic nod. "You don't need to worry. You're safe now."

"Can you find out about my husband?" she asked, craning her neck to see past Hannah. "He was in a really bad way. They should be rushing him to the hospital."

"Believe me, they're doing everything they can. Let's give them some space and get you checked out. As soon as I know something, I'll tell you. I promise."

Hannah guided her away from the backyard, around the side of the house to the driveway, where an ambulance was parked. The street, previously quiet and dark, was now crowded with vehicles: three squad cars, another ambulance, a fire truck, and several cars. A voice squawked over a radio. Across the street, an old man in his bathrobe stood on his front porch, hands in pockets, surveying the scene.

"Right this way," Hannah said, walking her to the back of the ambulance. The doors were wide open and she patted the edge. "Take a seat." After Sarah complied, she called out, "Can I get an EMT here? She needs to be checked out."

"No, really I'm fine," Sarah protested.

At the end of the driveway, a police officer stood questioning the young woman who'd called 911. Sarah heard her say, "I used to live in the neighborhood and I still keep in touch with Mrs. Scott next door. When I drove past and saw it was dark, I thought I'd check on her."

A former neighbor. Lucky thing she came along. The police officer handed Sarah a small bottle of water. Gratefully, she twisted off the top and took a swig.

A young guy in street clothes appeared. He said, "Hi, I'm Ethan. I'm one of the EMTs and I'm going to be checking you over, okay? Can you show me your injuries?"

"I'm not hurt."

"The blood on her clothing is not hers," Hannah said.

"Okay." Ethan nodded. "Let's start with your name."

She nodded. "Sarah Aden." Out of habit, she spelled out both names. Even though the night air was hot and muggy, she pulled the blanket more tightly around her shoulders.

Hannah left her side to talk to another officer, a lanky young man. The two conferred, with the guy talking briefly on his handheld radio. Sarah kept her eyes on them even while answering Ethan's questions.

When she saw the EMTs carry Gavin out on a stretcher, taking him directly to the ambulance across the street, she leapt to her feet. "Why aren't they bringing my husband out?" She didn't wait for Ethan's response, but walked over to Hannah.

"Where's my husband?" she asked. "I want to see my husband."

When two police officers exchanged a look, fear churned in her blood. Hannah said, "I'm sorry to tell you this, Mrs. Aden . . ."

"No." Sarah shook her head, took a step back, and put her hand to her heart. "Please no." She wanted to cover her ears, drop to the ground, and curl into a fetal position, but her body was numb and wouldn't move. She wasn't ready to hear what came next. It came anyway.

". . . but despite all of our efforts, your husband has died. I'm so sorry for your loss."

FORTY-THREE

Hannah had given her a clean T-shirt when they'd arrived at the police station, and Sarah pulled it on right away. They asked permission to test her hands for gunshot residue, something she readily agreed to do. Only then could she wash her hands and comb her hair. In the mirror, she noticed how haggard her face looked, as if she'd aged a decade in the last two days.

But really, what difference did it make how she looked now? Her world had shattered. Kirk was dead. No more anniversaries or days waking up next to him, rolling over to see him smiling in his sleep. Her view of a family life, with her as a mother, had also burst into flames. There would be no pregnancy, no baby, no dad coming home from work to scoop up an excited toddler. Without even realizing it, she'd mentally created a life that would never happen. All of that was over. Her mission to find the truth had led to two deaths and her actions were the impetus of those deaths. She was to blame and that was something she'd have to live with for the rest of her life.

Now Sarah sat at the same table where she'd looked over the report on her attack during an earlier visit. She didn't want to be here, sitting at the police station, but she didn't want to go to her empty house either. What she wanted was to rewind the clock and undo the last twenty-four hours. Wipe away everything she knew and go back to how it was before. If only that were possible.

Sarah ran a finger against the top of the table, wondering what would happen next. When a detective came into the room, he set a bottle of water and a box of tissues on the table in front of her.

"I'm sorry for your loss, Mrs. Aden. I know this isn't a good time, but I was hoping you were up to answering some questions."

He pulled out a chair for himself and took a seat. She hadn't seen him at the crime scene. He was good-looking: square-jawed with dark hair just starting to go gray at the temples. Old enough to have some authority. Young enough to have the vitality needed to do active police work. He'd introduced himself as Clint. It was a strategy, she surmised. Using a first name to put her at ease.

"Am I under arrest?" she asked.

"No, should you be?"

Mind games. Sarah had seen enough cop movies to know that sometimes innocent people implicated themselves when exhausted or confused, and she was both. Did she need an attorney? She wasn't sure. Kirk would know best, but he was gone and she was alone.

"Of course not," she answered. "Gavin's the one who pulled the trigger and killed my husband. He was going to kill both of us." Earlier, she had admitted to hitting Gavin with the crowbar, but that was in self-defense, and they hadn't mentioned charging her with that crime.

"If that's true, then the test we did for gunshot residue will show up on his hands and not yours, so you have nothing to worry about. In my experience, forensics always backs up the truth."

She thought hard. "I'll answer your questions, but I want to call someone to be with me while we talk." Without waiting for permission, she grabbed her backpack and opened the outside pocket, taking out her phone.

"Of course. Whatever makes you feel more comfortable."

With her finger poised over the phone, she thought about calling Phil and then discarded the idea. It was her first instinct, but she knew it was also a bad idea. He'd proven to be a good friend, and would come immediately, but how could she explain their friendship? Phil's name hadn't come up yet. Why get him involved at all? Instead, she dialed the number for the landline at her in-laws' house and prayed they'd answer an unidentified number.

"I'm going to call Kirk's parents," she told the detective after dialing the number. "They need to know."

On the sixth ring, Judy picked up. "Hello?" she answered cautiously.

Just hearing her voice made Sarah cry. Her throat constricting with emotion, she managed to get out the words: "Judy, it's me. Sarah."

"Sarah? Honey, what's wrong?"

In between sobs, she said, "Can you and Bert come down to the police station? Something terrible has happened." She reached for a tissue.

"What happened?" Judy asked, and Sarah, nearly choking from emotion, mutely handed the phone over to Clint.

"Ma'am? This is Detective Jackson. To whom am I speaking?" There was a pause and he said, "Judy Aden. You're Kirk Aden's mother?"

Sarah could hear Judy's voice, but couldn't make out what she was saying.

"I'm here with your daughter-in-law at the police station on Renner Road. There was an incident earlier this evening and Sarah would like you to come down to the station." He cleared his throat.

Again, Sarah heard murmuring from the other end of the conversation. Her heart sank when she made out Kirk's name. Judy wanted to know if something had happened to her son.

The detective said, "I can't disclose anything over the phone, but we can explain once you've arrived. Yes, I'll tell her. Thank you. Goodbye." He handed the phone back to her.

She felt her throat closing, but managed to ask, "What did she want you to tell me?"

"They love you and are coming right away."

"You didn't tell them about Kirk." She dabbed her eyes with a tissue and now gave him her complete attention.

"You don't give people news like that over the phone. Normally, we'd have a pair of officers go to their home to tell them in person, but that hasn't been arranged yet."

"I see." Sarah sat back and blinked. "When they get here, will you tell them?"

She couldn't imagine saying the words to them, seeing their faces, and having them know she had a role in all of this. Their son was dead because she had to snoop around in the past. They would hate her; she was sure of it.

"If that's what you want."

Sarah wiped away tears. "I would appreciate it."

FORTY-FOUR

FOUR MONTHS LATER

Answering a knock at the door, Sarah hesitated when seeing Stephanie Bickley standing across the threshold, her hands clasped together. "Mrs. Aden?" she said. "I'm sorry for dropping by unannounced. I would have called, but I didn't have your number." Despite her apologetic words, she stood tall, her hair braided in a single plait that rested on one shoulder, head held high. "Am I interrupting something?"

Only me changing the course of my life, Sarah thought wryly. The whole first floor of her house was stacked with moving boxes. At that very moment, Phil was in the kitchen, carefully wrapping plates in layers of bubble wrap. Because her new house was much smaller, she'd had to sort through her possessions judiciously. Choosing the furniture had been based on need and space, but the personal items were harder to select. It wasn't as simple as deciding what brought her joy. The last few months had been so emotionally tumultuous that even her wedding photos—once a documentation of the happiest day of her life—had become tinged with grief.

Now Sarah stood face-to-face with someone else who'd suffered badly. If Stephanie was here to rehash the past, she wasn't sure she could bear it. Her own load was too heavy. She couldn't take on anyone else's pain. "Actually, I'm in the middle of packing."

"I see," Stephanie said, but didn't move. The last time Sarah had seen her had been at the police station. They'd both given statements to the police, but hadn't spoken to each other. Sarah had been given a ticket for trespassing, but hadn't been charged with staying in the Caldwells' house, which would have been the more serious charge of breaking and entering. One police officer made a point to tell her she was lucky that way, but she didn't feel lucky. She didn't feel lucky at all.

Stephanie added, "It's just that my mom wanted to meet you. To say thank you." She gestured behind her and for the first time Sarah noticed a silver-haired woman in the passenger side of the parked car in her driveway. "I tried to tell her it would be awkward, but she just felt compelled to see you. She thought . . ." Stephanie closed her eyes for a moment and exhaled. ". . . it might bring you some comfort to know that you helped her. Helped us, I mean."

Sarah hesitated. "I'm not sure—"

"Just for a few minutes. It's important to my mother. She's been through so much." Stephanie put her hands together in a praying gesture.

"Of course." Sarah opened the door wider. "Please tell her you're both welcome to come in."

As if she thought Sarah might change her mind, Stephanie turned quickly and jogged to the car, swinging the door open for her mother. Assisting her mother out of her seat, she reached in to grab a cane. The older woman walked slowly, her daughter helping her up the step to the front door where Sarah ushered them inside.

"So kind of you to let us barge in on you," Mrs. Bickley said, leaning on her cane in the foyer. Her eyes widened as she looked Sarah over. "You're pregnant!"

"Yes, I am." Sarah's hand curved over her belly. "Five months." She hadn't thought it was that apparent, but glancing down, she saw that what had looked like a thickening waistline a few days before was now an obvious baby bump. When she'd first found out she was pregnant, what should have been joy was negated by having to plan a funeral for her husband and the ordeal of cooperating with a criminal investigation. She'd told her story to the police so many times she nearly had a breakdown.

There was no getting away from the pain. It manifested itself in so many ways. Heartbreaking grief at the loss of her husband. Fury at Gavin for murdering her husband, leaving her alone to raise the child she and Kirk had both so desperately wanted. Guilt at having played a role in Kirk's death. And worst of all, anger at her husband for having had a role in Jeremy's death in the first place. He'd had so many opportunities to come clean over the years and instead kept it quiet, to his own detriment, and now hers. There were times she felt as if his guilt had transferred to her.

The healing only began when Judy said, "Don't be so hard on yourself. You were a victim too." Both Judy and Bert were unbelievably kind to her. They could have blamed her, but instead they grieved alongside her. In that, she felt lucky.

She'd originally planned to move back east after the house was sold, but they'd begged her to stay. "You're family," Bert had said, wrapping her in a bear hug. "We already lost a son. We don't want to lose you and the little one too." All of their lives had been diminished. So she agreed to stay. The one thing she was firm on was moving to a smaller house. Her finances were in good shape, since her in-laws had found a new owner for the dealership and Kirk had a generous life insurance policy, so it wasn't money driving the move, but a need for a fresh start for her and the baby.

"Five months!" Mrs. Bickley repeated. "How wonderful! Babies are such a blessing."

Sarah led them into the living room, and then waited as they caught up, Mrs. Bickley taking halting steps down the hallway.

"I used to be much faster," Mrs. Bickley said apologetically. "I had a stroke a few years ago. I'm recovered for the most part, but my legs never got the memo."

"It's not a race. You're fine," Sarah assured her, gesturing for them to take a seat. "Can I get you something to drink?"

"No, we're not staying long, but thank you." Stephanie sat down next to her mother. "We appreciate you agreeing to talk to us. I know it's awkward."

"Not a problem. I'm glad you stopped by," Sarah said, clasping her hands around one knee. For some reason facing them made her nervous. Each of them had lost someone they dearly loved, but in Sarah's case her husband had a role in the Bickleys' misery. He'd known the truth and kept it from them. "I meant to write you a note telling you I'm so sorry for your loss." She'd thought about it so many times, but wasn't sure how it would be received.

Mrs. Bickley said, "I wanted to thank you in person for making such a large donation in Jeremy's name to the Mental Health Society. That was very generous of you."

"You're welcome," Sarah said, taken aback. "I thought it would be anonymous." She remembered checking the box and thinking the Bickleys wouldn't know. That it would be better that way.

"It was anonymous in that your name wasn't on the website, but Mom and I got the list of names," Stephanie explained.

"I see."

"It was so kind of you to think of us in your time of sorrow." Mrs. Bickley leaned forward, her hand on top of her cane. "It made me regret that we didn't do anything for Kirk's funeral. I'm sorry. I was only thinking of myself."

Sarah waved her hand. "You don't need to worry about that. If anything, I should be thanking you, Stephanie. Your photos went a long way in corroborating my story. It backed up the timeline, which was a big help."

The gun, as it turned out, had not been registered to anyone.

Luckily, the gunpowder residue on Gavin's hand was definitive. His defense? He'd said the gun was Kirk's, and that when threatened, he'd wrestled it out of Kirk's hands. He had to shoot him, he said, because he felt threatened. A lame defense, especially for someone in law enforcement, but Gavin was a convincing liar. He'd also said that they'd all arrived together and that Kirk had killed Clarice. Stephanie's photos proved otherwise, though, and also saved Sarah from being charged in assaulting Gavin with the crowbar. Her story, along with the pictures taken that night, made a solid case for self-defense.

"You're welcome," Stephanie said. "Just trying to do the right thing."

"One thing I've been wondering," Sarah asked, considering her words carefully. "Was it a coincidence that you were at Maggie Scott's house when all of this happened? You can tell me. I'm not in a position to make any judgments. You saved my life."

Stephanie shook her head. "Completely random. I'd love to say I had some premonition, but that's not the case. Just coincidental good timing." She tucked her hair behind one ear. "I do have a question for you as well—if you don't mind."

"Shoot." Sarah immediately regretted her choice of words, but neither Bickley seemed to notice.

"Do you believe Gavin's story—that Clarice killed Jeremy with the machete and that the three of them covered it up because they were afraid?"

"I wasn't there, of course," Sarah said, "but I can tell you that he basically said the same thing when I was down in the bomb shelter, and Kirk agreed. So yes, I believe it happened that way."

The local news had a field day with this story when it all came out. In Gavin's telling, it was an accident. Just a bunch of kids who'd had too much to drink and were playing around. According to him, Clarice had actually been the one at fault. She'd been waving the machete around and it struck Jeremy, slicing open his abdomen. He'd bled out in minutes.

"It makes me sick that he justified covering it up by saying they were just kids at the time. Just kids," Stephanie repeated, a bitter note in her voice. "They were old enough to know better. They knew what they were doing."

"Stephanie," her mother said, love in her voice. "Don't go there. Let it be."

"As you can see, my mother is more forgiving than I am."

"It's not a matter of forgiving," Mrs. Bickley said with a sigh. "I just can't let it devour me. There's a quote that has stayed with me over the years: holding on to anger is like grasping a hot coal with the intent of throwing it at someone else; instead, you are the one who will get burned. I'm paraphrasing, but that's the gist of it."

"Well put," Sarah said. There was a long pause and then she added, "All three of us are in the middle of tragedies we didn't choose. I don't know that I'll ever come to terms with everything that happened."

"You will. In time. It won't go away completely, but the pain will become manageable and you'll find things that will make you happy," Mrs. Bickley said, meeting her eyes with a kind gaze. "If it weren't for Stephanie here . . ." She gave her daughter a warm smile. ". . . I think I would have lost my mind a long time ago. And you'll have your little one too. You'll see. Having your baby will go a long way toward healing your pain. A new life is a miracle."

Sarah's hand instinctively nestled her stomach. "I needed to hear that. Thank you."

"Do you know if you're having a boy or girl?"

"It's a boy."

"How nice," Mrs. Bickley said. "There's nothing like having a son. Boys really love their mothers." After a long pause, she added, "You know, Stephanie and I ran into Judy Aden at the grocery store the other day. She and I used to be close friends when the boys were teenagers, but that all changed after Jeremy went missing." Her voice broke on the last few words and it took her a few moments to collect herself. "*Everything* changed after I lost my son. I would see Judy and Bert out and about and I'd go out of my way *not* to talk to them. They still had their son, and I didn't. Even making small talk was too painful for me. But seeing Judy at the store this time was different, now that we know the truth. I'm not sure that we'll be friends again, but we had a lovely conversation and I feel like a load has been lifted. So thank you for that, Sarah. You're a brave woman and you've helped me more than you'll ever know."

"You're welcome." It was the right response, but Sarah felt insincere saying the words. She didn't feel brave. Instead, she felt adrift and scared, but it did help to know that something she'd done had helped Mrs. Bickley find peace after so many years of pain. And maybe someday she'd find her own peace as well.

After a long pause, Mrs. Bickley struggled to her feet. "I do believe we've taken enough of your time. Thank you for speaking with us, Sarah. I wish you and your son only the best in the future."

Your son. Sarah felt a twinge of happiness. She'd been thinking of her little one as the baby, which was accurate, of course, but a son? The word brought an image of the Madonna and Child. Mother and son. A connection she'd have for a lifetime.

"Thanks for stopping by." Sarah accompanied the two women to the front door. "I'm glad we talked."

In the foyer, as they said their goodbyes, Mrs. Bickley pulled Sarah into an embrace. She said, "You take care of yourself."

"I will."

Sarah watched the women make their way slowly to the car. They were halfway there when Stephanie turned back, retracing her steps to the door.

"My mom would be appalled that I'm telling you this," she said, keeping her voice low. "But just between us, when we saw your mother-in-law the other day, she said her greatest wish is that you name the baby after Kirk. She said she'd never ask you to do such a thing, but secretly she and Bert are both hoping you will." She smiled.

"Oh." Sarah was taken aback. "I haven't really decided on a name yet."

"I really think you should name him Kirk. It would be such a great tribute to his father." She put her hands together, a show of impassioned plea. "The Adens would be delighted. Promise you'll think about it?"

Sarah caught the hopeful expression on her face and nodded. "All right, I promise."

"Please don't mention that I told you. I'd hate for Mrs. Aden to think I betrayed a confidence."

"Not a word," she said, miming the zippering of her mouth.

Moments later as the women drove off, they waved, and Sarah returned the gesture. When the car was out of sight, she closed the door, another chapter in her life put to rest.

FORTY-FIVE

We drove away from Sarah Aden's ritzy upscale house, Mom sighing with contentment. I knew this exchange had brought her some measure of closure. As for me, not so much. I couldn't help but notice that nothing in Sarah's home looked like it needed updating or repairing. The walls were free of scuffs. The flooring could have been on display in a showroom. And then there was Sarah herself. Even pregnant and in the midst of packing, she'd looked calm and collected. Her pretty face was flushed pink with exertion, giving her a healthy glow. She was dressed casually, wearing jeans and a V-necked T-shirt, but still somehow managed to look elegant, ushering us inside with the grace of the First Lady at the White House.

She'd been so nice it was difficult to resent her. Not impossible, though.

When I saw her come out of the bomb shelter so many months ago, I was relieved it was her and not Kirk, or worse yet, Gavin. When everything came to light and the facts were finally made known, I was euphoric to know the truth, and better yet, to know that two of the three suspects had met an untimely and gruesome death. A bit of poetic justice to balance out my family's suffering. It seemed right that Gavin would be going to prison. The other inmates were going to love having him in their midst. For the first time, I felt a bit of peace, and some gratitude to Sarah Aden for her role in revealing what had happened to my brother. She'd done it at great personal cost to herself, not that I cared all that much about that aspect of it.

At one point, I thought I'd turned a corner. It wasn't until Mom and I ran into Judy Aden at the grocery store that I knew that the corner was actually a circle and I'd never be clear of it. The two exchanged condolences and apologies while I stood there in aisle six, only half listening. Somehow, I'd become a bystander in my own life. Sure, I'd come to terms with what had happened to my brother and felt like a measure of justice had been meted out, but I still wasn't ready to extend an olive branch. As I said, my mother was the more forgiving of the two of us.

In quick time, Judy and my mom had a conversation that covered all the years and laid all of the suffering to rest. I tapped my toe impatiently, distracted by an elderly woman standing behind Mom and Judy, surveying the spice shelves. They were arranged in alphabetical order, but judging from the way she searched the display, she wasn't aware of this. My mind shifted from her when Mrs. Aden said, "I do have one piece of news, a bit of happiness in all of this: Sarah is having a baby." She beamed. "I'm not supposed to tell anyone, but I can't seem to help myself. She's nearly five months along." She clasped her hands together in delight and I felt my blood boil.

"How wonderful!" Mom exclaimed, truly meaning it. "A grandchild. Do you know if it's a boy or girl?"

"A boy." Judy Aden could not stop grinning. I wanted to smack her. "Bert and I can't wait to hold the little guy. God is good."

God is good.

I was running this earlier conversation through my brain when Mom's voice floated over from the passenger seat. "Penny for your thoughts?"

"Nothing really. Are you glad we stopped in?" I flicked on the turn signal and took a sharp right out of the subdivision.

"Very glad. I wanted her to know that despite everything I didn't hate her and I wished her well. I didn't want that sitting out there."

Typical Mom. Always wanting to put positive energy out into the world. Good thoughts, good words, good deeds. "I'd say you accomplished that."

"Just one question. When you ran back to the house, what did you say to her?"

I didn't have to look at my mom to know her brow was furrowed, concerned I had dropped some kind of spite bomb. "You would be impressed at my good manners. I was very nice. Just thanked her for letting us drop by unannounced. Said that it was important to both of us." I glanced in her direction. "Honestly, I wasn't entirely sure she'd let us past the front door."

"I thought she would," Mom said with certainty. "I just had a feeling." I'd paused at a stop sign and now proceeded to cross the intersection. The movement must have seemed sudden because she reached out and grabbed the dashboard like she did when I had my learner's permit and I'd accelerated too quickly. Old habits die hard.

For all of her insights, Mom never could have guessed what I'd actually told Sarah. Never in a million years. What I'd said was unplanned, and yet somehow as perfect as if I'd spent all night scheming to find a subtle, yet agonizing revenge.

The seed of the idea started that day in the grocery store. Hearing about the baby brought emotions to light that had been, I found out, only superficially tamped down. How could these two women be so joyful when my brother was still dead? Worse yet, this woman's son was part of it all and my mother was congratulating her on her new grandchild? Did she not realize that the Adens were still coming out ahead of us? There would be no grandchild in my family. Jeremy was dead and I was stuck in my mother's house, the one left behind. The family life raft. I would never find happiness or have children of my own.

To add insult to injury, I had to listen to my own mother telling Sarah, "There's nothing like having a son. Boys really love their mothers." *What?* As if I was nothing. As if having a devoted daughter was a consolation prize.

No. This was not right. Not right at all.

While Mom had waxed poetic about the joys of a son with Sarah, I thought back to the rest of the conversation in the grocery store. After Judy had announced it was a boy, I couldn't resist making a comment. "Maybe she'll name him Kirk."

Judy's face dropped in horror. "Oh, I hope not. I mean, it's up to her, but that would be heartbreaking. A constant reminder." The old woman surveying the spices finally found what she was looking for, plucking a jar of cinnamon off the shelf and adding it to her cart. All that time and trouble for a little jar of cinnamon.

I said, "You'd probably get used to it eventually, and start associating the name with the new baby." I didn't have any preferences in baby names either way, but it was satisfying to see that I'd struck a nerve.

"No." Judy shook her head. "I'd never get used to it and it would be a knife in my heart. I think the baby needs to have his own name and identity. That would be best."

"If it comes up, you can just let her know how you feel," my mom offered.

Judy sighed. "Bert and I talked about it and we're not going to offer any opinions about the baby unless she asks. We already talked her out of moving back east. We don't want to be overbearing."

Hearing Kirk's name would be a knife to her heart. I smiled thinking of what I'd done. A small retribution, but for now it was good enough.

FORTY-SIX

Sarah found Phil in the kitchen, surveying a lineup of small appliances on the island. Most of them had been gifts from her mother-in-law, high-end machines designed to make life easier. In actuality, she'd only used most of them once or twice, and then afterward tucked them away in a cabinet, forgetting she even owned them. She looked over the collection: an espresso maker, juicer, two Instant Pots, a mixer, bread maker, and a food processor.

"Any of these coming with you?" he asked as she entered the room.

Sarah took a seat at the counter. "Only the juicer and food processor." She imagined both would come in handy with a baby. Her son.

"Can I take one of the Instant Pots?" he asked, eyebrows raised.

"Help yourself."

"Cool." He nodded approvingly, resting his hand on the larger of the two. "I've been eyeing one of these bad boys for a while, but couldn't justify the expense. I have to say that rich people's castoffs are better than anything I can afford."

"I'm not rich," she said, giving him a smile. "I just don't have to worry about money."

"That, Sarah Aden, is the exact definition of rich." He sat on the stool next to her. "I have a confession to make." He exhaled loudly. "I was eavesdropping on you and your visitors." His soft features formed an apologetic expression. "I'm sorry."

"No need to be sorry. I should have included you."

"It's probably best that you didn't. It seemed pretty personal."

"It was an odd visit. I was a little worried when I saw Stephanie at the door, but they were nice. I guess it's good that we talked. Now if I see them out in public, it won't be so awkward." She tapped her fingers on the counter. "One weird thing. After Mrs. Bickley went to the car, Stephanie ran back and told me—off the record—that they'd run into my mother-in-law at the grocery store and she told them that they want me to name the baby Kirk." Sarah's curved fingers rested on the crest of her stomach. Baby Kirk? It just didn't sound right. She continued, "Judy said they won't say anything to me, but they're secretly hoping I pick that name."

"Do you want to name him Kirk?" As usual, Phil pared the issue down to its core.

"No," she said, shaking her head sadly, "I don't. It's probably the last name I would have thought of on my own. But they lost a son and if it would make them happy . . ." She sighed. "I guess I could get used to it."

He reached over and clapped a brotherly hand on her shoulder. "Look at you, being all martyr-ish. I say, it's your kid. Name him what you want."

"You think?" She met his eyes.

"I do. It would be a nice gesture, but there already was a Kirk Aden. Let your son have his own identity. Plus, you don't even know that Judy said that. Stephanie sounded bitter to me. For all you know, she made the whole thing up."

She tilted her head to regard him quizzically. "I can't believe she'd outright lie about it. I mean, why would she?"

"Oh, Sarah." He shook his head and laughed. "You're too good for this world."

FORTY-SEVEN

When the trial came to a close, Gavin was convicted on two counts each of first-degree reckless homicide and an additional charge of hiding a corpse. He was sentenced to seventy-four years in prison and twenty-eight years' extended supervision.

Seventy-four years. Ridiculous, he thought.

In retrospect, he'd have thought the trial would have gone better. It was his word against Sarah's. He was the chief of police and she was, well, *what* was she? The brain-addled wife of a privileged guy whose parents bought him a car dealership, that's who she was. Not even from around here, while Gavin had a lifetime of friends, co-workers, and relatives in the area. The number of people who owed him favors in law enforcement could fill a page.

His lawyer was incompetent, that was the problem. Attorney Brett Hughes, supposedly the best criminal lawyer in the state, had failed him big-time. At first, Hughes seemed like he'd be the hero in this story, talking smack about the case lacking a motive and Gavin's impeccable record of conduct.

"Not even a parking ticket," he'd noted almost gleefully. "And you're a smart guy, the chief of police. Why would you kill two of your best friends from high school on someone else's property? I'd like to see the defense build a case around that one."

Gavin imagined he'd be cleared of the charges, and then afterward, the two of them would go out for drinks, toasting his success. Hell, he even planned on picking up the tab.

The situation, which had started out well, quickly went downhill. At some point, Gavin saw an almost defeatist shift in Hughes, a change from wanting to get his client cleared of charges, to talking about reducing the length of his sentence via a plea deal.

That damn prosecutor, Tara Green, now she was a real ballbuster. Somehow, she'd found out he was in possession of the machete, which threw suspicion on his version of events regarding Jeremy's death. Bert Aden identified it as being the one he'd owned when Gavin and Kirk were in high school. Bert claimed he knew it by the distinctive pattern, but admitted it was possible there existed more than one machete with that appearance. Attorney Green used this to discredit Gavin. "Why would a man sworn to uphold the law display a murder weapon in his home?" she'd asked the jury. She also harped on the gunshot residue on Gavin's hands and showed Stephanie Bickley's photos on a large screen, the silencer on his gun clearly in view.

"Premeditated" was the word that reverberated around the courtroom. "Prepared" was the word he would have used, something he'd acquired from his years protecting the community, and he wanted a chance to say as much. He had a whole speech planned, but his attorney advised against it. "Let me do my job," he'd said.

What a putz. Why had he listened to him?

Gavin, given the chance to speak at length, would have brought up other topics as well. Why weren't Stephanie and Sarah charged with any major crimes? Both of them had trespassed on private property and Sarah had disturbed a crime scene. Seems like there was enough blame to go around, but he was the only one who caught some flak.

The fact that he'd been driving a squad car that night turned out to be problematic as well. The prosecution posited that he was using his position as police chief to circumvent the law. His revised take on it? He'd been about to leave work, but first returned a call to an old friend. Kirk had been frantic, sure that Sarah was at his old house, and Gavin, being a good friend, left immediately to help him. He'd been in such a hurry that he hadn't switched cars. The fact that he was in the squad car was a mere timing issue.

As for the rest of it? In his mind, the alternate version had unfolded like this: Sarah had been in a homicidal rage after finding out that Kirk and Clarice were having an affair. When he and Kirk arrived at the scene of the crime, Sarah was in the bomb shelter, having already killed Clarice, who she'd lured there under false pretenses. After they arrived, she killed Kirk right in front of him, and she would have killed Gavin too if he hadn't overpowered her and taken the gun away. Then she knocked him unconscious with a crowbar. With enough reasonable doubt and a little help from the guys in the lab, they could have eliminated the gunshot residue issue altogether. Made it inconclusive. The photo evidence could have been cast into doubt as well. It was dark. He could have been holding a flashlight. He presented this version to his attorney, who did lay out the story during closing arguments, but even to Gavin's ears, Hughes's presentation was less than compelling. It was all in the telling, and the idiot didn't tell it correctly.

Gavin had kept his temper in check almost until the end, but after the prosecutor maligned his character saying he'd shown no remorse, he'd blown up at Hughes during their next private session.

"Why would I have remorse for something I didn't do?" he'd demanded. "You need to point that out."

"Look," Hughes had said impatiently. "I've told you this already. You need to adjust your body language and facial expression if you want to appear sympathetic." Gavin had years of experience reading people and it was clear: Hughes had given up on him.

And now he was stuck at the Dodd Correctional Institution, a maximum-security facility for adult males. A place he used to send people and now he was the place's most eminent resident. To make matters worse, Natalie hadn't come for a visit the day before, as she'd promised. He hoped she wasn't giving up on him, but then why would she? The two of them were solid. When he'd met her, she was working the night shift in a warehouse. With his help, she'd started her own business, a popular fashion boutique. He'd saved her from a lifetime of grunt work and she owed him for that.

None of this was his fault. Like any teenage boy, he'd fallen prey to Clarice Carter's seductive advances, and it had all unraveled from there. Despite her deplorable personality, she'd been great in the sack, and that long-ago summer, sex in the bomb shelter had been intense. He and Clarice had always made it a point to enter the Adens' yard via the park. They'd been careful when opening and closing the metal doors. Kirk's parents never suspected a thing. They'd joked about what a great setup it was. So nice of Bert Aden to provide them with a cot. So much better than the beanbags Kirk dragged in from his family's rec room.

Having sex there had gone a long way toward making him feel like he had an edge over Kirk instead of the other way around. It might have been on the Adens' property, but Gavin was the king, since he was the one getting his rocks off doing things with Clarice the other two guys could only dream of. Kirk had denied desiring her—said he only saw her as a friend, but that was clearly a lie. Whenever Clarice made a flirty comment or touched him, even innocently, Kirk's face flushed bright red. Jeremy fell into a different category. His lust had taken on a form of adulation. He'd followed Clarice around, gazing at her adoringly. He always made a point to reserve the comfortable beanbag for her, and constantly offered to get her cold drinks. So needy.

That fateful night, Clarice had arrived at the bomb shelter drunk, not that it mattered to Gavin. Their sexual encounter had been fast and hot. Clarice had no modesty at all and would strip off all her clothes without a second thought. The first time she did it, he was both shocked and pleased. She'd never worried about the two of them being caught. When he mentioned they should be careful, she'd laughed and said, "Live in the moment and go for the greatest pleasure, that's my motto."

Say what you would about Clarice, but she knew herself and stayed consistent to her values. Or lack of values, depending on your point of view.

They'd just finished having sex and were still lying together on the cot when they heard the bomb shelter doors open and the sound of talking. Two voices. Kirk and Jeremy. The lantern had cast enough light that he was able to find his briefs and jeans on the ground and pulled them on in short order. Clarice hadn't moved a muscle. She stayed stretched out on the cot, completely naked. He tossed the crocheted throw at her and she sighed and covered herself with it. In retrospect, her reaction made it seem like she wanted to get caught.

There was a confrontation, of course, something that delighted Clarice. And then, since she was sloppy drunk, she had to start playing around with the machete. The way Jeremy and Kirk stared at her, you'd think they never saw a naked woman before. Both of them tried to get her to put the machete down, without success.

Gavin saw that neither of them was going to be able to get control of her. Pansy asses. "You got to be kidding me," he'd said, pushing past them and grabbing her arm.

Clarice had yelped. "Stop! You're hurting me." She pulled away from him, not releasing the machete.

"Leave her alone," Jeremy yelled, and rushed in to help her.

What happened next was a blur, both in real life and later in his memory. As he tried to restrain Clarice, she struggled out of his grasp, throwing herself forward and away from him. He reached for the machete just as Jeremy moved into their path. In a flash, the blade sliced through the front of his shirt and plunged into his abdomen. Jeremy staggered back, and the machete, stained with his blood, fell to the ground.

Looking back, Gavin regretted not taking the machete away from her earlier. He was the biggest one in the group and the only one not unnerved by her lack of clothing. He should have taken action, he knew that. Still, the weapon had been in Clarice's hand at the time it struck Jeremy. Clarice blamed him, of course, because that was her way. Nothing was ever her fault.

After the machete made impact, Jeremy had staggered backward. Before he could fall, Kirk grabbed him under the arms and lowered him to the floor. Jeremy clutched his stomach, the blood spurting between his closed fingers. So much blood. Gavin had seen the crime scene photos his dad had brought home and knew how ugly things could get, but this was far worse than anything he'd ever seen or imagined.

"What have you done?" Jeremy said, his eyes wide.

Clarice took a step back. "Oh my God!"

Kirk looked to Gavin and said, "I'll go get my folks."

"No, wait," Gavin had said, buying himself time to think. "Not yet." He took one of his socks and pressed it tight against the wound. On the other side of Jeremy, Kirk crouched, a terrified expression on his face. Clarice had retreated back to the cot, suddenly sober.

Jeremy looked him in the eye. "I don't want to die."

"No one's going to die," Gavin reassured him with false bravado. "We're going to stop the bleeding and then we'll take you to the hospital." Silently he willed the blood to stop, but within seconds the sock was saturated, and still it seeped through.

For years he was haunted by the pathetic sound of Jeremy crying out, "Mama!" right before he took his last breath.

"Damn," Gavin had said, when he realized Jeremy was dead. "He's gone." He'd stood up, looking down at the knees of his jeans, which were stained with blood.

Kirk had shaken his head. "No." He leaned over the body. "Jeremy, hang in there. I'm going for help." He stood up.

Before he could leave, Gavin had grabbed him roughly by the arm. "He's dead, Kirk. Dead."

Kirk ran his fingers through his hair. "He can't be dead. He was fine a minute ago. I mean, we were just talking to him." He was hyperventilating. "We'll call for help. They'll bring those shock paddles."

Gavin shook his head. "Defibrillators? No, it's too late. That wouldn't work. He's gone."

"But they bring people back all the time!"

"Not this time," Gavin said.

Kirk staggered backward, leaning against the wall. "I don't believe this."

"He's really dead?" Clarice said, her voice a screech. "Oh my God, Gavin, you killed him!" She started gathering up her clothing and began getting dressed.

"*You* killed him!" Gavin had said, pointing a finger in her direction. "You had to pick up that stupid machete."

"Why was he even here in the first place?" Clarice had asked Kirk accusatorially. "You guys never come out here at night."

"His dad beat him up," Kirk said, his voice flat. "He was going to spend the night out here."

"Why here? Why not in the house?" Clarice asked.

"He didn't want my parents to see his face. His dad gave him a fat lip." Kirk slid to a crouch, hiding his face in his hands.

The three of them argued then, Kirk making a case for telling his parents, Clarice insisting she'd done nothing wrong. The pair of them had been useless. If it hadn't been for Gavin and his clearheaded thinking, they'd all have been arrested that night. Worse yet, they'd have been tried as adults and sent to prison.

Gavin came up with the only sensible solution. "Look. No one expects Jeremy home anytime soon. Did anyone see you with him?" He looked to Kirk, who shook his head. "We have the perfect opportunity here. I say we wrap the body in plastic and bury it somewhere. If anyone asks, we say we haven't heard from him."

He presented such a foolproof plan that he hadn't expected any objections, but Kirk, as usual, was full of them. Finally, Gavin settled it once and for all, telling them all the ways the law would interpret what had happened and how they'd be prosecuted.

"Even if by some miracle we aren't charged and convicted, this will ruin everything. Your scholarship, Kirk? Gone! Anyone you want to date, Clarice, will know you as the girl who killed a guy. This will follow us for the rest of our lives."

Seeing them hesitate, he added firmly, "We're doing it my way or else I'm pinning it on both of you. My dad is the chief of police. Who do you think they'll believe?"

"But it was an accident," Clarice wailed.

"It doesn't matter. Murder is murder. You killed him, Clarice."

That shut her up. In short time Kirk had retrieved one of the blue plastic tarps his dad kept in the garage. They wrapped poor Jeremy up inside it. Gavin was the brains of the operation and he came up with the brilliant idea of burying Jeremy right where he lay.

"Your mom has been wanting to seal this thing up forever," he said to Kirk. "You're going to tell her you agree with her, that we've outgrown it. We'll fill it up with dirt or something and lock it up. Jeremy will have his own crypt."

"What if she wants to know why I suddenly want it filled in?" Kirk asked, trying to hold back tears.

"You'll think of something," Gavin said. "You're smart."

Kirk *was* smart, but Gavin was smarter. It had been his idea to leave the note in the Bickleys' mailbox. Jeremy kept his notebook on the shelf in the shelter, so Gavin ripped out a sheet of paper, grabbed a pen, and mimicked Jeremy's awkward printing. On the way home, he dropped the folded sheet into the Bickleys' mailbox.

When he'd left, Kirk had been such a blubbering mess Gavin was sure he'd spill the beans, but as it turned out, Gavin was the one whose resolve was tested. When he got home that night, his dad was sitting at the kitchen table, sipping from a can of beer. His mother, he surmised, was already upstairs fast asleep. Normally, Gavin would say good night and head up to bed, but on this evening, his dad put out a hand to stop him.

"Gavin," he said, looking him up and down. "What's new?"

His dad noticed the stains on his knees and the dirt on his shoes. Nothing ever got past him. Gavin, who was calm and collected when among his peers, couldn't hold it together under his father's scrutiny. Chief Bill Kramer was nobody's fool.

"Nothing much." Even he heard the waver in his voice.

"Where've you been?"

"Just hanging out at Kirk's."

"What's new over there?"

"Same old, same old." He took a deep breath. "His mom has been wanting to seal up that bomb shelter for the longest time. Kirk's thinking it's a good idea. We've all outgrown it, and it's sort of a death trap."

His dad raised one eyebrow. "*A death trap?*"

"The stairs are crumbling and it's not well ventilated."

"I see." His dad turned back to his beer.

And then Gavin said good night and headed upstairs. He threw out his clothes from that evening. His dad never brought up their conversation again, but when Jeremy was reported missing, Gavin could tell that his father guessed what had happened by the way he handled the investigation. When it came time to check the bomb shelter, his dad took him along and sent him down to make sure Jeremy wasn't hiding there. By then the smell was terrible, but Gavin somehow forced himself down the stairs and was able to come back up and truthfully report the shelter was empty. Afterward, Gavin's dad told the Adens he'd inspected the shelter himself.

"I recommend you seal it up pronto," he'd said. "It's unsafe and doesn't meet code."

Once the bomb shelter was locked and covered, Gavin felt that the whole episode was behind him. Jeremy was gone, of course, but he'd always been more Kirk's friend than his. Gavin was able to move on and would have continued living his best life if not for Sarah Aden. Some people just didn't know how to mind their own business.

Crime committed. Crime covered up. Crime revealed. It had been buried for so long but unraveled quickly at the end. Even though he was now incarcerated, Gavin knew this wasn't the last word on the subject. Nothing was forever. His years in law enforcement had taught him that new evidence could be uncovered. Convictions could be overturned. It wasn't common, but it happened. Persistence and confidence were key, and he had plenty of both. He just needed a better attorney, and another shot at presenting his case.

The Dodd Correctional Institution was a temporary address, as far as he was concerned.

He sat at breakfast staring at a bowl of tepid oatmeal next to a glass of milk. He desperately wished for a cup of coffee with cream and two sugars, but that wasn't going to happen. He was hungry, so he spooned oatmeal into his mouth, but nothing about the meal was appealing. All around him, men perched on stools bolted to the floor and ate. If they spoke at all, it was quietly. No one wanted trouble this early in the day.

Across the table, a guy named Rod gave him a nod. "Hey, Chief, how's it going?" Rod seemed affable enough for a guy who'd killed a cashier at a gas station mini-mart for less than two hundred dollars, but Gavin wasn't letting his guard down.

Everyone there knew he'd been a chief of police and that alone had made him a target. He'd only been here two days and already he'd been threatened, spit on, and punched in the head.

"Going okay," he said, lifting his spoon.

"It's hard at first," Rod said. "But you'll see. Things work out for the best."

Gavin nodded as if agreeing, but mentally he balked. Things work out for the best? That was a laugh. He wasn't going to get settled in, if that's what Rod was suggesting. Right now, Natalie was working on hiring a high-powered attorney to appeal his conviction. He'd already outlined all the ways he could counter the prosecutor's arguments.

Before long, he'd be a free man.

Taking a sip of his milk, he ignored the stares in his direction. These miscreants had nothing better to do than try to make him uncomfortable. Well, it wasn't working. Setting the glass down, he raised his gaze to Rod, who was looking past him.

Rod smiled at someone behind him and said, "Hey, Starkey."

Starkey? Gavin felt the hairs on the back of his neck stand on end, but the blade was at his throat before he could even react. The makeshift weapon sliced his throat in a few seconds' time.

The oatmeal never got eaten.

EPILOGUE

Sarah carried her son on her hip and strode across the expansive, neatly manicured lawn. They went past headstones marking the lives of strangers, all of them greatly missed by those they left behind. She finally set the toddler down when their destination came into sight. Liam, still clutching the bouquet of flowers they'd purchased earlier, took off, his chubby legs carrying him straight to his father's grave.

"Liam Anthony Aden!" she called out, quickening her pace. "Wait for me."

By the time she caught up, he'd already placed the flowers on the grave, kissed his fingertips, and pressed his hand against the stone. He'd learned the gesture from watching her do it countless times.

Her son. Such a sweet little guy.

They came out to the cemetery every week, weather permitting. She knew her in-laws visited the grave site as well. They didn't discuss it, but she found the notes and flowers they left behind, something she found both endearing and heartbreaking. She kissed her own fingertips, and pressed them against the marker, which had been engraved: *Kirk William Aden, Beloved*

Son, Husband, and Father. Judy had been pleased, but surprised to see that she'd chosen the word "Father" when she'd ordered the memorial. Sarah suspected it was because the baby wasn't born at that point. But Kirk was Liam's father and always would be.

Emotionally she'd been on a journey since Kirk died. Besides the usual emotions of grief, she'd also felt robbed, as if her previous memories had been tainted. Her view of her husband as a kind, loving man had become marred by the knowledge that he'd once covered up a heinous crime. How could he do such a thing and still go on living his life?

She'd tried to explain her feelings to Phil, who'd gently said, "It sounds like you're having trouble forgiving Kirk."

His words nudged something in her memory, something Mrs. Bickley had said about forgiveness: *Holding on to anger is like grasping a hot coal with the intent of throwing it at someone else; instead, you are the one who will get burned.*

Sarah repeated these words to herself whenever she felt bitter or depressed.

It took time and counseling, but eventually she decided to try and let go, for the baby's sake if not for her own. She still had conflicted feelings on occasion, but ultimately she decided that Kirk—like everyone else on the planet—should not be defined solely by one act, no matter how horrendous. Framing it that way didn't excuse what he did, but it allowed her to keep her cherished memories and have the hope that someday she could move on. And she wanted to do just that.

She'd been shocked to hear at the trial that Gavin had concocted some kind of alternate scenario in which she was the actual killer. She'd also heard that he planned on appealing the case, but the legal counsel her in-laws hired had said not to worry about it. "His ridiculous story is never going to fly" was the way Bert relayed it to her.

The fact that her father-in-law was irate on her behalf made her smile.

She sat down cross-legged in front of her son, who was pull-ing at blades of grass. "Liam Anthony, what are you doing?" She laughed when he showed her the grass clutched in his tiny fist. He was so clearly and irrevocably a Liam it was hard to believe she'd ever considered naming him anything else.

For weeks she'd gone back and forth between any number of names, including Kirk. She tried talking to her growing belly to see if the baby would respond to any one name more than another. She felt foolish doing it, even though she was alone at the time.

In the weeks leading up to his birth, she had a terrible time getting a good night's rest. The baby seemed to be most active just when she was finally sinking into sleep and all of his in utero gymnastics only contributed to her constant need to go to the bathroom throughout the night hours. Sometimes she felt lucky to get a solid two hours at a time.

It was during one of her rare deep sleep episodes that she'd had a vivid dream. In it, she walked into the kitchen of her new house and came upon Kirk, who sat at the kitchen table along-side a little boy she instinctively knew was their son. The child, who had to be about four years old, had a pencil in his hand and was concentrating on getting something down on a piece of lined paper. Kirk glanced up and gave her a smile, then returned his attention to their son. "That's it," he said encouragingly. "Now you've got it. Show Mommy."

The boy lifted the paper and she saw that he'd printed the words "Liam Anthony" in shaky letters. "Look!" he said in an excited tone. "I wrote my name."

"Of course you did," her dream-self exclaimed. "Great job!" She moved closer to Kirk, who looped his arm around her waist. When Sarah woke up, the joy of being a family was with her, and her husband's touch lingered.

And she knew her son's name would be Liam Anthony.

After a few minutes, Liam lost interest in the grass, and she decided it was time to leave. Standing up, Sarah brushed a scattering of fine green blades off the front of her shirt. "Time to go home for lunch, Liam." The promise of food always got his attention. She took his hand and they began to walk toward the parking lot.

They were nearly to the car when they approached an elderly gentleman coming from the opposite direction. A stranger with a friendly smile. "Beautiful day," he said with a nod, leaning on his cane.

Sarah glanced down at the top of Liam's head of unruly hair, and the dimpled hand that clutched her fingers, and smiled. "Yes," she agreed. "It's a beautiful day."

A LETTER FROM KAREN

Dear Reader,

Thank you for choosing to read 214 *Palmer Street*. I hope you enjoyed the story within these pages. If you did enjoy it, and want to keep up to date with all my latest releases, just sign up at the following link. Your email address will never be shared and you can unsubscribe at any time.

https://www.karenmcquestion.com/

Sometimes you'll hear authors say they got an idea for a book from a dream. In my case, the premise for this novel came from something similar, but more disturbing.

Throughout my adult life, I've had a repetitive nightmare during times of great stress. I'm always in a house, usually my childhood home or the first house my husband and I owned, and I know *I'm not supposed to be there*. I'm very aware that the new owners could return any minute and discover my presence, something that frightens me. Throughout the nightmare, I try to leave but never can. Sometimes it's because I can't locate my shoes or there's a blizzard outside or I can't find the door. Once, it was because the strap to my purse was caught on a chair.

While awake, these scenarios sound ridiculous, but believe me, my unconscious mind found every one of them terrifying.

It wasn't until I was partway through writing 214 *Palmer Street* that I realized the idea for the story—a woman is in a house and isn't supposed to be there—came from these very nightmares. Funny how the mind works.

If you've enjoyed this novel (born from the terror of my nightmares), I'd love to see your thoughts in a review. Positive reviews serve as fuel to keep me going, so thank you in advance for any kind words you might choose to bestow on my book.

All my best to you,

Karen

 facebook.com/kmcquestion

instagram.com/karenquest

ACKNOWLEDGMENTS

I wish to thank the team at Bookouture for their work in getting 214 *Palmer Street* out into the world.

A vote of gratitude goes to early readers Charlie McQuestion, MaryAnn Schaefer, Barbara Taylor Sissel, and Michelle Watson. As always, your suggestions are valued and appreciated.

Kathy Aden and Phyllis Jones Pisanelli, I hope you don't mind that I borrowed your last names for this novel. Thank you for being supportive readers and insightful reviewers.

To my family, Greg, Charlie, Rachel, Maria, and Jack McQuestion, you give my life love and purpose and I appreciate you more than I can say.

And last, but never least, I need to acknowledge the readers who make it all possible. I cherish your reviews and messages and am glad you enjoy my books. As long as you keep reading, I'll keep writing. Thank you for giving me that privilege.